THE COMPANION

Lorcan Roche

THE COMPANION

Europa
editions

Europa Editions
116 East 16th Street
New York, N.Y. 10003
www.europaeditions.com
info@europaeditions.com

Library of Congress Cataloging in Publication Data is available
ISBN 978-1-933372-84-6

Roche, Lorcan
The Companion

Book design by Emanuele Ragnisco
www.mekkanografici.com

Cover photo © Getty Images

Prepress by Plan.ed – Rome

Printed in Canada

CONTENTS

THE COMPANION

To my wife Nicola & our daughter Piper

BOOK ONE

Don't believe a word, for words are so easily spoken . . .
And your heart is just like that promise, made to be broken.

PHIL LYNOTT, *Don't Believe a Word*

URGENTLY REQUIRED: Mature, responsible person to act as **Big Brother/Companion** to young man with Muscular Dystrophy. Ideal applicant will be courteous, kind and considerate. Will also be able to lift heavy loads. Keen interest in music, especially British 'prog-rock,' an advantage. Live-in option available for right candidate. A non-smoker who speaks English as his first language. Experience pref'd.

NYC, June 11th

The ad is in *The Voice*.

Then, after a little while, a voice is in the ad.

Sounds exactly like the bloke who played the evil-baddie in *North by Northwest*, you know him yes you do, silver hair, real refined, *shite*, what's this his name is . . . ?

Mason, James.

And this is what James Mason is saying, softly: *Trevor, you should endeavour to respond. On the contrary, it will not be a waste of a subway token and will not involve your faith in humanity further being broken. My dear boy, this is for you. Believe me.*

And I do. So I read the ad over and over again. And the chaos of the street retreats as if someone slowly is sealing one of those steel hatches in a submarine, you know the kind where you have to twist a squeaking, rusting wheel. And it's as if a great weight is being lifted . . .

'Hey, buddy! Do me a favor—take the paper home. If you have a home.'

This is not James Mason. No, this is the newspaper vendor, a bag of fifty-year-old bones in a wife-beater vest who thinks he's real Scorsese. He's standing there chewing imaginary gum giving his spiky old jaw a right good workout, and he's making it pretty obvious he's expecting me to move on, pronto.

But I'm in no hurry, none whatsoever.

'Hey buddy, it's free. Ya don't need to fuckin' *mema-rize* it.'

Do you ever look at people and wonder, *Now, if he or she was a bird or animal, what would they be?* I do. I always ask myself, real fast: *fish or fowl, bird or beast?* Maybe they're doing exactly the same thing, I don't know. Mostly I think people—especially Americans—are asking, *Gee, I wonder what this one can do for me? Make me some more money? Get me over my date rape experience? Clear up any doubts about my false memory syndrome?*

Truth is, you never really know. Dogs have the upper hand. They just go around behind, have a sniff and think, *No way. This is one uptight, anal-retentive hound.*

Anyway, the old scrote with the hedgehog stubble, he'd be an ankle-biter of some description, something vulpine and sly that goes around in packs pulling down by the painful tail gnu or gazelle who've been separated from their mates in some terrible, blinding dust-storm. Or maybe he'd be something that slithered along on its belly and got made into a belt. Either way, say if I was in Tanzania driving a Land Rover with big bull bars and he slunk out of the bush like a secret, and I could see his fishing line whiskers all silvered in the headlights—maybe with something not quite dead dangling—there's no chance I'd lift off the gas, not the fuckin' slightest. *Squish.*

Smiling at people you think are weird or wonderful, or smiling at completely the wrong time, is an excellent thing to do—it really can be quite unnerving.

I smile at Fox Face who, far as I can see, wears soft little leather gloves because he doesn't like touching other humans, unless of course he's got some sort of skin disease. People who handle money all day often get skin complaints. It's true—money really is dirty.

He doesn't return the smile, just wrinkles his evil weasel nose and I'm thinking, *Yep, definitely the type that'll get riled real easy*. So I take the corner of the one page I require, hold it up like a doctor with an X-ray and let drop the rest which hits the deck and fans out as if it has a will of its own, like those calendar shots from Frank Capra movies where forty years pass in seconds flat and everyone gets flour fecked in their hair and talc lashed on their cheeks. Naturally, as I walk away he's screaming blue murder telling me what he'd like to do to me if he was '*twenny* years younga,' yeah right. People like him need to take a long look at themselves in the mirror. Still, they're good for a laugh and sometimes if you're not feeling so magnificent you can use them, like stepping-stones, to lighten and brighten your mood. To turn the moment round.

I met this interesting guy once—well, quite a few times actually—who had this amazing Filipina secretary with a really calming voice. He explained how, with a modicum of effort and imagination, we could devise our own comedies with the rest of the world as unwitting co-stars, hapless extras, how most of us failed to realize how enormously entertaining days could be and that we really didn't need to sit like toadstools in front of TVs.

I agree. Wholeheartedly.

People answering telephones should really be more circumspect and careful.

The woman who picks up barks at some sort of servant. 'It's for me, put it down,' then she coughs like an outboard engine that's all backed up and flooded. 'I wasn't expecting, *splutter,* anyone to call. So soon.'

'Oh. If it's not convenient I can—'

'No. You have a nice voice, *splutter.* Where are you from?'

'Ireland.'

'Ed's father and I went to Ireland on our honeymoon, *splutter.* That was a long time ago, however.'

'Eh, right.'

'Would you like to tell me about yourself?'

'Well, I'm mature and responsible. I'm also courteous, kind and physically very strong. Plus, I'm really into British progrock.'

'Ed doesn't weigh that much. Sometimes you'd have to be able to lift him. And the chair. Together. Not often though.'

'I'd manage.'

'I don't suppose you have any experience working with people like Ed, do you, *splutter*, hon?'

I tell her how I'd only recently been working at the Central Remedial Clinic in Dublin teaching *English and Appreciation of Poetry* to 'you know, non-able bodied men and women of all ages, shapes and sizes.' I think maybe she's going to ask what poets I'm partial to, which is probably what an Irish person would ask, although to be honest they're getting kind of brusque over there too and everyone's walking around in Italian suits acting all European and being terribly serious into tiny fuckin' phones.

But all she wants to know is what sort of problems the Clinic people had to contend with.

'Let's see. Eh, some of them had MS and related motor neurone diseases. Others had Muscular Dystrophy, naturally. Then there were some Spina Bifidas, plus a whole host of NTDs.'

'NTDs?'

'Neural tube deficiencies.'

'Oh. OK. Ed was right as rain when he was born.'

'That's good. Well, I mean it's not *good*. It's a pity he was OK and then got sick.'

'Yes it is. It's a living tragedy.'

I tell her there were quite a few with Cerebral Palsy and that at least two, if not three, had Freidrich's Ataxia, plus this one other guy had the quite rare Guillian-Barré Syndrome which, I explain to her, is the disease the dude who wrote *Catch 22* caught. She doesn't seem familiar with the book, however, and I'm pretty sure it wasn't her who worded the ad.

I'm thinking of all the people in my class, trying to retrace their thumbprint faces—hard, because quite a lot couldn't lift up their necks while others were screwed down into the chairs all kind of skewed and they looked at you from odd angles. You know when you're sitting in a Nissen hut with a night watchman somewhere and the coals are burning away in the little primus thing and you can't really see him properly because there's a kind of mirage effect going on? Or when you had a perspex ruler and spent the whole school day looking through it? Well, that's exactly what teaching at the Clinic was like: you might just see someone's nose and maybe their right eye blurred plus a corner of their mouth drooping, and you had to be real careful about walking around talking because you'd get all this shifting and sighing as they tried to follow you sometimes a tiny flinty elbow someone hadn't got great control over would fly high and get someone else upside the head.

I'm thinking of all of the laughs, especially at the start when this one guy Redmond, or Edmond, who had this incredible speech defect on top of a lot of other problems—including a head that was permanently positioned sideways—started rocking like a disturbed creature at the zoo, then screaming *eek eek* like a fuckin' bald eagle. I hadn't a clue what he was trying to say, something about a *badly cooked erection* until this other one who could decipher him better explained that I never *looked at him directly.*

There was this big silence, *shite*, and all the other ones who felt the same were nodding away in unison *yes, yes, yes* trying to lift up their flower-pot heads, and I was right on the spot. Glued to it.

But it's OK I didn't panic. I simply said, 'Yeah you're right, but there's a very good reason why I never look at you directly,' then I left a pause while I tried to think of the reason, and started walking in and out between them fast, causing total fuckin' mayhem.

Finally I said the reason was that he, Redmond or Edmond or whatever his name was, was 'one weird-looking, alien-headed motherfucker who could land a wheel-on part in *Star Trek: Voyager* any day of the week simply by sending in a Polaroid.'

They all fell about the place, with two notable exceptions, literally collapsing with laughter. And Edmond started bucking like a bronco, there was even a tear rolling down his sideways face, plus this Pyrenean mountain dog slobber coming out of his permanently wide-open mouth. I went over and tightened his straps as he grinned and drooled, spittle was bouncing up and down like elastic on his chin, so I caught it and wiped it, and the poor fucker was trying really hard to bring his sideways head around and his little arms were coming up with the effort. He said, '*Newt a bunny guy, nut nore bed id too gig for nore, nore mody, end nore nore bands gluck like hay hay hay hay be hone on. By Doctorfrankin time. In a botch op op op op up a nane.*'

'Course all this took him quite some time to say, especially the bit about the botched operation up the lane, but fair play, it was pretty funny especially when I used the same hands to tickle his bony, brittle little body. Anyway, it really broke the ice and I started looking forward to going to work for the first time in my life, even if there were two of them I was going to have major hassle with, you know the type: they won't laugh at anybody else's jokes and they sit beside each other every day sniggering, like demented hyenas.

One of them was this tiny, deformed creature called Dalek; he was only three and a half foot high but made up for it with some serious fuckin' 'tude. His sidekick was much bigger and was called The Captain. I'm telling you, these two really were a nightmare.

The Captain was the only one who could decode Dalek properly and Dalek was forever whispering things in The Captain's fat ear. Then The Captain would roar his head off like a donkey in the middle of a field and if you said, 'Do you mind telling the rest of us what's so hilariously fuckin' funny?' he'd say, 'Sure, no problem.' Then he'd leave a big pause and you'd say, 'Well?' and he'd smile and say, 'Your stupid-lookin' potato head' or maybe 'Your shiny fuckin' moon face, alright?' and he'd wink at Dalek who had this demented grin (bit like the dwarf on *Fantasy Island*) plus this bizarre light emanating from eyes that looked like they'd been lifted from a curly-horned ram on the side of a mountain in Kerry.

She's telling me about Ed's 'off-the-scale intelligence quota'—*yeah right*—and his 'special emotional needs,' which, let's be honest, each and every one of us has. But I'm not really listening, I'm checking around to see if Fox Face isn't coming running with a machete or machine gun, you never know in this fuckin' place. And what I'm really thinking about is the Clinic, and the field trips into the bog where we'd fleece these dozy rednecks in their sleepy village shops, cleaning them out completely.

We had this contest to see who could shop-lift the biggest item and I was way ahead, having stroked a big roll of tinfoil which just about fit under the long leather coat no one ever believes really *did* belong to Phil Lynott. Then Dalek and The Captain robbed a turkey, don't ask me how, stuffing it up the front of an anorak and Dalek was declared the winner on weight plus the fact he had no arms to speak of, just these scary platypus paws which had a puppet-life all of their own. When I pointed out the tin foil was in fact longer, they got together and pulled the bird by its feet and neck until it stretched out like a cartoon, which sounds much easier than it actually was.

They all wrote glowing reports about the day trip, even Dalek, describing in detail how easy-going I was, how strong I was when I was lifting them on and off the bus, how relaxed and safe they felt in my company, etcetera etcetera. When the

Committee called me in sat me down and offered me a full-time job obviously I couldn't refuse, even if working with a load of armless, legless and sometimes hopeless people wasn't exactly what I had in mind staring out the window as a kid I used to see myself as some sort of Shining Hero saving people, maybe getting mildly disfigured in the process, possibly even suffering hypothermia like the little Dutch boy who stuck his finger in the dyke (and I mean dam-like construction, not lesbian female, alright?).

She's banging on about Ed's twice-weekly physical therapy, the noble way he endures pain, blah blah blah. But I'm right back in the creaking barna building with its makeshift ramps which used to get all slidey in the rain and I can see his face clearly, and OK I admit he *was* handsome in a predictable, Gabriel Byrne kind of way. And this is The Captain who'd got both arms right up to the shoulder and both legs right up to the knee ripped off in a thresher in County Carlow, the one who'd been the Star Performer on the local hurling team, and who from the moment I walked in hated me with all his fuckin' might.

Isn't it odd how people's minds spring so swiftly into action like steel traps, and isn't it weird how hard it is to prise them back again?

She begins a fresh bout of spluttering and I'm thinking of the metallic throat noises Dalek used to make, especially after eating his liquidized alien baby food, and of the essay he wrote with the black wand attached to his oily, pimply forehead: what he thought of the Clinic and the other spastics in the class, what he'd like to do to me if he could only become fully-formed for five fuckin' minutes, *incredible shit*, page upon fantastic page made all the more amazing by the amount of time he must have spent creating it. I mean, his poor neck must've been fuckin' knackered.

I gave him a B+, said he could've tried harder, you could see him and The Captain trying not to laugh when I handed back the homework. I like being able to make people laugh. It's like that quality of mercy thing, isn't it?

Traffic is distracting me. There's a wino who definitely has fleas. You can actually see his mangy coat *moving*, and he's rifling the little silver slot on the phone next to mine which is futile. He'd be much better off recycling cans. And it's as if he's reading my mind because there he goes terrorizing a trashcan, mumbling and tumbling shit out all over the sidewalk.

He comes back to the phone, lifts up the receiver and listens, probably imagining he's some Wall Street exec in pinstripes with a stiff white collar and the thing is, his eyes are disturbingly blue and clear. Like God's.

Flea Man starts bashing the head of the receiver off the shiny steel plate hissing about stocks and bonds, and I know it's silly, but this makes me inordinately happy because I was right about what was going on in his swamp fever mind in the first place, and I'm probably laughing a bit because she's going, 'Hello, what's going on, hello?' So I tell her, 'It's OK, I'm calling from the street.' Except she just says, 'Oh, I see,' as if I'd just told her I was occasionally incontinent.

And the banjaxed phone with its blue and yellow circuitry exposed looks like it really might have been sinister when it was alive, and Flea Man might have had good reason to attack it. And I really need to take control so I enquire after Ed's reading habits pretending to be real impressed, *oh really*, when she mentions Simone de Beauvoir and Jean Paul fuckin' Sartre, two frog writers I really can't abide.

I get the interview back on track, telling her my father is a professor *emeritus* which is true, but which basically means he's retired and is a bit of an asshole who still likes to call himself a professor, like those Wing Commander blue-blazer-and-cravat types who live in tea-shop villages in England. Now it's her turn to be real impressed. Suddenly she's asking how would I feel about coming up to sit with Ed 'for a spell.'

And words are standing out on their own, which isn't good. I need to listen to complete sentences.

She gives me the address slowly and carefully as if she were talking to a ten-year-old, and it feels as if I'm walking into a new future as I descend the steps of the subway; my heart is lifting, which is nice—it's been heavy and low for a while—which reminds me, I hate that Eleanor Mc Evoy ditty 'Only a Woman's Heart Can Know.' I mean, did you ever hear such sexist *shite* in all your life? You really think men my age living in hostile, incredibly expensive cities don't have hearts that sink like suns, particularly as beautiful, kind-looking Asian women walk by dripping in jewellery with fat baldy bastards trailing after them, grinning like pumpkins at Halloween?

The young black dude with the starched white shirt in the glass booth says nothing as I slide my crumpled dollar across he slowly slips the token into the wooden bowl made smooth by tens of thousands of similar transactions. When I say 'thank you' he nods, smiles and holds up the novel he is reading: *The Philosopher's Dog*. Don't ask me why, but I get the old fluttery sensation in my chest; it's as if he's part of some elaborate Christopher Nolan movie (*Memento*) where everyone's trying their level best to reveal these incredibly important clues, except I haven't a breeze what they're all banging on about. It's like the time I passed a phone ringing steadily in the street near my building—I swear to Christ I could hear it all the way up the stone stairs even as a slow train trundled past I was thinking, *Hey, maybe it was for you. How the fuck do you know it wasn't?*

I suppose what I'm saying is, if you allow your mind to bend a little then the possibilities are infinite and endless whereas if you decide it's all logical and ordered and *things like that simply cannot happen* then you're ruling out all kinds of magical stuff. For instance: when I was a kid, I found a blue plastic bottle down on the beach. Wrapped up watertight inside was a handwritten letter from some decrepit old dear in Australia. I remember my father telling me not to get my hopes up high when I was writing her back. To be fair, he let me sit in his office, a *major* fuckin' deal, he even helped compose the letter, listening to classical music, drinking overly diluted Miwadi.

Six or seven weeks later when a brown paper parcel arrived at the door he had to admit I had more faith than he did. Meredith Baxter was the name of the lady and she was nearly ninety, with incredibly bad spidery writing. Meredith had sent me a boomerang—not one of those imitation ones that never come back, but a real one made of hard black wood with little white drawings of birds and snakes on. Her letter explained how it was *the genuine article,* how she'd seen an Aborigine boy the same age as me hunt with it.

Took quite a while, maybe even months, but in the end I could make that yoke land smack-bang in the middle of my palm. I remember it took some vestige of me with it as it travelled through the air. Seriously, my blood used to hurtle forward with the delight of flight; it's much the same sensation you get when you see your dog hunting down a big pale hare in the dunes.

When my father pitched it into the sky, however, we both knew it wouldn't make the same singing sound, we both knew it wouldn't come thwacking back. Why? 'Cause he'd already admitted defeat. And you'd be amazed, or maybe it's *appalled* at how many times we do that especially as we shake someone's hand or gaze into their eyes for the very first time.

When the black guy says, 'Watch the closing doors,' his voice is gentle, almost like a friend giving advice. I really wish there were more people like him using tannoys, bullhorns and public address systems in the city sometimes it's as if there's this constant barking effect going on in the background. *Christ,* imagine what it's like living under the commies with no peace or quiet as you sit on a park bench there'd be some demented lunatic telling you through a loudspeaker how wonderful your life was, how extraordinarily fuckin' lucky you were to be living and working in Vietnam, Cambodia or Estonia. And you'd have no choice, none whatsoever; you'd just *have* to carry tiny, homemade pliers concealed about your person at night and to go out snipping and clipping the carelessly dangling wires. Well, maybe you wouldn't, but I definitely fuckin' would.

I have a thing about voices. I mean, let's face it, in the grand scheme of things they're incredibly important and whereas I may not have been first-up in the queue in the Good Looks Department, my voice is unusually easy on the ear and, apart from my hands, nearly always the first thing strangers remark on.

The summer after I left school I worked in a factory in Germany and every morning when I went to the U-Bahn there was this woman's voice that used to smoothly announce, '*Gleis zwei, bitte zuruck blieben,*' which means Platform two, please stand back. Nothing to get too excited about, obviously, but it was a real nice voice, calming, and pretty sexy, too. After a while I used to quite look forward to hearing her say it, so eventually I went searching for someone in a position to tell me who in the hell she might be.

As you can imagine, however, Germans—especially Germans working underground all day—aren't exactly the most romantic people on the planet. In fact, they all looked like fuckin' moles with walrus moustaches attached, and they just brushed me aside pretending they couldn't understand my *fabrike deutsche*, telling me as they frog-marched me out like a shoplifter, that it was just a tape, not a real person.

I have to say, if the same thing happened in Napoli instead of Stuttgart, the dusty old blokes in uniform would have taken it upon themselves to hunt down the studio where she'd made the original recording and I'd have gotten her number, phoned her up and had a nice long chat, maybe even met up for a glass of cheap Chianti. And it wouldn't have mattered what age she was or how many chins she had; *no*, what mattered was on the day she was asked to lean in towards the microphone she'd put a bit of herself into it, she was probably smiling, maybe even flirting with the sound engineer, daydreaming of somewhere with warm clean sand she could bury her painted toenails in. It's the same with cooking by the way—put a little bit of love in, it always tastes much better.

Train doors hiss and crack open in New York sometimes it really is like an episode of *Star Trek*; you never know who the fuck is going to make his or her entrance. This time, it's the turn of a greasy guy in a stinking combat jacket who starts hollering he's a Gulf War vet, how the passsengers have no choice, they have no fuckin' choice, they *have* to cough up some goddamn money, if it wasn't for him and brothers like him they wouldn't be sitting there reading their papers and devouring their celebrity magazines, they'd be reading the fucking Koran, they'd be down on their knees praying to Allah eating falafels, baba ganoush, all sorts of bugs and shit. He keeps shoving this chipped styrofoam cup into their hot flushed faces; you can see they find it completely overwhelming. They scramble around in their purses bags and wallets like little rhesus monkeys, some with black faces. For his part, he looks like a big ape all hunched up, even swinging from pole to pole—all he's missing in his fist is a bright yellow Chiquita banana.

Here he comes, right up to me, and what does he do? He shoves the begging bowl at me screaming, 'You have no choice

man, you have no fuckin' choice.' This guy's breath would flat-
ten a horse, *Christ almighty*.

I fan the foul air in front of my face and he steps back a frac-
tion to repeat the line, only not so loud. Isn't it weird how a
tiny little gesture can change absolutely everything? The wind
is out of his sails now he tries to do this bad thousand-yard
stare, except one of his eyes starts getting bigger as if someone
has an invisible straw in his ear which they're blowing softly and
steadily. The iris in his yellowed old eye is ringed by a creamy-
coloured corona, it's all flecked like Donegal tweed and it's clear
the guy's liver is shot, probably his pancreas as well. He
blinks the big bad wolf eye three times then shuffles away
leaving behind a really nice stink, *gee thanks, bro.* You can see
some of the people who handed over their hard-earned cash
are pissed off all of a sudden he doesn't look quite so big or
brutal.

The sound of the subway's steel wheels is strangely soothing, probably because I'm going somewhere *specific*, and I'm
sitting there trying to remember the names of British prog-rock
bands: Pink Floyd, Genesis, Yes, with the beginnings of a grin
growing due to the fact I'm experiencing one of those excellent
tapocketapocketa moments where you're not afraid to see yourself in a brighter future. And I'm nodding away thinking, *Yep,
you're dead right there, Trevor. It's not healthy to have no real
focal point to the day, now is it?*

The doorman is West of Ireland, looks a little bit like
Samuel Beckett, another scribbler I'm not exactly head over
heels about, but for a little guy he has a good grip and a
straight gaze. At least it isn't one of those ones that peer into
you and try and figure out what you're made of, as if people
have a clue just by fuckin' *looking*.

He asks me what I need to know, so I say what is there to
know, and he tells me the husband is a Supreme Court Judge,
works a *helluva* lot. The mother, 'Well, ya'll see for *ya-self*.'

I ask him about Ed. He says he hasn't clapped eyes on him in nearly a year. 'Poor kid wen' *ovah* the park last July, or maybe it was August, for some John Lennon memorial thingimmy, got bit by a bee or insect, received some God-awful throat infection. For a while there it was touch and go. Yes indeed, touch and go.'

Then there's a pause, which happens quite a lot when you meet someone new but it's nothing to worry about, it's just time being compressed by unrealistic expectations. He looks down at his shoes which are incredibly shiny, almost as if they were made of patent leather, except they're not. Then finally he shakes his grey head slowly.

'Poor mite, poor unfortunate little mite,' except he keeps looking at the floor as if the solution to the mite's medical problems was written in invisible ink there. Another pause as he raises his eyes up, then he does this little whistle thing like an old-fash-ioned kettle. 'Phew. Jesus H. Where'd ya get the hands?'

So I tell him, 'From my grandfather on my mother's side who was a blacksmith and who boxed Golden Gloves for Ireland back in the days when that actually meant something.' And he says, 'Yeah, when men were men and Yamaha made *pianahs*.' I smile, mostly because of the way he pronounced pianos, except he believes I'm marvelling at the sophistry and artistry of his phraseology so he says it again: 'When men were men and Yamaha made *pianahs*.'

Then he reaches up, he puts his arm halfway around my shoulder and pats me twice. When I ask does he do everything twice, he goes, 'Why do ya ask, kid?' And, even though there are loads of other examples, I tell him he said the Yamaha thing twice, then tapped me twice, and he says he doesn't know, *Jesus*, he's never thought about it. Maybe I'm right, maybe he does.

'Well, if that's the case your wife is pretty fuckin' lucky.'

He laughs—it's quite a nice sound really—then he tells me I'm all right for a guy from Dublin, if indeed that is where I hail from, so I say, 'Yes it is' and with his hand still perched upon my shoulder he walks me to the lift. Before he disappears he says, 'Just be yourself kid, just be yourself,' which is kind of weird, I mean, he doesn't know me from Adam and *he* did most of the talking.

The lift guy is a super-creep, says nothing the whole way up, just delivers this oily, fake smile like a weasel in a red jacket, you know the one that hid behind the tree when Pinocchio was on his way into town. When he opens the old-fashioned, wrought iron door to their floor I say, 'Nice fez!' then I wait half a second before adding, 'If you're into those old road movies with Bing and Bob, ya fuckin' jackass.'

Like I said, you should never be afraid to turn the moment round.

First of all I meet the Judge. If you like, you can put those little titles underneath, you know the ones from *The Good, The Bad and The Ugly.*

Il Judgo is small and neat like an old car he smells of wood and leather. He looks a bit like that real old actor who always smoked cigars and once played God. *Burns, George.* I say 'Pleased to meet you' and in return he says absolutely nothing. He's one of those people with negative energy, black holes that suck you in, the type you feel less well after talking to, even for just a few seconds.

He gazes at my chest as if something's written there in ancient Aramaic then clears his throat, *he-hem,* to announce in a dead sea scroll of a voice, 'I hope you'll endeavour to contribute something constructive to Ed's, *he-hem,* existence.'

And he didn't say anything to me when I greeted him, so fuck him, I'm not saying anything back, *he-hem*. He realizes this, turns on his heel, walks into his office and shuts the door sharply a voice down the corridor calls, 'Is that you hon, is that the Irish boy?' So I shout 'Yes it's me' and she replies 'Come on down,' which is what they say on game shows, isn't it?

I'm suddenly very nervous which isn't good because I can get this bird's wing thing fluttering about in my rib cage and sometimes I need to laugh out loud, except it's not *my* laugh, it belongs to a much smaller person, plus it can be quite high-pitched like a bat she shrieks, 'Wait!' Then her voice gets calmer as she tells me to stop at the door, please give her a moment.

I can hear swishing noises within, maybe curtains being pulled and I'm bending to peek through the keyhole when I remember the last time I did that, so I just stand there staring down at the insistent, thin tracks of a wheelchair. Finally, she tells me all ceremoniously, 'Come!'

I enter slowly pinching my legs through the pocket lining, *Don't laugh, ya fuckin' eejit, don't laugh.* And I don't, because sitting up in the bed is the *fattest* female you ever did see, big as a Mac truck, with these huge mammaries hanging out over the top of the crimson duvet like human heads, and I don't mean Papua-New Guinea shrunken ones either.

She's looking me up and down, down and up. Then she pats the bed, *sit.*

For a while we just look at each other, which is only natural because she's the mother and I'll be protecting her cub, hopefully. I smile and take in her gargantuan size, her long grey hair like the Chewing Gum Chief in *One Flew Over,* her cold blue eyes, that incredibly mean little mouth. Then I let her examine me as I take in her room.

Considering all their dosh it really isn't anything to write home about, all chintzy with too many patterns clashing. It also needs to be hoovered and despite one of those old perfume bottles with the little balloons attached being right by the bed it has a pissy sour smell, which means she's even lazier than she looks—and no disrespect to fat people, but she looks pretty fuckin' lazy—or else she has a whole tribe of cats sleeping alongside her.

There's a TV on its side in one corner, a TV upright in the middle of the room on a dresser with overflowing drawers, and a third TV on its side in the far corner. She weighs so much that if she lies down in one direction she doesn't want to have to shift again. Her arms are as big as my legs and I'm not exactly the Road Runner, plus you can see these blue veins twisting like rivers across the terrible topography of her tits. Tossed in a ball on the carpet is a massive pyjama top with these absurd little Pierrot clowns grinning away on it and you wouldn't believe the nightie she's just struggled into, *Jesus*.

There's a long pause as she scans the room through my eyes; I love it when silence engulfs you, when it flies into your ears like two kites with old-fashioned tails and paper messages attached which you'd really love to have time to read, and you can hear your heart nice and steady, you can even see her tongue move like some great slow sea creature Jacques Cousteau didn't know was hidden under the sand.

Her over-inflated head tilts to one side, she swallows and it's obvious she's getting ready to make an important speech, like some corrupt old Senator on his last legs. 'Ed's nineteen. And he's a miracle. Doctors been telling us ever since he was seven years old, he had but a year to live. But *mah* Ed defies them, every second of his precious life.'

She's putting on this fake Southern accent and I'm trying not to laugh, *stop*, because it sounded funny when she said '*mah* Ed defies them' as if her head defied all the Humpty Dumpty doctors with the boiled-sweet size of it, plus this ticker tape title has started running under her Zeppelin boobs: *El Grosso Fuckin' Piggo*.

I get the giggling under control, but for the life of me I can't stop staring at her melons and I'm wondering was it Charles Dickens, a writer I really like, who called it 'the attraction of repulsion'?

She catches me staring and the old bitch rubs one big tit with a blood-red fingernail, lazily tracing the outline of the areola which is the same size as the top of a sandcastle; if you look close enough it even has carbuncle-lumps like tiny seashells you might use as sandcastle windows, *that's* how fuckin' enormous this whale woman is.

'Ed hasn't got much time left. And, *as a consequence*, we need someone kind. *Ah* mean to say, you most certainly look strong, but are you kind?'

'Yes ma'am.'

''Cause we've had some cruel boys here in the past. Selfish, cruel boys who had hard, hard hearts. Do you have a hard heart?'

'No ma'am. I don't believe I do.'

She peers into my eyes to see if this is true, then there's another pause which I also enjoy, in fact the only ones I don't are the churning windmill ones that occur when you're unable to make a major decision about your life, or when you're shagging someone and the pause and the blank stare indicate it isn't going as swimmingly as you'd like. And what I'd like to know is, why can't women just tell you what they want instead of trying to communicate like antelope with their darting brows and eyes?

Speaking of which, right now she's using her pink pig ones to draw mine down towards the V of her Diana Dors negligée and I'm getting a crick in my neck from *not* looking. It's as if I'm in an episode of *Batman* and one of my arch-enemies has produced this huge magnet to try and draw me in, *nnnnghnooo.*

'*Eh*, I'd like to meet Ed now, if that's OK with you?'

'Don't you want to know how much the position pays?'

I tell her it's obvious she has a lot of love for her son, and she says 'yes' in this little-girl-lost voice. *Yes*. Then I say it is abundantly clear that she wants him to be happy at the end of his tragically short life.

'Yes*, ah* most certainly do.'

'You want someone who is physically strong, but who has a kind heart?'

'*Ah'll* settle for nothin' less.'

'You want someone mature and responsible?'

'Yes.'

'Someone sensitive?'

'Yes.'

'Someone with a high intelligence quota, just like Ed.'

'Yes.'

Then I leave a pause—it's a brilliant one altogether—and finally I say, 'Well Ma'am, in that case I'm sure the position pays exceptionally well.'

And you can see by the way El Grosso Fuckin' Piggo is narrowing her eyes and flaring her thick, square nostrils that she's suddenly not quite so sure what to make of me. And because she is no longer in complete control she looks past me towards the open door and says in a real dismissive way, 'I'll let him know you're coming.'

And all of a sudden she no longer sounds like Blanche du Bois, in fact she sounds exactly like the permanently pissed off cow I share an apartment in Astoria with who constantly leaves these little notes lying around all the time. I'll tell you something for nothing, if you find one of them first thing in the morning it can ruin your entire fuckin' day even if you have what I like to call a Victor Mature voice saying, *Don't let it get to you, pal. You have your health, you have your whole life ahead of you, it's just a scrap of paper with some sexually-frustrated cow's squiggly fuckin' writing on it.*

Miss Piggy picks up this antique little phone by the bed, it was probably in the apartment from day one, and already I can hear another one tinkling down the corridor. It takes an age for him to answer. Then finally she says, 'Ed, hi, it's your mother.' *Well who else was it going to be, Naomi fuckin' Campbell?*

She sighs as if me and her had been at it hammer and tongs, and says, *sigh*, 'The Irish boy is on his way,' *sigh*, as if I'm no longer present. I thank her and tell her it was very nice to have met her, but she's lost all interest; her hand is already reaching for the remote. And as I'm walking out the door and down the narrow corridor I realize I'm doing my breathing exercises which means I must be on the verge of getting angry. The reason, I reckon, is sheer bad manners.

Old sow never even bothered to ask me my name.

2.

*I*nhale. Hold. *Now, let the negative energy out.*
That's better.
People are like clocks or musical compositions—they all have different rhythms. And although at times I jabberwock (i.e. talk *way* too quickly for my own good) my basic rhythm is kind of slow. Think cello or oboe. As a result, *as a consequence,* when things start spiral-staircasing downwards, when other men stand there with their traps open catching flies, it really isn't that difficult for me to step in and assume control. Or what looks like it.

Example: when I was in India we had this driver with a bandage over one eye and yellow pus seeping out from under it—fell asleep and got bit by a tree spider, I'd say—and he had this infant on the front seat beside him, quite beautiful actually, with black mirrors for eyes and silver bracelets on little ankles that jingled when you picked him up and tried to stop him from crying, which was exactly what this lovely, incredibly healthy-looking older American woman was doing. You could see she was doing OK, *no problemo*, but that didn't stop old Gunner Eye from looking over his shoulder every two fuckin' seconds, no matter what was coming at us.

And then I heard it. Like a record on the wrong speed, a 45 on 33, whispering, like Ray Winstone or maybe Bob Hoskins. *Oi, this is it Clever Trevor, this is one of those fucking situations.* And the voice is sort of sing-song, but very reasonable and calm, and it says that the *fucking towel-heads never fit new brake pads on any of their fucking vehicles and if they do, they probably fit the fucking wrong ones,* now he has my attention. *I mean, you've seen 'em, Trev, Indian mechanics. Hunkered down on the side of the road, roll-up in one hand, iron bar in the other. Tell me, what are they always fucking doing?*

I don't know. What are they always doing?

What they're always doing, Trev, is beating the shit out of some vital fucking bike, car, or let's-fucking-face-it, bus component. Now, as you've already clocked, our driver has only one eye in his head. The baby is distracting him, as is the fucking hippy American bird who, to be fair, is only tryin' to fucking 'elp. But the thing is, Trev, if you was sitting up a bit closer you would hear the unmistakable, not to mention highly fucking unwelcome sound of metal on metal. So, what you have to do now is ask yourself a question.

He leaves a pause, quite a tense neck one, and I have to ask, *What's the question?*

Do you or do you not like being alive?

He laughs and I'm out of my seat, walking up the aisle of the lurching bus, listening and nodding as he follows.

See, it doesn't fucking matter how many times he's thrown orange flowers or brass farthings out the fucking window. Because truth is, mate, you fucking like being alive, right?

I have to admit, there've been a few times when I wasn't entirely convinced that I liked being alive all that much. But we all feel like that from time to time, right? I mean, they're just moments or moods, or maybe they're seasons . . .

Earth to fucking Trevor. Would you like to ask the audience? Maybe phone a fucking friend?

I'm at the very front now, the driver is looking up at me with his one good eye and yellow pus really is seeping. The baby is screaming and the American woman isn't helping anymore because she's crying too, her tears falling on the baby's face. I put my hand on the driver's shoulder and it sinks a bit, like a plunger in a coffee pot, as if he is very, very tired. Then I tell him as calmly as I can that maybe it'd be best for all concerned if I took the wheel, just for a little while.

There's always that moment, when you don't know if what you're doing is rational or right, when the universe stops spinning and the gods stop playing snakes 'n ladders with our lladró lives and they lean forward wondering if he'll scream into my face, *Get back to your seat you big, bloody, stupid-looking foreigner!*

Except he just smiles up as if he, too, was aware that Death, or its first cousin, Permanent Disfigurement, was waiting around the next bend. He lifts his bare black foot off the accelerator (did you ever notice how brown-skinned people have jet-black feet?) and he starts grinding down the hurting gears, nodding his head from side to side. 'Yes my friend, you can take the wheel now, but only just for little while.'

We stop. The peace is glorious. The American woman is saying 'Thank God' over and over. Thank God. Thank God. I fire up the bus gently. The steering wheel is huge and sticky from his pink, sweating palms, and it really is a piece of shit this bus. And Bob Hoskins was right, there are practically no brakes, and the huge red speedo needle is hopping all over the place, so *nice and easy does it.*

This other more modern bus, which was honking at us from behind, overtakes in a red cloud of cough dust and the American woman comes up and kisses the top of my head softly. 'Thank you, whoever you are.' She says she was praying for someone to act, to intervene, that she was convinced we were all going to die, but that God had answered her prayers.

That's when I tell her to keep on praying because we have no brakes worth talking about and there's a big steep hill up ahead. She laughs and says, 'OK, I'll get back to work, I think I may have Him on the line.' And before she turns to sit back down she asks me my name and where I am from, and I tell her. 'Thank you so much, Trevor from Ireland.'

Then she asks me, 'Are you a believer?,' and I say out loud for the whole bus to hear, 'Yes, I most certainly am.' And I'm sitting there, driving the big old creaking wreck, happy to be alive, but at the same time I say to myself quietly, *I know He's up there all right. I know it because I can feel Him. Watching. Judging. But not fuckin' participating.*

As an adolescent I became convinced that God had taken an instamatic photo of me when I was still a womb-wet newborn. It was still developing as He was passing it round to his cronies and they began asking *So, Yahweh, what's the Grand Plan for this fellow?* when one of them, probably a Protestant, smudged me with his thumb.

Then, as the Proddy handed back the photo, God stared blankly at the square of paper he was holding and declared: *No plans in hand, boom-boom!*

It'd be funny if God turned out to have a really shit sense of humour and everyone in Heaven avoided him and his awful afterdinner jokes.

Anyway, I always felt I was the unnecessary part that rattled in the box after the gift had been assembled. I was forever breaking things accidentally and if I played with other kids who occasionally came to visit—the sons of other professors, say—they ended up getting injured or knocked over backwards with their thick glasses half on. Then there were the muted whisperings behind closed doors about my *lineage,* and the age gap between me and my ugly sisters, not to mention the fact that we resembled one another in the way that chalk and fuckin' cheese do.

And I admit I definitely spent way too much time alone as a kid, and a dog and a boomerang are not compensation enough for a yearning that would well up inside whenever we went out driving and passed estates where ordinary boys built tree houses and dreams with their determined, earnest little posse of friends.

I was equally convinced as I grew up that all my doubts, fears and uncertainties about who and what I really was, all my endless worries, were trapped in my wide, stupid, frontier of a face where nothing could be even thinly disguised. I hated looking at myself in mirrors especially first thing in the morning, and nothing ever fitted in department stores. I suppose that's how I developed my compulsive hatred of neat, perfectly turned-out shop assistants and the way they always made me feel blurred, *vague*. Like in the original *Star Trek* when they're bringing Kirk or McCoy or Lt. Uhuru back on board and the transporter device starts acting up and you get the coming and going, that awful fading and re-animating, and you don't know whether they're going to make it off the doomed planet in time. Well you *do*, but you don't.

When I was thirteen or fourteen there was an incident behind the school shed and I believe that's the time I stopped speaking for almost a year. I say *believe* because I find memory very confusing altogether, especially family and childhood stuff, what I refer to as the *tadpole material* of our lives, the untrustworthy messy fuckin' frog spawn. I mean, let's face it, it's way too easy for anyone with any brand of an imagination or any kind of emotional problem to selectively edit or sneakily rewrite events to suit their own complicated agenda, their therapeutically, pharmaceutically recreated version of themselves, just like a little dictator. And even if you get some professional help years later, it's sometimes impossible to go back to the original pond because it's been left high and dry, bereft of any teeming, telltale clues. *Hey*, maybe you've filled it in and built a Happy Family theme park over it.

I'd be reluctant to say that my silence had to do with just one particular thing, with the rich kids screaming in the school shed, my skin erupting violently, or my voice breaking at the boy scouts' crackling fire. It was more a feeling of sands shifting within, of creaking components rearranging themselves, of various voices competing for the microphone in my head; and then one part—the soft, malleable child part—falling away slowly, like a lunar module. And the other adult part failing to attach itself to the rocket ship right away.

Prolonged, elastic panic. What seemed like years of waiting for heart and brain to desist, hiss, and finally slow down. I shot up and sprouted out. My feet and hands seemed to acquire a will and a rising, threshing temperature all their own. I was at least three times stronger than any boy my age, at least as strong as any man my size. You may think that's an immediate advantage, but it isn't, because no matter what happens, no matter how many of them wait, like jackals, outside the changing rooms grinning, no matter how many of them snap open your metal locker and throw your personal shit, your diary, your drawings all over the floor and you're picking up the wet pages of your soggy life, it's always a case of *but look at the sheer bloody size of you.* You're constantly in the wrong. You're an *animal, a tyke, a throwback.*

To what, Dad?

I'd seen my first porno pictures where there was all this spunking up on tits and faces, what they call *the money shots,* and in the shiny magazines the sperm was Moby-Dick white. I'd been whacking off a lot, I mean, what else do you do after school when you've been moved down the country and you don't know a single soul except the local doctor with his little leather bag, the priest in the confessional and the butcher who gives you scraps for your dog? So, I used to beat my meat. A lot.

My sperm came out snot green.

I got it into my thick skull that I was an alien. Yes I know that sounds ridiculous, and it is, but I was fourteen for fuck's sake. I became converted by the idea that I was not normal, that I was not *of this world*, that I was in fact a brother from another planet, that as soon as I had sex with a girl all of this would be announced to the world. There'd be this big investigation and international manhunt, they'd find my diaries and capture my confessor and make him talk, and he'd tell them what I said I'd like to do to my sisters, you know the sort of thing, making them drink twenty litres of tepid sea water, wrapping them up in barbed wire, forcing them to roll down steep hills, *fast*; what I'd like to do to my old fella and his pipe *puff, puff and what precisely is your point, Trevor;* my piano teacher and her metronome which seemed to have built into it the beat of other boys acquiring friends steadily. Then the beat of feet retreating as I approached.

They'd put me in this program where I'd be studied and where they'd do that *X-File* stuff . . . *Bend over, open wide, does this bit come off? Sorry. Jeez Pete, look at this, the guy's hands are kinda like flippers, let's put him in the water tank, see how fast he can go.*

And you know that ringing you get in your ears, real high and pure, almost like computer music? Well, I was getting that quite a lot in those days and was convinced it was my old alien buddies trying to contact me, or send me some Pharaoh-coded message that I was no longer able to decipher, having hung around with my pooch for too long.

In the end it was really unnerving me and I developed a very short fuse and like I said I was becoming embroiled in quite a lot of fistfights and just because you win, or emerge unscathed, it doesn't necessarily mean you enjoy it. And I used to get physically sick after some swimming races what with the rank smell of chlorine, the bayonet screams of the crowd as you twisted your head up for hot, competition air. Then, afterwards, flip-flop thoughts slapping cold wet tiles: *Please, no smart comments in the shower. Please, not another round of carpark fuckin' aggro.*

I couldn't take it any longer, the pressure-cooker singing. I couldn't sleep, which isn't good for the short fuse either, and eventually I stole into my mother's room, woke her, and told her what was eating me up.

When I finished she just laughed her tits off, which I felt was *incredibly* inappropriate and she said I was perfectly normal, that my father had snot green spunk too and sure wasn't I here, larger than life, sitting on the bed beside her?

'Aren't ya a right eejit, Stretch, worrying yourself sick about something as ridiculous as that?' Stretch was her nickname for me and I hated it as I felt I *had* been stretched, maybe a bit too far.

Ma tried her best but she failed to convince me because as far as I was concerned there was a high probability the old man was not my real father, and we'll get into all that stuff later. But even if he was, there was a pretty good chance he was an alien too and the alien nation we belonged to were kind of like cats in the way that parents and offspring didn't really bother to get to know one other.

You know what I mean: your cat has kittens so you give one to the neighbours down the road outside Mass one Sunday on a velvet cushion, and one year later you have a red lemonade and Marietta biscuit tea party to reintroduce the clan. You have all the little kids from the road come in to watch, you maybe even charge a few pence admission, so what? And you do a speech about families and reunions and there's unrealistic expectation in the air, very fuckin' unrealistic. Because right away the mother cat tries to knock the shit out of her own son, hissing and spitting, her electric tail standing up like the pole on the back of a dodgem car.

Ma was stroking my head, saying it was crazy how I let these things build up inside, *fester,* but that at least I was talking again.

Her voice sounded fake however and she *had* been an amateur actress in college, she might even have won some silver medals for her performance in Tennessee Williams way back when. But she wasn't winning any now in her lilac, overdone room.

When I sat up and looked at her she just smiled and said, 'What?' when she knew what I was trying to ask. I kept staring and willing her, *Come on, Ma, for fuck's sake*, but it didn't work because she just smiled and said, 'What, son? Go on.'

I wanted to. I wanted to scream, *Is he or is he not my fuckin' father?* but the words got trapped and nothing came out except my milk-sour, anxious, adolescent breath, because my stomach was in a state of high anxiety, had been for quite a while.

I ended up seeing this gentle old country doctor in a rambling house full of Buddhas, plants and stone statues way up in the Wicklow hills. He told me I reminded him of a giant turtle from the South Seas—he even promised to help me come out of my shell. It was pretty embarrassing having to jerk off into a little specimen jar and have the contents sent off to a lab in Dublin. I had stored up a lot of this stuff (not sperm, but notions, ideas, doubts) and I just couldn't stop talking; during the vow of silence my voice had changed register and it sounded awesome, really heartbroken, like Iggy Pop on a *bad* day.

He listened sometimes he'd smile and nod, and I'd smile and say it was OK if he wanted to laugh, that I found it all kind of ludicrous too. I told him I'd taken the not-fitting-in concept and basically run a bit too far with it. In the end he would just laugh his thick wool socks off, especially when I talked about my sisters and my old fella.

He said comforting things to me, that it was a great gift to be able to make people laugh and that on a more serious note it was perfectly acceptable to think strange thoughts about family and authority figures, *look to Aristotle*; that he would be very surprised indeed if any single notion that entered my head was not a notion that some other fine young man, or indeed some nice young lady, was not having about his or her father, or piano teacher, or swimming coach. And that if I didn't enjoy the swimming, I should give it up altogether, *throw in the towel*, because doing things we don't like creates internal strife that could lead ultimately to repressed rage. But actually I did enjoy it because in and under the water I was in my element, I could feel my massive hands pulling like oars on a galley full of slaves and with each stroke I drew ahead of the competition, with each kick of my clown feet the distance between me and the rest of the world both lengthened and diminished.

I was the one in control, breathing.

And I didn't feel odd, disjointed, or distorted. In fact, sometimes I felt quite beautiful, like a porpoise or a white dolphin.

And before you go and say there's no such thing you should read up a bit on your sea- and ocean-going creatures because there are white dolphins in the Amazon; the most amazing thing about them is they're born completely blind.

It was the gentle old country doctor with the yellowed cellophane holding his specs together, the crooked smile and the tiny glass of golden whiskey at his patched elbow who encouraged me to start devouring the same books my family did, to 'level the playing field.' And it was he who told me that my opinions were just as valid as theirs, but if I wanted to be a 'true counter-revolutionary' (here he winked and I knew she'd told him and we'll get to it later) then I had to get stuck in again, become a part of things, that too many young Irish men sat on the fence with their inherited fears and ancient, inferiority complexes only to become permanent 'hurlers on the ditch.'

Actually, he had quite a few good phrases such as 'you're talking pure tarmac now' and 'I think the rainwater's getting in again.' Anyway, in his own quiet undemanding way he really urged me to show them what I could be. And I did start studying after that and it was amazing the way my grades began to soar, not in every single subject, fair enough, but in enough to make my egghead sisters think twice before they began to blow trumpets at the dinner table.

It didn't put paid to their embarrassing pictures in the *Wicklow People* however. And when I explained to them that they should exercise a bit of restraint on the old PR front they just looked at me aghast as if I had no right to even utter the word *restraint*. I explained to them that I could've had my mug shot in the local rag every other week since I was constantly winning medals and cups for swimming, even setting the odd Inter-Provincial record, but I mean, after one or two stories the readers get the message, don't they?

The oldest one, she just smiled and said that winning 'trinkets' for mere sporting achievements—as opposed to earning distinctions for academic excellence—was, well, so *Bolshevik*, 'rather like comparing chess to draughts, or the construction of the Pyramids at Giza to the erection of a rudimentary bungalow in Cavan,' or some such patronizing shit.

Then I'd have this excellent Jimmy Cagney voice in my head urging, *Why don't ya shove dat baked potato into her noisy gob an' seal it shut foreva?*

I knew more about restraint than they imagined.

Relax, we'll get to Ed in a minute and he'll still be there waiting at the end of the corridor, I mean, it's not like he has a court appointment with Judge Judy now, is it?

And I agree, all this hopping around is tremendously distracting and chaotic; but you see that's because it's a human life being laid out here, pal. *My* life. And I reserve the right to step in and out of my past and present, in and out of my memories and mishaps, like a demented céilí dancer. Don't worry. You'll get used to it. Like old Fyodor Dostoevsky says, man gets used to everything: lies mounting; the debt to compromise accumulating as we settle for less and less, especially in ourselves; watching dreams dissipate; watching people curling up and dying; watching people walking away and feeling all manner of things sliding, especially *hope* and *control*.

Yeah, those two in particular.

Ed's room reeks of medicine and ethyl chloride, the stuff they dab on your nipples before they pierce you. It also reeks of Death. He is incredibly thin, like a communion wafer, and unbelievably pale. David Bowie (circa *Low*) heroin-chic pale.

His hair is long, thin and straggly. It makes his already elongated face look like it is in the process of melting, like Swiss cheese, only with eyes for holes. His are weak and watery. He is so frail it is frightening.

No one at the Clinic was this small (bar Dalek, obviously), and if you insist on an animal, it's a white church mouse with a soft blue rug draped across its knobbly knees.

'Hi. I'm Ed.'

'How's it going, Ed? I'm Trevor.'

'Mum says you're. I. Rish?'

'That's right, yeah.'

'Where. A. Bouts. Are. You. From?'

'Dublin. But my family lives in Wicklow.'

'Wick-low?'

'It's out in the country. The sticks.'

'The other. Guy who. Was. Works here. He's from Scotland.'

'Really?'

'Maybe you could. Meet. Him. Later?'

'That'd be nice. Thank you.'

The 'thank you' makes him squirm. As he smiles you can see his teeth need *serious* attention, which means bad breath is going to be an issue, but you can't blame Ed: you can only question the diligence of the other so-called companion.

Back at the Clinic I had become obsessed with oral hygiene and initiated a campaign of letters and phone calls to the Eastern Health Board, sometimes as many as twenty a day. It ended with them delivering 150 electric toothbrushes along with a handwritten note: 'You win.'

Ed has questions written on a sheet attached to one of those metal clipboards people used to carry around to make themselves look important. His knuckle-hands shake when he lifts it.

'We should. Get. Started.'

'OK.'

'How. Many. Brothers. And sisters do. You. Have?'

'No brothers, more's the pity. Three sisters, all much older.'

'Do you get. On. With. Them?'

'No.'

'Oh.'

'Sorry. Maybe I should've lied?'

'No. It's good that. You. Were. Honest.'

'Yeah, honesty is always the best policy.' A pause as he scans the questions. He has very few eyelashes left. 'What sort of. Music. Do you. Like?' 'I have pretty varied tastes. What do you like?' 'Rick. Wakeman. Ever. Hear of. Him?' 'Sure. *Journey to the Centre of the Earth.* I think I still have that one at home. On vinyl.'

'You like. Yes?'

'Yes.'

He smiles, so do I. 'I really like John what's-his-face's voice.'

'An-derson's.'

'Yeah. It's very, you know, distinctive. In fact, I genuinely believe "Owner of a Lonely Heart" was a minor fuckin' classic.'

See the white church mouse swallow palely, and smile. See the coated, discoloured teeth. Hear the grey gums click, and stick. See the tiny eyelids, which have little blue veins like the ones that run across his mother's tits, jump. And quiver with delight.

See me play him like a pin-ball machine he lights up inside. 'You. Really. Like. "Owner. Of a. Lonely. Heart?"'

'Yeah, I really do.'

He squirms and worms around in the chair; it's clearly his alltime favourite ditty. And I'm lying through my teeth, obviously, I mean, I hate that kind of turgid, overblown *shite*. But you'd swear someone had just informed him he could rise up like Lazarus, walk out the door and start a career as a fuckin' pole dancer. And in his next breathless sentence he calls me 'man' and suddenly we're getting on like a house on fire, except I'm not being me, I'm being this upbeat, hippy-dippy version of me. But that's OK, we all lie in order to get work or put some food on the table, or achieve some easy sex, and in the grand scheme of things it's no biggie, now is it?

Ed has a Pink Floyd poster over his bed, you know the one with the big inflatable pig floating over this industrial chimneystack in Europe, so I think of his mother, obviously. Then I ask, 'Ever been to a Pink Floyd gig, Ed?'

'No.'

'Oh, OK.'

There's a pause as he tries to play it cool, except he can't. In the end he blurts out kind of high-pitched, 'You?' 'Just the once, yeah.' 'Where?' 'Stuttgart.' 'Cool.' 'Yeah. But it was a long time ago. I was just a kid really.' 'Tell me. Please.' In that *please*, there's quiet desperation. 'There was this huge wall on stage, right?' 'Right.' 'And thousands of people from all over Europe are sitting there smoking dope and dropping Egyptian Eye acid. And next minute this voice rings out—Gilmour, or maybe it was Waters—and it asks, "Is there anybody out there?"'

'Wow.'

'And it echoes around the stadium. *Is there anybody out there, out there, out there . . . ?* The place erupts like a tidal wave and this East Berlin chick with racoon circles painted under her eyes and cropped blonde hair—sorta like Daryl Hannah in *Bladerunner*—who'd been dancing real aggressively on her sweeney . . . '

'Sweeney?'

'Sweeney Todd. It means . . . *on her own.*'

'OK.'

'So, she's dancing on her sweeney, real fuckin' firestarter stuff, and she's freaking out the clogs and sandals brigade.' 'Clogs. And. Sandals. Brigade?' 'Come on Ed, get with the programme. Hippys, man.' 'Hippys. Right.' 'Anyway, she launches herself at me and starts playing serious tonsil hockey until I discover there's a tab on her tongue, which I swallow, then we trip out together. Sparks fly and static crackles every time we touch. All the bricks in the wall come tumbling down and a guy on stilts with a big Medusa rubber head comes out—he's the Evil Headmaster—and we sing at the top of our lungs, "We don't need no education, no dark sarcasm in the classroom, hey teacher, leave those kids alone."'

'Fuckin'. A.'

'Yeah. And the communist girl is holding my hand up as if I'd won the Grand Prix and she keeps circling underneath, smiling up with these painfully honest eyes and the thing is, you can really be yourself man, I mean there's no need to pretend.'

'Cool.'

'Yeah. And you know what's even cooler?'

'No?'

'Next morning when we wake up she puts her hand in under the scratchy bri-nylon pillow and takes out the remains of this fat joint. She lights it, takes this huge toke, *ppphhhhhh,* then she starts the day off singing, "We don't need no educa-tion," except her voice is really deep and sexy, you know, from all the horny stuff we'd been doing the night before and . . . '

Poor jerky Ed is nodding his head like one of those little toy dogs you sometimes see on the dashes of cars in suburbia and you'd swear he'd been there holding his pink plastic lighter up in the air—impossible, because with his wire-hanger arms he wouldn't be able to lift a feather, not for more than five fuck-in' seconds.

But mostly it's impossible because I've never been to a Pink Floyd gig, and because I've never shagged any communist girls. And before you go and get all judgmental, what you need to realize is: a companion must be able to paint pictures, must be able to open windows on other worlds, maybe even worlds that don't exist. Why? Because the one that Ed and his kind find themselves trapped in, like slow-winged insects after sum-mer has slipped away, isn't exactly a barrel of fuckin' laughs, now is it?

I lived with this smiling guy for a bit in southern India, lead-ing him around on a little silk rope while he sang these excel-lent, ancient songs to passersby.

I couldn't pronounce his name so I just called him Sockets, which seemed fitting because he'd been born without eyes and in their place had these huge, sunken holes in his face. He called me Mister Bigman almost immediately after we'd shaken hands and he'd measured my head with his hot brown mitts.

Sockets could do weird things with his mouth, little fire-cracker *clickety-clacks* of the tongue, ululations, vibrations. He could also open his mouth wide as a hippo. I remember his tonsils well: pink rubber stalactites. I ate what he ate, drank what he drank, and we spilt everything fifty-fifty. (When I was leaving I gave it all back, obviously, secreting it away in his Dick Whittington bundle, though for days after I was worried sick he wouldn't cop and would let it all drop. Being blind, like.)

I tell you one thing, for a skinny little bloke he could really chow down and I never saw anyone take such good care of their teeth. They really were snow white. He was forever cleaning and picking at them, and if he wasn't chewing parsley or mint he was rubbing some powder stuff into his gums. Still, I reckon if you were born without eyes you'd take pretty good care of your remaining bits.

Sockets was either the best actor I'd ever seen, and I've seen some good ones, my mother included, or else he was without doubt the happiest guy I'd ever stumbled across, always whistling or humming or practising his scales, although I really do believe that singing for a living gives you some kind of natural high, increasing as it must the levels of serotonin in the brain, turning dopamine neurotransmitters on like a steady little tap. Take those big, lush opera singers. Divas. They always look permanently post-coital whenever I see a photo of one of them I always think they'd make wonderful wives: great in the sack, incredibly competent in the kitchen, the sort of women who have amazing soft skin, excellent taste in La Perla underwear and who laugh out loud with their rich, musical voices at least one hundred times a day.

Which, you have to admit, would be really kind of nice.

Anyway, I used to observe Sockets going about his business, lighting little fires, brewing up, chowing down and humming away in the shade. Eventually I figured if he's happy, and he genuinely seemed to be, then there was really no good reason why I shouldn't be. I mean, everyone's mother dies sometime, right?

I was being inordinately careful not to bang on about it until we got to know each other better, basically because I think it's a cliché, you know: 'Lonely, Befuddled and Bewildered Irish Man Misses his Dearly Departed Mother.' So, without getting into the whole shebang right this very second, let's just say that my mother and I got on *extremely* well, that she was one of those excellent people with whom time never drags its heels, one of that rare breed who doesn't suffer the urge to be all serious and grown up the whole fuckin' time.

OK?

3

Four days a week to begin with, then he'll increase it to five, sometimes six, if that's not too much of a problem. And when the other guy is away, I might also have to do nights. But you know, maybe nights might suit someone like me since they pay more, due to the *anti-social as-pect*.

I'm trying not to laugh because I'm thinking, *Well it's not exactly going to be a rave during the day, now is it?* And I break out in this big smile, which fades when he says,

'Can you. Start. Right. Away?'

'What do you mean by *right away*?'

'To. Morrow. Morning.'

'Jesus. *Eh*, I could make a few calls, but . . . '

'It would. Mean. A lot.'

'I may not be able to make it first thing.'

'That's. OK. Takes me a. While. To get. Moving.'

'OK.'

'Say, eleven?'

'Eleven bells. OK.'

'One. Last. Thing. Do you. Ssss-smoke?'

'No.'

'Good. I can't be. A-round people. Who. Do.'

'I understand.'

'My dad will talk. Money. And. Ssstuff. With. You.'

'Great.'

'There's one. Thing. You need. To. Understand.'

A pause, which he controls by staring at the pedals.

'He's paying. You. But I. Will be the. One that. Will. Fire you. If. It doesn't work. Out. OK?'

'OK, Ed, but I see no reason why it won't.'

He says nothing; in fact, he seems to be having difficulty operating his neck muscles. Then at last his head rises up, like a snake being charmed from a basket. He looks straight at me. His pupils go big, then suddenly small, like a jellyfish with purple veins out in the cold, grey Atlantic. And if you cross him, he'll be one of those creatures that rolls up and becomes spiky and impossible to communicate with.

He yawns artificially, then waves his stiff wrist on the handle of his chair, like a crash test dummy after a simulated car crash, as if to say, *Hey man, all of this is nothing really, just a minor detail.* But in those weak, watery eyes he can't conceal a single, shallow emotion; you can see straight off the bat Ed is a very poor liar.

Then again, you would be too if you didn't get out in the real world very often.

It's not going to be easy looking after someone rich and spoiled like Ed. It's never that easy looking after anyone, though personally I believe looking after yourself is hardest. I mean, you know *exactly* what your brain and body demand, you know *exactly* what not to give them, yet for some strange reason it's really fuckin' hard to nourish them consistently. It's like keeping goldfish: if you empty too much of the dried fly stuff on the surface you think, *What the hell?* but then you come back to find the fuckers bellyup and bloated with these little ropes of spiralling shite dangling from their fish asses so they look like underwater balloons someone suddenly let go of.

Sockets was particularly pleasant and easygoing, but even with him you could see occasional doubt sprout. He'd wake up, stretch and call out my name. There'd be a tiny bit of fear in his voice, and I'd say nothing, then he'd call out my name again. 'Oh, Mister Bigman?' And there'd be an increase of anx-

iety in it, he'd maybe sniff the air or wait a moment before calling out again. And this time there'd be an element of desperation in it. 'Mister Bigman, my friend, I know you are there hiding,' and still I'd say nothing. Finally, I'd laugh out loud and
say, 'Over here, Sockets, you baldy blind bastard.' Or maybe
I'd say, 'Hey, Sockets. No point sniffing around for me when
all you can smell is your own fuckin' parsley breath.'

Or I'd say nothing at all, just wait, and eventually throw something at him, maybe a pebble, or my big flat sandal. It would
hit him on his little Malteser head, *boink*, and he'd smile, a
huge big electric thing, like neon. 'I knew all along you were
there, my friend. I knew all along because, you see, I have more
than a degree of faith in you.'

He banged on about Faith, Hope and Charity quite a bit,
but he was a good friend, which means he didn't judge. Sometimes when I got plastered on cheap beer or stoned out of my
tree and began to wail like a fool, or if I got angry about my
family and started roaring abuse at the stars, he'd calm me
down, make up a nice soft bed beneath a Bunyan tree, maybe
even place some special lineament or herb on a tiny little pillow that he carried in his bundle.

'Thanks, Sockets. You're a gentleman and a scholar.'

It was quite easy waking up all hungover and ashamed the
next day beside a blind peasant who would later be pulling like
a goat on the rope when he got panicky on a crowded, sticky
street. You certainly felt less self-conscious than you would if,
say, you'd made an ass of yourself at an after-hours party in the
Village full of designers, writers and poets with vintage clothing and pneumatic Eastern European girlfriends with perfect
skin, remarkable English. And astonishingly cold lips.

To be honest, the only thing I *didn't* like about Sockets was
the way he'd hunker down in the dirt to take a light brown
dump, right in fuckin' front of me. But then again he wasn't
the only one in India who was fond of doing that.

India wasn't exactly all fun and games and a lot of people might be envious of me, you know, out there in the big wide world travelling around with my knapsack on my back; but the truth is it can get pretty lonely and there are plenty of days you'd pay a lot of cash to have a proper conversation, no flowery eighteenth-century English, no false laughter from someone looking for a tip, no repeating the most simple, elementary things, over and over again.

Like your address—as if they were ever going to visit.

We don't realize it, but we have quite a lot of space in the Western World, and it can be quite hard when everyone insists on standing with bits of themselves rubbing off you in post office, railway and bus queues, and you have to remember they're all wearing the sheerest of cotton, and let's just say not everyone had the same standards of hygiene as Sockets.

I was starting to feel undone. I mean, there was always someone pointlessly beating some oddly shaped drum, or blowing into something that looks like a bugle but sounds like a nanny goat screaming. I remember one searingly hot day when I got lost and stopped to look at my guidebook I was surrounded suddenly by all these smelly little mahogany people who seemed to have their own fan club of oversized horseflies and gnats. Their carved hands were all over me, pulling at the book, breaking its spine, and how the fuck could they help me when none of them could read or even speak fuckin' English?

I let out this roar. *'Get the fuck away!'* It frightened even me, and everything seemed to suddenly go quiet, as if God had hit the volume button on his remote control in the sky all colour leached from the orange sun. Bangra music from clapped-out taxis was suddenly snapped off. People scattered. Black birds with red beaks flew silently from dead trees.

And I knew it was time to go somewhere, and just put the head down.

I'd been at this moon party in Goa, which was probably quite beautiful five hundred years ago, and I'd been smoking *charras*, this Indian shit, without much of a buzz coming on when all of a sudden I felt incredibly ill at ease, not just the old dry mouth and rapid heartbeat which we all get, but this terrible lead weight attaching itself to the heartstrings, as if loads of Lilliputians had clambered into my chest with ladders, ropes and mallets and were hammering and heaving my heart down into my boots. Except that I was in my bare feet.

This white South African Rasta man with cheap beach tattoos was trying to pass me a bottle of hooch and I hated the way it felt when he touched me, repeatedly. So I told him to stop and he said he was just trying to be neighbourly, and I told him to shag off back to South Africa and try to be neighbourly with some black people for a change. And my feet seemed suddenly to be made of clog wood and they looked like big puppet attachments and I was scared stiff to look at my hands.

It was all a bit much, the bassline of the music ripping into me, all these skinny Aussie and English women with their eyes closed gyrating in the MTV moonlight, and I started running, really pumping the thighs hard. After an age, I found a place behind a rotten old rowboat where there was no one smoking, or fucking, or sucking bits of each other, or drinking hot beer, or rolling spliffs, or splitting up for the fourth time in two weeks.

I lay down and looked up into the 2D sky—cheap pyrotechnics and unconvincing shooting stars—and I heard teenagers laughing behind the black scudding clouds, like Beavis and Butthead. I sank into the sand.

And the sinking feeling, it stayed with me, clung to me, hung around me like a smell, the feeling of the world being some kind of perverse joke, a grotesque, ridiculous fuckin' cartoon. And I went on the move again, holding onto tickets and chits on bockety trains and lurching buses in places no one ever inspects such things, basically because I felt I had to prove I'd paid in to the horrible, universal fun fair.

When you're feeling like that, you invite short breath and illness, and you try to breathe in and out through your nose because it has little seaweed hairs that can stop dirt and foreign bacteria lodging in your sore throat. And you can't relax around other people, especially ones with huge coldsores on their lips jabbering in foreign tongues, you always feel you've misplaced something, your hands keep flying in and out of your pockets, like yellow cuckoos.

And the best thing you can do is to check yourself in some-where that used to be a palace or the home of some Raj, some-where with air con and satellite, proper toilets that you don't have to squat over, and intelligent staff who whisper and avert their eyes, who sleep on little mats outside your huge teak door, who check on you night and day, who make mint tea without being asked, who close doors gently.

And just wait it out. Patiently.

Except the thing was, by some freak coincidence—and this is hundreds maybe even thousands of miles from the lurch-ing bus—who the fuck is staying in the hotel? Only the hippy American. She spies me with the manager one morning and starts sending notes up to my room, and baskets of overripe fruit. I detest bad manners, so I make one brief public appear-ance.

She invites me to swim with her in the pool, which sort of brought me back to life. Then she insisted on buying me din-ner and I can't really remember what happened except I drank way too much and began talking up a storm.

It finished with us back in her room, her holding me, telling me it was OK, let it all out, 'That's it Trevor, there is nothing to be ashamed of,' as if she had a clue what I was bab-bling about because, as usual, I'd left out quite a lot of background material and quite a large percentage of the truth. We must have sat there for about four hours with her just rocking me and afterwards she told me I needed to have more faith in myself, that I was a very, very good person. But look, if someone thinks you've had a hand in saving them from destruction, they're not going to listen to your stories properly. It's like when see your girlfriend acting in a play and you won't admit, you *can't*, that it's total crap and she's incredibly false, shrill and transparent. You try to pretend that the set is realistic when really it's fuckin' laughable and it keeps moving. You can see the other actors getting ready to make their awkward entrance. You can hear them stepping over each other's lines. And really it's amazing how easy it is for us humans to kid and cod ourselves, to hoodwink and hide inside, holding onto the little bits of so-called truth we need, bite-size, convenient, *twisted*.

I remember drifting off to sleep in the arms of the American, her stroking my shaven skull, telling me there was no need to be afraid, it didn't matter who my father was, that I was one of the good ones, 'one of the truly sensitive ones.'

When I woke she led me into the bathroom where she'd lit a hundred candles and run this really hot bath with scented oils and she sat there on the edge anointing my head, which you have to admit is pretty weird.

She said she knew by looking into my eyes that I was a 'benign and positive force.' And like I said earlier, people know jack shit by looking into your eyes. Anyway, mine were closed because the oil was stinging, and before that they were full of water from crying, and before that they had goggles on in the pool because you can't trust Indians with chlorine, and before that they were red from drink and drugs, raw from dust and sleepless nights.

The American bird with the soft, glowing skin was wrong, way wrong. Of course it matters who your fuckin' father was.

Of course it matters how you feel about yourself deep down. Of course it matters if you're scared.

Especially if you're scared of yourself.

Ed flicks his hair with his right hand, then eventually his left. *Fly away Peter*. Pause. *Fly away Paul*. Pause.

As he twitches in the chair the fabric of his pale Levis catches and two sweat patches become visible on the black vinyl seat beneath. *Jesus*, the poor bastard's thighs are the size of curtain rods.

'I guess. That's. It. Then.'

'Sorry?'

'You're. Hired. Con. Gratulations.'

'Thanks.'

'See you. To. Morrow. Eleven. Bells.'

'OK. Thanks again. You won't regret it, Ed. Good luck.'

I stand and he smiles at the size of me, as if I'm some kind of exotic pet. Then he imitates the *good luck* the way Americans do, turning the phrase around in his mouth like a pebble. You can see he loves having foreign people around, loves the way we speak, we're probably like little laboratory experiments. As I walk out I hear him pick up the little phone slowly he tells his mother not to take any more calls—he is 'very, very tired.'

Except, the old sow must still be sore about me outwitting her because in the tiny earpiece I can hear, 'You sure about him, Ed?'

He pauses before saying, 'I'm sure.' She says something else about me but he reminds her how it was *she* who picked the Scottish fuck, 'And look what he. Turned out. To be.'

Feels quite strange to be standing out here in the corridor listening to their voices I'm thinking the pair of them are like children with empty tin cans and a length of twine running between the rooms I can almost hear the ghost of a wan, sickly child; as you can imagine, his laughter hasn't been heard pealing in the longest fuckin' time.

The door of the Judge's room opens. He steps out into the corridor, looks at the open door of Ed's room, then the open door of his wife's, then to and fro, like someone watching slow mo' tennis. Each time he turns to the side these loose tent folds of flesh on his neck sway; *he's* the real sea turtle eased from its shell. Finally he shakes his weary head once, twice, three times. Then he sighs and steps back in.

Without a single, solitary word.

The cook is in the middle of doing her thing when the little phone rings. She answers it, sighs, and points at a chair. She turns her big, broad back and starts muttering darkly as she produces a willow-pattern plate, piles it high and places it before me.

'Thank you.'

'Uh-huh.'

She's got a little layer of cheese, then breaded veal, then a little layer of ham, then more veal. There are sweet potatoes and yellow corn with tiny red peppers mixed in. Everything is piping hot and it tastes amazing, except she just stands there, *staring*. She's one of those people that isn't in the least bit bothered by silence, and neither am I, save when I'm the only one eating and a jet black stranger is watching.

Finally, after a long pause, she says it's real nice to see someone enjoy her food, but it's been ages since I've had a home-cooked meal and I'm probably shovelling it in a bit too fast. It's like when you're in a fancy restaurant and the waiter asks, *And how are you enjoying your Dover sole, sir?* just after you've lobbed in a huge forkful, which is a roundabout way of saying my mouth is jammed and I'm forced to just nod enthusiastically and wave my fork as if to say, *Mmm, this really is lovely, yes indeed, absolutely smashing.* But all she does is nod her big heavy head and say, 'U-huh.'

After I finish I sigh out loud and tell her there's a distinct possibility that her breaded veal was one of the finest bits of nosebag I'd ever had the pleasure of. She seems to like the word *nosebag.* In any event she smiles and says, 'Nice of you to say so.'

But it's too casual. So I say, 'No, I'm deadly serious, you can really fuckin' cook,' and she says she knows that already but you can see from the cheshire grin on her big black face that she really likes being complimented.

Then again, I don't ever remember meeting a human being who didn't, apart from The Captain, who had serious issues about his essays being patronized by a moon-faced, overgrown fucker with no formal training, no letters after his name and no halfway plausible stories as to how he'd ended up with a bunch of freaks and deformed geeks in electric chairs in a creaking, leaking shack at the edge of the fuckin' universe.

Or words to that effect.

The cook gets me a beer—Red Stripe, Jamaican stuff—plus one for herself. You can see she's strong because when she flips the lids with the opener tied to her apron she doesn't miss a beat.

'So. What *you* good at?'

I say that I honestly don't know, which isn't true because there are a number of things I'm good at such as long-distance swimming and cheering sick people up. When I worked as a DJ on hospital radio after my shift was over I'd stroll around the wards, I swear to Christ some of those rheumatic old farts really and truly *adored* me. It's just that I have this rule about blowing your own trumpet, probably comes from overexposure to my sisters: I wish Americans had it too.

'Well?'

'Well what?'

'You gots to be good at somethin'.'

'Do I?'

'Uh-huh.'

'I'm good at getting into trouble.'

'Shit, I know that jus' by lookin' at you. You jus' outta the army?' 'No.' 'Jus' outta jail?' 'No.' 'You from Ire-land?' 'Yeah.' 'You one of them terrorist-types? Gonna blow the place up? Send Ed and his chair sky high?' 'Maybe.' '*Maybe*, he say. What you work at last?' 'I was a waiter.' 'Don't look like no waiter.' 'Really. What does a waiter look like?' 'Smaller. Neater. Faster on his feet.' 'Yeah, well, wasn't exactly my finest hour.' 'What happened?' 'A fat guy in a leisure suit clicked his fingers at me.' 'Shit, I know that deal. You like to get high?' '*Eh*, sometimes. Not really. No.' 'You some kinda religious freak?'

'No.'

'You gonna move in when Scotty leave?'

'Is he leaving?'

'Sure is.'

Maybe Ed's a better liar than I thought.

'So, you gonna move in?'

'I guess so.'

'Why?'

'Beggars can't be choosers.'

'*Beggars can't be choosers.* Where you at now?'

'Astoria.'

'Shit. All them Greeks.'

'Telly Savalas was born there.'

'Who?'

'*Kojak.* It's a very old detective series. On TV.'

'I know it. Ain't that old.'

'Well, he plays the baldy lieutenant. With the lollipop.'

'He a Greek?'

'Well he ain't fuckin' Irish, now is he?'

She laughs—it's an excellent sound. 'No. And he ain't Jamacian, that's for sure.' 'No. He's an extremely white, bald Greek guy whose suits have very loud linings.' 'And whose face have a lollipop stuck up in it.' 'Yeah. That's the guy. He had a hit single once.' 'Yeah?' 'It was called "*If.*"' 'Shit, I could write me that: if only I'd listened to mama, if only I'd studied in school, if only I hadn't taken the easy way out, if only I hadn't been a fool.'

There's a bit of a pause as we sip and stare. The whites of her eyes are unnaturally clear; I'd say she uses some sort of super strong drop and that's when I spy the half-smoked joint on the sill.

'Want some free advice?'

'No such thing.'

'Maybe. But you move in they own your lily-white ass. Wake you up middle of the night if Ed wants to take so much as a leak, an' most times he can't squeeze more'n a drop from that miniature dick a' his. Send you out to the all-night pharmacy ain't a goddamn pill in the world gonna help that fucked-up rich boy. You got a girlfriend?'

'No.'

'You some sort of over-growed faggot?'

'No.'

'Good. You want some of my pie?'

'What is it?'

'*What is it*, he say. Gettin' fussy already. Blueberry 'n apple.'

'I could be tempted.'

'Yes child, I believe you could. What's your name anyway?'

'Trevor.'

'Trevor. Pleased to meet you. I'm Ellie.'

She holds out her surprisingly small hand. When I hold out mine she slides her palm along, real slow, and our skin makes this excellent sandpaper noise, only softer. It's the first time I've actually touched a totally black person (Sockets was light brown, like good firewood) except of course for this Nigerian woman on the last bus home from Dublin who had this incredible corkscrew hair like *Bride of Frankenstein*. It actually had currents of electricity running through it.

I'm smiling now, partly because of all the fuckin' fuss on the bus after I'd touched her hair and she screamed and everyone presumed I'd said something racist in her ear. But mostly I'm smiling because of the way Ellie said *my pie* as she stood up and rubbed the tops of her thighs with her small, strong hands. You can see even though she's a good bit older that she really enjoys flirting and when she catches me examining her big old ass as she bends over at the oven she gives it a little shake, like an otter doing construction work at a dam.

Ellie says she reckons there might be one or two things I'm good at, but sneaking a look sure as hell ain't one. If I want to look I should just be straight up about it. Be a man. But she's only pretending to be annoyed. Really she is chuckling away, in fact she's having a rare old time to herself. I'm sorely tempted to ask for a swift hit off her joint, but I need to know someone *properly* before I can get stoned with them and remain, you know, comfortable in my own skin.

She puts down the pie and a clean fork. As I tuck in she puts her chin in her hands and whenever I look up she is staring.

In the big saucer eyes there's nothing but warmth, maybe even acceptance. And when she smiles it's one of those that leaves you no choice; you have to forget your cares, the pissy smell, the jellyfish eyes and the unsettling fact that so far no one has asked for a reference or even mentioned the fuckin' word *experience*.

Ellie asks me, '*How it is?*' I tell her that without a shadow of a doubt it's the finest piece of pie I've ever eaten. To prove it, I scrape the plate clean, then hold it aloft and lick it making *numyum* noises. She slaps my leg, tells me I'm a crazy Irish fool, a jughead, maybe even a crackhead, who knows. 'Some pretty weird peoples worked here.' Then she gets me another beer.

When I light up an after-dinner smoke she starts imitating Skippy the Bush Kangaroo, going *tsk tsk tsk* as she puts on the extractor fan and opens the little window. She turns around with a sea-shell ashtray in her hand she makes these big blow-fish eyes *you better not let them find out*, but I just exhale as if to say, *Fuck 'em*. And that's when she sparks up her little joint, blows out blue smoke, says, 'Yeah. You right about that, Clever.'

When the Judge calls me in to talk money she says not to be *'timidated*, not one little bit. That he's a real mean little sono-fabitch—'whatever figure he come up with, jus' look him in the beady eye an' multiply it by two'.

'Remember, Clever. What you think of as money, they think of as change. Chump change.'

I tell her relax, I'm not easily *'timidated*, except she's star-ing straight at my crotch while removing a bit of grass from her piano-key teeth. She sees me swallow then all of a sudden she just bursts out laughing, her shoulders shaking like Tommy Cooper. As she touches my cheek gently she says, 'I'm jus play-in' with you, baby. Princip-lee 'cause I like you. OK?'

'OK.'

And I haven't even started, not officially, but already this is looking like an excellent job possibly even better than the Clinic where some days your ribcage would ache from laughing at the things they said they'd do to their relatives and carers, if only they could lace up a pair of hob-nailers or wield a blackthorn stick for sixty seconds.

And sometimes they'd get so frustrated trying to talk about their pent-up emotions that they'd tie themselves in knots. One day, one badly-bearded bloke who cut himself a million times whenever he shaved, just gave up in mid-sentence and started imitating Bruce Lee instead, screaming *hiiii-ya, hiiii-ya,* doing this Woodie Woodpecker movement with his head. And in our imaginations we could see sandalled nuns and soutaned priests, disinterested doctors and cynical social workers flying through Chinese paper walls, one white-coated uppity doc getting his whirly stethoscope wrapped round his neck in tune to a whistling cartoon effect.

And The Captain is staring at me waiting, so I say, 'OK, if you got the use of your arms and legs back for one day, and one day only, what would you do with them?' And it wasn't as if there was a strict syllabus I had to adhere to, alright?

'I'd play a game of hurling, let them know who was Boss. After, I'd enjoy a nice, slow pint. Or two. Then, I'd drive up this leafy lane that runs behind my father's farm . . . '

I'm thinking, *Christ where's this going?*

'I'd park, put the handbrake on, then I'd turn to her and touch her face with my fingers, gently. I'd run my hands through her brown hair, softly. I'd hold her there against my chest for as many hours as I had left. That's what I'd do, alright? Are ya happy now, ya dozy fuckin' cunt ya?'

No one said anything for five full minutes I could feel this lump in my throat, as if it were cement hardening. Then he nodded slowly and I walked over, except it was one of those extremely long ones, like when you're walking down a hospital corridor after hearing bad news. I leaned down and hugged him, except hugging someone with no arms really is hard, seriously, you don't know if you're overdoing it or when to let go or anything. The Captain seemed relieved though, and he whispered, 'I'm sorry, Trevor' into my ear.

So I whispered into his, 'Me too.' But then I added, 'Even if you had two arms, I'd still kick your culchie ass 'round the fuckin' barna with my two tied behind my back.' He laughed out loud, and the awful thing was he owned this perfect set of Tom Cruise teeth.

Anyway the others, especially Dalek who hero-worshipped

the guy, saw that The Captain and I were finally destined to be friends. And there was this lovely release of tension. That was the great thing about the Clinic: when you stepped out after a day's teaching, it wasn't just that you realized how fortunate you were to have all your bits and bobs intact. No, you were nearly always empty of Fear. And if Fate put something in your way, some small opportunity, say a good-looking bird at a bus stop in the rain when you've an umbrella and she doesn't, then you wouldn't have to think twice, you really wouldn't give a shite if she said, *Eh, no thanks all the same.* You might even do a little jig in front of her, hopping up and down off the kerb singing a makey-up song about being all warm and dry under your brolly while she stood there doing a pretty good imper-sonation of a drowned rat.

I'm serious, when you work even for a little while with real-ly sick people, people at times too tired to eat or smile or lift up their heads or hands, when you arrive in late one Monday and everyone is all eyes down like dray horses, and they tell you that over the weekend someone you really liked *slipped away peacefully,* and there's another empty chair to contend with, well, that's when you realize how crude and abrupt this shitty life is. And you decide *formally* inside your head that you will never go in for regrets recriminations or any of that wishful thinking crap.

The little phone tinkles once again. Ellie stands and says, 'Uhhuh, uh-huh,' bit like a distracted Elvis Presley.

Then she hangs up and says the Judge wants to see me in his room. As I'm walking out she adds, 'He also say he had to ring his wife who didn't know you'd disappeared, then he had to ring up Ed who guess correctly you in the kitchen, eatin'.' But like I point out, what's the Judge getting all het-up about, it's not like he's calling long-distance now is it?'

And you can still hear her cello-laughter playing all the way down the hall she is calling things out 'bout the slippery Irish, how they been pullin' wool over people eyes for *hunnerts* of years, yeah, all the corruption in Boston, Philly, Chicago—you name it—slippery Irish always be at the *epicentre* of it.

The Judge doesn't invite me to sit, so I do.

He slides across a two-page document then produces a really nice fountain pen, one of those ones that can write upside down in an airplane. And because he expects me to sign on the spot I tell him I'll take it home and study it, if it's all the same.

That's when his grey eyes flash, and I wonder how much of him is left in Ed, and is that what's keeping him alive, *sheer fuckin' determination?*

'Normally, we pay fifteen dollars an hour.'

I'm excellent in these situations that basically involve just staring at the other party with a frank and honest face. It also helps if you visualize yourself as younger and more innocent, say an altar boy, or a tragically drowned version of yourself in your communion suit; if that's not working just picture this golden light around you, like in a painting by Leonardo.

'There are, *he-hem*, certain considerations for night and weekend work. As well as national holidays.'

Still I say nothing, just smile benignly. And to give Il Judgo his due, he's pretty good with the old silent treatment; it's like that scene in another spaghetti western, you know the one with the musical watches playing. So I'm smiling, and he's staring back, and the watches are tinkling, and in the end it's me that silently says 'uncle,' which I have to admit is extremely unusual but I was starting to get a right rictus pain in my cheek.

'Thing is, your Honour, the situation we find ourselves in is anything but normal.'

'In what respect?'

'In respect of the fact that your son is dying, sir. And needs someone with, you know, special talents.'

'And you're confident you possess such, *he-hem*, attributes?'

'Yes.'

'You have particular qualifications in this area?'

'Yes.'

And it depends on what you mean by *qualifications*. I mean, I don't have a piece of paper stating that I'll clean up puke and crap, or that I'll mop sweaty brows with distinction, or hold damp hands at night, or listen without judging to dreams that will never unfold. But then I'm not aware of any universities handing out such certificates in the first place, are you?

There's a bit of pause. I'm not sure who's in control of it but whoever speaks next will lose.

'*He-hem*. In that case, shall we say twenty dollars an hour?'

'Sorry, but this is not a situation I feel comfortable haggling over.'

'I see. Then without further ado, I propose twenty-five dollars an hour.'

'Forty. And forty-five for night and weekend work.'

'Thirty. And thirty-five for weekend and night work'

'Thirty-five, and forty for weekend and nights.'

'If you insist. I also propose a trial period. Six weeks?'

'Again, I have no wish to appear difficult or, you know, contrary . . . '

'But?'

'But the nature of this work is well, quite intimate and intense.'

'And?'

'And, both your son and I will know in a very short period whether or not it is going to be successful.'

'I see. What time frame do you suggest?'

'Three weeks.'

'Agreed. However while the probationary period is ongoing, your salary will be, shall we say, fifty per cent of the full amount?'

'No way, José.'

'I beg your pardon?'

'I'm sorry, that's not possible, your Honour. You see I have prior financial commitments.'

'Might I inquire as to what those commitments are?'

'Certainly . . . '

And of course I leave a little pause so as his imagination— if the little fucker actually has one—starts running away with itself.

'I'm helping to educate one of my sisters. Back home.'

You should see the look on his face.

'*He-hem*. Well, that is indeed laudatory. In that case, shall we say seventy-five per cent?

'Agreed. Full amount to be paid retrospectively once the trial period ends. Successfully.'

'And if it doesn't?'

'It will.'

He's smiling now, in fact I'd say it's the most fun the guy has had in a long time. He says, 'It's always refreshing to encounter someone who knows the true value of their work,' so I say 'And this work being practically *vocational*, it is especially valuable.'

He coughs and says, 'Indeed, *he-hem*, point taken.' Then he says he will trust me to keep a meticulous record of my hours, and that he believes that concludes our business for the time being unless of course I have anything further.

I say, 'Actually, I've a few things I'd like to get off my chest. How many people have worked here? As companions?'

'Quite a few.'

'More than a dozen?'

'In the last three years, yes, I'm afraid so. Yes.'

'How long do they last, generally?'

He winces. 'You make them sound like light bulbs. Generally not too long.'

'Why?'

'Ed is . . . '

He looks over at me now he is no longer Il Judgo and the silver pocket watches have ceased to chime in the desert there is no bearded Clint, no Indigo, no Colonel Mortimer. There is just the father of a pathetically sick, impossibly sad young man. He puts his hands to face, he covers his little cave of a mouth as if he were about to scream; it's abundantly clear he is at his wit's end and he hasn't a clue what to do except, unlike his fat fuckin' wife, he's not all dismissive just because he's no longer in the driver's seat.

He takes his hands away and stares at his dainty doll fingers. 'Ed is . . . difficult.'

' 'Course he is, sir. I mean, I'd be pretty difficult too if I was his age and saw that I'd been cheated.'

'Cheated?'

'By Life. By Death. By the Man Above.'

'*Ah*. Is that how you perceive it?'

'Yes it is. How do you see it?'

'I'm not sure.'

He sighs and takes off his glasses then he polishes them with a little yellow cloth and you can see he's the sort of person who likes to have books to refer to, rules and regulations to adhere to and he's not nearly as tough as he'd like people to think, though to be honest I wouldn't like to appear in front of him.

Sometimes small men can't help being vicious with bigger ones.

He leaves his glasses off, looks up and asks me my name, so I tell him and he says, 'Well, Trevor, as you can imagine it hasn't always been particularly easy here in this house,' or maybe he says *abode,* but anyway he looks over at the oak-panelled door and lets you know he's referring to both his big huge wife in her sick bed, and his tiny little son in his chair.

And I can't help but feel sorry for the dusty old bookworm, but at the same time I'm determined to take him for every nickel I can.

'I can't promise it will work out. That's as much up to Ed as it is to me. But I'm genuinely good at this type of thing and I swear to you I will use all my available resources to try and well, lift his spirits. If you know what I mean.'

'I know precisely what you mean.'

He sits his glasses back on his soft little caterpillar head, except his dry-skin ears are so small he has to feel around for them like someone playing Blindman's Bluff. Then he says he is, in general, a very able, a very *he-hem* capable man, but he is not sure he ever possessed that ability, and here's where his little insect mouth whispers as if he were in chapel—*the ability to lift spirits.*

'It's easier when you're not blood.'

Which isn't strictly true.

'That's very kind of you, *em,* Trevor.'

'I'll sign now. If you like.'

He passes the pen, I sign, and it feels very symbolic, like some sort of age-old ritual—he even blows on the signature. He thanks me and when I stand he seems genuinely relieved, he's even trying to smile up at me, although all he manages to do is add a few more wrinkles to his forehead. And the problem with guys like him is they cut themselves off from ordinary people so much that they lose sight of the fact we can have this balming effect on each other, and even if it's only temporary, what the hell.

And you can see by the new set of his shoulders that he feels lighter and not so bogged down in the mire. And when I ask him for an advance, 'just to keep me going, like,' he nods, slides open his desk drawer and takes out a huge leather-bound cheque book. *Excellent.*

He asks my surname without looking up and he's writing now with real gusto genuinely enjoying the act, his hand coming up in the air at the end of his signature like a long-haired conductor in Vienna. When he passes it over it's for $500 and I'm thinking, *yep*, there'll be some good times ahead negotiating the terms for not paying it back, because I have no fuckin' intention. There might even be the odd afternoon sherry, a vintage port, maybe a nice Cuban cigar. *Monte Cristo. Romeo and Juliet.*

And I can't stop this gleeful grin breaking out, *shite,* I wish I had more control over these things because he exhales sharply through his nose as if he's just woken up to the fact he's been conned by Antonio Vargas—you know, the guy who played Huggy Bear in *Starsky and Hutch,* or by some other jive-talking street hustler with Foster Grants, a wide brim hat and loud yellow flares on.

He stands up with no eye contact whatsoever, then he starts imitating one of those white boiler suit guys out on the runway with the paddles waving me out as if I were this big huge blue-bottle at a family-picnic, not that he's had too many of those in his time.

Then the crab apple-faced wanker tells me to shut the door behind me.

So I'm out in the corridor again, except this time I notice there are no tyre tracks from Ed's room to his and for some reason this makes me unbelievably sad, plus there is the sinking realization that I have no one to spend this money with or on; it's as if there's a little elevator inside my chest, someone's just stepped in and pressed 'b' for basement.

Some days you can hear your heart descend.

All the way down to your boots.

This time it's my eyes that close and have their spidery fine veins exposed. I sigh and ask myself: *Self, what are you doing here? What exactly are you trying to prove, and who are you trying to prove it to?*

Don't worry. It's just one of these bad moments. And bad moments pass like cars on the freeway without their headlights dipped. Anyway, it's not like I'm the only person in the world who asks himself those types of questions, now am I? And sometimes it helps to realise that the thoughts you have swimming around inside are thoughts that others most probably have too. Except, sometimes it's difficult to prove that, isn't it? I mean, there is no way of actually knowing unless you stand on a street corner in a suit with a survey: *May I have a moment of your time please ? I wonder, have you ever felt completely and utterly vanquished, even for a day? Ever felt it's all a pointless, uphill fuckin' struggle? Ever resorted to physical violence when the old brain gets too hot and bothered? I wonder: do you lie to yourself on a regular basis? Twist reality in order to keep marching on? And one final question if I may: how often are you confronted by Truth? I mean, do you ever find Him sitting there patiently at the top?*

Let's get a few things straight before we go any further; if you don't start un-knotting the little lies by the time you tackle the big ones the whole thing will have started to tilt.

For the record, the Committee at the Clinic never called me in nor sat me down to offer me any kind of full-time fuckin' position: They called me in to fire me.

On the way up to Ed's apartment I never told the little oily elevator guy he had a stupid hat on—I merely *thought* it.

And sometimes I'm not sure if thoughts actually exit my mouth as words and phrases or stay stuck up inside. I've often uttered things out loud that I was convinced I'd kept contained, and vice-versa. And you're not sure therefore if you've managed to turn the moment round, or just got stuck in its eternal creaking and twisting.

And I never worked as a hospital DJ, OK? I just said it because it seemed to back up whatever claim I was making at the time. Call it a white lie, an embellishment, a spoof, a spin, whatever; truth is we all do it.

Interesting question is *why?*

I used to think about being a hospital DJ quite a bit though and sometimes at the Clinic that's what I was like. A DJ spinning yarns, keeping them distracted from snide reality. And if you ask me there's nothing wrong with lying to sick people, nothing wrong with running out a harmless spoof to a class full of people with no arms, no legs and no dreams to speak of.

Some of the other teachers at the Clinic lied to themselves about the real reasons they were there. In the draughty staff room they sat around, giving out shite about the facilities and the lack of investment, the ancient fax machine, the *poor recompense.*

Sometimes when I was filling the kettle, I'd say, 'Well if it's so fuckin' awful, why do you stay?' and they'd say, 'Oh, but it's easy for you, Trevor. You're on a short-term contract,' then once I'd made their tea and handed it to them they'd say the real reason they stayed was because they loved to teach, loved to *impart*, loved to *give something back.*

Bollocks.

They enjoyed the fact that they were standing up without callipers or crutches, the fact they were walking without canes or aids or talking without stammering or drooling or their heads drooping or quaking.

They liked it because they had *power.*

I know what I'm talking about: sometimes when the class were dribbling all over themselves at something I'd said or read aloud from my diary I'd feel it in my heart, and I'd stop and stare down at my hands—I swear to Christ more than once they were actually shining, a kind of mossy, brassy ancient gold.

For a while when I was young I thought I had healing hands. I imagined these posters of me in a white suit on lamp posts across Ireland telling people I was coming to their village soon, that anyone with psoriasis or eczema or shingles, anyone with mysterious spots or pustules appearing on their face or forehead should break open the piggy bank and get ready to be saved, *Hallelujah*.

4

Walking along Madison thinking, *I'd love to be a simple person with a straightforward workaday job*, a plumber or plasterer, someone who whistles while he works, his (one syllable) name embossed on the side of a vintage Chevy van. Someone who fixes things, who comes from a laughing family who'd sat around playing board games instead of puffing on pipes and arguing Greek philosophy, pretending they liked one another.

Someone normal.

Sometimes you see these couples—I've just passed one—and they're not the drop-dead gorgeous ones with chiselled features and Swedish au pairs or Mexican maids, or satin skin and racehorse shins. They're not the ones with Farrah Fawcett teeth or 500 dollar haircuts or clothes that fit perfectly. The ones I'm talking about are everyday and unassuming, but when they pass you feel this aura of *durability.*

He has his son perched on his surprisingly wide shoulders, while the bright-eyed mother casually holds hands with their smiling, freckled daughter. They've bought her one of those little red twirling windmills and it is visibly generating happiness.

Every single object they witness is *imbued.*

With possibility.

They've been blessed with ordinariness, they're content with their lot, not absurdly seeking miracles or popping pills or desperately trying to reinvent themselves. They're not dreaming of another life. They're not applying for reality TV or plastic surgery makeover shows, not paying disengaged doctors to half-listen, not shagging sad secretaries in crotchless undies. They're not running first thing in the morning from who and what they really are. And when things go wrong—when money's tight, when the kids need braces, when the van needs a new transmission—they sit in the kitchen, talk calmly, hold hands and work things out. And when they make love later, they are able to look inside each other because nothing is hidden. No one wears a disguise.

They have so much it makes your heart race and your feet refuse to go any farther and your brain gets stuck on a really simple question: *What is it they have that I don't?*

The guy sees me staring at his little girl, his wife. He unhooks his son, steadies himself and begins to stare back. Except suddenly he seems to understand what's in my heart, because he winks, 'What's up, bro?' And in three little words he bestows upon me the no longer absurd possibility that some day I will have what he has.

I too will radiate capability. Calm.

Fuck's sake, Trevor, you don't even have a girlfriend. Get on with the fuckin' show.

There's a bit of palaver at the Chase Manhattan, you'd swear I'd demanded the keys to the Kingdom of Heaven. And I should've got the Judge to make it out to cash since the teller is one of those hatchet-faced old bags with big hair like Margaret fuckin' Thatcher she gets a real buzz out of saying, 'No.'

I ask to see the manager, so she presses a button and out comes this Puerto-Rican guy who hasn't entirely left the streets behind. He's shaking his impossibly smooth bald head, looking at his tacky big wristwatch as if it was the middle of the night. 'I'll have to ring the Judge. You sure you wanna do that?'

'Yes.'

He's on the phone now, describing me. I can see him smile and bite his big lilac lip like an angel fish at something Il Judgo has said, then he tells the woman with the hair to give me the money after which he struts away like a peacock with his pastel pink shirt on. You'd swear he'd just solved the Arab-Israeli conflict.

She counts out the cash as if it was coming out of her personal piggy bank and when she's finished, I take it and count it over again. *Slowly*. She asks is there anything else she can help me with and in terms of boredom in the voice she could give Ellie a real run for her money. I tell her yes, actually there is one other thing and she says, 'Go ahead.' So I say, 'Well, I hope you don't mind me saying this'—I look at her nametag—'Mabel, but your stupid ass hair would make a terrific nest for a flock of fuckin' seagulls or a big fat minah bird. Seriously, you should think about renting that Marge-Simpson mess of yours out to the Bronx Zoo since a lot of storks and pink flamingos find winters up here very tough going indeed.'

She doesn't bat an eyelid, just whispers through the glass, 'You keep taking those pills now, you hear.'

As I'm walking away, wondering who came off best in the encounter, she calls after me in a sing-song voice that's incredibly irritating, 'Have a nice day now!'

And she very nearly wins, except I turn around and say even louder, 'Hey, love that hair!'

No contest.

Then I start laughing out loud because I have this image of Mabel running after me, challenging me to a dance-off. And it turns out she's into body-popping and was one of the original Michael Jackson *Thriller* dancers so I'm forced to do this elaborate Michael Flatley routine, jumping over trash cans. In the end, people in the street call it a draw, me and Mabel bow, smile at each other and walk away, happy.

Strolling along, thinking, *Nice to have a few bob again*. Weird how having no money saps your strength; you feel as if someone has strapped a sadistic band on your back and they're just waiting until you get to the corner, and it's all a bit of a strain, and you're forever counting out your paranoid change feeling incredibly guilty for not leaving tips in ancient aluminium diners in Astoria.

I pass this black guy twice my age. He's wearing a little coloured hat, like a wizard. He's squatting on the sidewalk with every single thing he has left in the world laid out on a threadbare rug.

I'm not good in these sorts of situations.

When he looks up, he has the saddest moo-cow eyes with these huge baby doll lashes attached.

There are *Life* magazines from the sixties and seventies with amazing pictures of JFK as a child inside, and battered books including one called *The Dangling Man* which is an excellent title altogether. Beside it there's a record player in a box with a busted handle, leaning delicately against that a copy of the Stones' *Sticky Fingers*. Underneath there's another album called *Ramshackled* by some guy I've never heard of, Alan White, and you won't believe what Squatting Guy says: White used to be the drummer in Yes. I'm thinking, *Maybe I'll buy it for Ed*, so I put it back down. I don't want to appear too interested.

Squatting Guy has a stained, antique-lace tablecloth, a paperweight with a butterfly trapped inside, which has a hairline fracture, and this decrepit, dusty old typewriter. I hear this schmaltzy *Waltons*-type voiceover saying that some of the saddest acheybreakey letters home to Egypt or Ethiopia or Zaire—or wherever the fuck he comes from—were delicately tapped out late at night on this trusty old portable. How he was paying his way through medical school working as a doorman in some yuppie building. How he had a major falling out with some Aryan bitch because he failed to inform her that her personal trainer would be five minutes late. How she wielded her influence with the building manager and the Aryan Residents' Committee. How she had him canned because basically he never smiled like a good *professional* doorman should. How he always had his goddamn nose stuck in a book when she was outside in the rain struggling to get out of her cab with three bags full of designer-label shopping.

I try to stop myself touching the typewriter, but I can't. The *g* and *d* keys aren't working very well he says, but other than that it is a most reliable machine, a Remington, which is, *in point of fact, the Rolls-Royce of typewriters*. He stands up as he says this and nearly topples over because his little stick-insect legs have gone to sleep beneath him, which means he must have been there for the longest time, maybe even forever.

There are lots of medical texts with their backs broken and I have this incredible urge to ask him, *What went wrong? Was there a precise moment in Time where you felt it all slip-sliding away?* But I know if I start getting into it I won't be able to stop and what I have to remember is, *I've only just got myself sorted.*

With his open palms and moo-cow eyes he invites me to make him an offer, but I tell him, 'Nah, it's OK.'

He looks at his filthy toenails and worn-out sandals. You can see in his heart he doesn't really expect anyone to buy his old junk, so that's when I tell him I'm interested in Alan White. He picks up the LP as if it were a Stradivarius. With bone-thin fingers he slides out the inner sleeve, slowly, then the record, and it's like new (or else he's spray-painted it with some lacquer shit). Even so, I ask him how much and he says, 'What about five dollars?'

'What about it,' I say, and he says 'OK, my friend, what about four?'

I know it's cruel but I leave a tiny little pause before saying,

'Actually, I think that's way too little for such a rare and unusual long player.'

He doesn't understand, he thinks I'm taking the piss and his chest collapses in on itself with a little, sad sigh. I give him a twenty and tell him keep the change. His chest swells out again, in fact he becomes very excited altogether and tells me to take something else, *please*, take the typewriter, get the two keys fixed, write some nice long letters home, yes? I'm thinking, *Actually, I don't really write that many letters home but if I did I'd use email, thanks all the same.*

Then he does the strangest thing: he takes my hands in his, which are surprisingly cold, leathery and old; he kisses them twice with his parchment-dry lips and says in a Hammer Horror, Egyptian Mummy kind of whisper, 'The money you have given me will return to you one thousand fold. Allah and the honourable Elijah Mohammed will see to it henceforth they will travel with you. You are my friend. You are my saviour also. Yes, my friend, all this is true.'

Which you have to admit is kind of overdoing it. I don't really know what to say, so I just go, 'Thanks very much, you are my friend also,' and put my hand on his shoulder—*shit*, the guy really is cold.

He smiles bravely. I don't know why but I always expect black as well as brown people to have perfect teeth, but he doesn't. In fact they're yellow and soft-looking, like eggs, another reason the Aryan bitch might have wanted him to hit the road, jack.

'Sir,' he says, 'you need to realize something,' except he leaves a huge fuckin' pause that makes me feel extremely ill at ease.

Then at last: 'You need to realize, you are a good man, a kind man.'

I'd much prefer to keep moving, to re-enter the tumult of people chewing mobile phones, only that would be phenomenally rude.

He's blathering on about riches of the soul, how Heaven will reward me for my great act of charity. *Jesus,* I really wish he'd give it a rest because there's always that thing in the air in New York, isn't there? I mean, they're always tuned in eagerly awaiting The Second Act in The Universal Freak Show. And I really don't appreciate it when guys in expensive lightweight suits start staring as if I had two fuckin' heads and to be honest it's been a right rollercoaster of a day emotionally speaking, what with Ed and his mother, plus the whole bizarre experience of sitting on the side of her bed, which reminded me of sitting on the side of my own mother's.

By the way, it was my mother who first showed me how, if you sprinkled a bit of love on top of the other ingredients, you could rest assured someone at the table, usually my old man, would nod, tap his mouth three times with his napkin and say, 'This is delicious darling. What was it you put into it?' To which she'd answer, and not always in such a sweet and gentle voice, 'A dollop of love and a little bit of understanding, dear.'

A gay guy in a silver spacesuit that once belonged to a much bigger person hands me a flyer for Studio 54 which says all drinks are half-price, fuck it, why not?

It's half-empty, just your usual assortment of losers and daytime boozers, they all look like extras from a David Mamet movie, you know, Joe Mantegna-look-alikes with fake Rolex watches and grizzled chest-wigs on display. One guy even has a match moving about in his mouth, left to fuckin' right, right to fuckin' left.

Another has forearms like Popeye; a set of worry beads lies idle on the sticky tabletop beside him.

Rules of the house: *No one talks to anyone else.*

I order a beer, the barman is a total dickhead, he lists off about fifty brands and I'm standing there thinking what would be nice when he says, 'Take your time, I got all fuckin' day.' This other guy on a high stool laughs out loud, like Santa Claus.

I say, 'Rolling rock,' with no *please*, which is unusual for me. He gets one, pops it open without looking, then he slides it over, except when I go to pay the prick moves down the counter to the register and I have to follow like a little lost sheep. I pass over the flyer but he just picks it up, crumples it, throws his bug-eyes skywards.

'No discount on beer, just shots 'n cocktails. *Capiche?*'

I hand him five dollars and he says something under his breath as he slams the register. I have my hand out, but he slaps the change down and this always pisses me off: I can feel tingling in my feet, like nettles stinging, and I have to be extremely careful it doesn't spread to other parts, so I sit well away. *Relax, don't let him get under your skin, you have a job, you have 500 bucks in your pocket, you're on forty an hour into your mitt, plus any accommodation problems you're currently experiencing are shortly to be sorted, you'll soon be living rent-free on Madison, eating like a fuckin' King, OK?*

The place is like a graveyard it really is dead, until the barman and the guy on the stool, the one who laughed out loud, start moving ashtrays and glasses with a flourish the barman wipes down the counter, *excellent,* they're getting ready to arm wrestle.

I'm one of those people who truly appreciates free entertainment, you know, Do-Wop singers snapping ebony fingers and harmonizing, '*In the jungle, the mighty jungle, the lion sleeps tonight*'; unicycle-jugglers in the park, hovering like gigantic hummingbirds; apprentice break-dancers with skid marks on their backs. And you've no idea how much I love to spy little learning-curve scars on the hairless arms of Chinese fire-eaters. To be honest, I even get a buzz out of bridge-and-tunnel types arguing over carspaces on Madison; as their fingers twitch like gunslingers, as they pretend to reach for non-existent guns I fuckin' love it when rich kids in hoodies walk past trying hard to be something they can never be.

(Black)

Anyway, the one who isn't the barman is some kind of re-tired athlete or ex-ball player, I'd say. And although he's carry-ing a few kilos round his middle he's still got the precision of movement that can only come from standing in the middle of a field with thousands of paying-punters looking, you only have one chance to connect.

He lights his cigarette with his left hand he takes a sip from his whiskey glass, immediately blowing long plumes into the other guy's mush. You can see straight away he is cocksure, and also pretty strong: His right hand hardly falters all the while he is playing head-games with the barman who looks like a seri-ous steroid-abuser. 'That it huh, that your best shot, huh, that all you fucking got?'

It's plain to see he can thrash Mr Abuser with his right or left, doesn't really matter. He knocks back the dregs in his glass and orders another with a fuse-sized finger up. Then he starts looking around like a bear in a Rocky Mountain campsite, stiffly left, then here we go slowly right, *Doobey, doobey doo, where's the next lovely trashcan at?*

He has to shout a bit—you can see he was a real asshole in school—but after a degree of goading and personal insulting he gets to take on a few more punters, including Match-in-the-Mouth who, to be fair, Ed would probably beat. Then comes the guy with the forearms, Mr Worry Beads; he's a different kettle of fish entirely.

Worry Beads is one of those people that are completely and utterly silent, as if sealed off in some kind of invisible vacuum-pack. He's probably suffering from some strain of continuous low-grade depression like a lot of folk on the west coast of Ireland where it never stops raining for more than twenty seconds and no one's clothes get properly aired, which has to be a contributory factor because you're going around damp on your High Nelly all day reeking of turf fires and dung. Anyway, although he will eventually lose, Worry Beads is making Ball Player work pretty hard; if you do that Steve Austin thing with your eye you can zoom in on this lightening-fork vein starting to pulse at the side of Ball Player's temple. You'd be very surprised how heavy and tired your arm can get after two or three bouts, and soon it will be my turn, so I let the tell-tale tingling filter up my legs and into my belly, then into my hands, and you're right: the fucker behind the bar did burst my bubble, and sometimes no matter what you say to yourself the gnawing rat feeling won't go away.

Abuser is sweeping up as I walk slowly over and ask for another. He says without looking, 'One Rolling Rock comin' right up,' except he keeps on sweeping for three fuckin' minutes, so I say, 'Actually I'd like to hear that list of yours again, only a bit slower this time please,' which really gets his goat. So he's standing there reciting, like the school dunce: 'Amstel, Dos Equis, Corona, Heineken, Miller, Bud, Stella . . . ' and I'm not listening because of course I'm going to have another Rolling Rock. I'm also busy sending Ball Player this excellent, faintly-amused-by-your antics look.

Which he falls for, hook, line. And sinker.

'Ya wanna shot, huh?'

'I think I'm safer with a beer. But thanks. Most generous.'

He calls me a 'mook,' whatever that is. And that's when I say: 'You know what Pops, I'd welcome a shot at the title. But why don't we make it interesting, say fifty of your American dollars?'

He's laughing like a drain now he's looking straight at my balls as if I'm going to fish them out and wrestle with them. Then the gobshite throws his dyed-black head back for even more effect. *Ho, ho, ho, what would you like for Christmas little boy?* And if you peer way, way up in his nostril hairs you can see these ancient grains of cocaine lodged there, I'll tell ya one thing, he won't be laughing in a minute.

'Hey Petey. Big kid here wants to put fifty bucks down.'

Abuser stops and says, 'There's one born every minute, why not make it an even *hunnert*?'

So I say, 'You know what Petey? You're dead right. Let's rock and roll.'

Ball Player wastes no time, he lifts his little hard-boiled egg of an ass up, puts his hand round into his back pocket, retrieves his wad and puts his money down. 'One hundred bucks, let's see the colour of yours kid. Ya better not be talking through your asshole.'

I really, really want to say, *Actually, the only person who's talking through his hole is you*, but I don't, I just take out my money, peel off the nice crisp notes and add them to his. Then I hand the pile to Petey the Pea Brain.

You can see Ball Player is a little surprised by this, but it suits him fine. *Hey, no problemo.* Then he asks me am I ready, and you should always make them wait, so I say 'Actually, no I'm not.' And I don't know why but I put on this Northern Ireland accent which I use to tell Abuser to fetch me a pack of Marlboros 'if it's not too much fuckin' bother, that's the chap, aye, step lively.'

Except he doesn't.

They're suddenly looking at each other as if to say, *Ya think it's fair to take this moron's money, maybe he was only let out for the day?*

Eventually Abuser takes the money off the counter, folds it and puts it in his shirt-pocket, then he brings me my smokes.

I crack my knuckles carefully. Then I place the beer bottle within easy reach, just in Casey.

Ball Player grins like a salmon shark and sets his big arm up there on the counter, making sure to show me the bicep moving like a python under the black silk of his sleeve, *Ooh I'm so scared, help me mammy.* I'm feeling very giddy now mostly because the guy is completely clueless, I mean, he's so busy jerking his head this way and that way at the people who've gathered around trying to tell them with his low-voltage eyes, *Hey you guys, watch how I make mincemeat of this punk,* that he doesn't even register the size of my hand.

Until it engulfs his completely.

That's when you need one of those strange Coen brothers' shots where the camera travels in behind his eyes, and you see the toilet of his Little-Italy brain flushing away the Tough Guy routine.

Before we've even begun, he has lost. And I'm recalling this embarrassing slow-motion date where the sister of one of the people at the Clinic asked me out, and before we'd even finished our starters I knew it wasn't going to work because everything in her life was sweet, ordered and sorted, and everything in mine was the opposite.

Ball Player has real power in his arm, and some in his wrist, but not too much in his hands. I can feel the little bones meeting and greeting each other in there under the tanned skin, *Hi-ho, hiho, it's off to work we go.* I'm thinking of Mass and the best part where the priest used to say, 'You may now offer each other the Sign of Peace,' which I really used to enjoy, especially the time Ma and I were seated right in front of our neighbours who were always 'officially informing' us that our dog was doing his dumps in their garden, which was exactly what I'd spent hours training him to do with a torch and a rake that I'd used to poke holes in their hedge. After three or four nights, all I had to do was hit the spot where I wanted him to squat; it was as if we were planting steaming little landmines. *Mister Whippys.* When he emerged to cut the grass you could hear the idiot-husband fucking and blinding like a madman I used to run upstairs to my mother's room, throw open the window, then we'd laugh ourselves silly at the sound of his Briggs-and-Stratton stopping and starting. The odd time if we listened *really* hard we could hear the blades slowing and squelching, it was probably the best sound in the whole wide world, her laughter.

I remember breathing in to give the neighbour's hand a right fuckin' squeeze, *Peace be with you, too.* His pencil neck and pointy head went engine red and, bar one other episode, we never heard zilch from him again.

Ball Player is starting to suffer now. Once the bones begin to pop, they can't stop. *Firecracker fingers.* If I wanted, I could keep his hand there for maybe another ten seconds and he'd never be able to hold a baseball bat or even a fuckin' fork again, not properly. But I let him off easy, well sort of, just bang his baby knuckles down on the counter. It's the sound of a big fish hitting the wet deck of a trawler, *wallop.*

One of the spectators, Match-in-the-Mouth, I think, says: 'He ain't got hands—he's got catcher's mitts attached to his friggin' wrists. Kid's a goddamn freak.'

Everyone's staring now there's a deadly silence, if you listen closely you can hear this high whinny, then hooves coming hard as Chaos comes in on his charger. And because Ball Player is the type that will *definitely* swing, I grab my beer by the neck and move around to his left, fast as I can. Liquid runs down my fingers, incredibly soothing after the lava-lamp heat of our hands.

He half-stands, half-slides his ass around to face me, except his bar stool makes this whoopee-cushion sound. *Fuck it*, I can't hold it in any longer, I just burst out laughing. His head is all purple veins lifting out; he is like an old bull who's been made a holy-show of by a matador from Palookaville in a silly borrowed costume. He also has this weird, yellow alligator-glow in his eye and I wonder, *If I let the fire spread from my hands up into my neck and face is that what I'd look like?* Nah, I'd probably wind up looking like a giraffe on acid.

He's lifting his foot onto the lower rung of the stool beside him, hiking up his trouser leg. He's got these really sad red-and-black cowboy boots with little ropes and lassoes stitched on, *shite,* there's a black handle sticking out the top.

Backing away carefully, I'm thinking, *Wasn't such a good idea to hand the money to Abuser, now was it? And why have his hands got so busy under the counter all of a sudden.* Time slows down, in fact it gets dug in like a WWI soldier in a trench. My heart speeds up. Sweat above my eyelids is about to fall in and make it hard for me to see this woman—who was there the whole time, but who I didn't notice because her red hair was camouflaged against the tacky leatherette of the booth—stepping up: 'Relax Gordy. Ya don't wanna go an' get barred all over again, now do ya?'

She has this slow way of asking questions that makes you think very fast, and when she moves you understand that in some Midwestern town fifteen or maybe just ten years ago she used to stop traffic on her way to the ice cream parlour.

'Why don't ya sit your ass back down again. Huh?'

There's something in the air between her and Ball Player, she definitely has some hold over him, probably knows he needs to dress up as a baby or hold a rattler in his fist before he can rise to the occasion.

She smokes a bit as she pushes him back down on his stool. 'Kid beat ya fair and square. Shit happens.'

She extinguishes her cigarette in the ashtray by Ball Player's elbow as if someone's jellied eye is staring up, *squish-squash.*

'Hey Petey. Quit stallin'. Pay the kid. The rest of yiz, why don't ya go back to the rocks you crawled out from *undah?*'

Abuser steps forward with the money much like a sentry who wants weekend leave, *yes sir, sergeant major sir,* and the rest of them slink back like extras in a Frankenstein movie.

She lights up, smokes some more, then puts the money down on a table near me. She really has an excellent walk.

Everyone is staring at the cash, you'd swear it had turned into a million. I trouser the money and try hard to stop myself grinning as Ball Player looks away in disgust. I move off very fast with my beer still in hand, then I retrieve Alan White and from a safe distance take a big swig from the bottle; you wouldn't believe how parched my throat is, or how cold and slow the liquid. I'd really love to finish every amazing drop, it tastes of Victory and Ancient Greece but I have this image of Petey holding me from behind in some piss-stained lane with broken glass dancing all around while Gordy arcs these big, stadium shots into my gut, *Not such a fuckin' wise-ass now, huh kid?*

And I've been down, way down, in a piss-stained lane before (and we'll get to that later, too, don't worry) so I'm out the door, *Warp factor fuckin' ten, Mister Scott* and I'm laughing my tits off as I run down the street humming the original *Star Trek* theme, except it's quite hard because the first few notes are high, very high indeed.

I'm not in the next bar, nor the next one, but the next one after that, way, way down the block, some imitation Irish kip with a neon shamrock outside and a barman inside who should've been in *Darby O'Gill and the Little People.*

He has these tomato-ketchup cheeks and a little roundy belly like a beach ball someone just let the air out of, but the best bit is this freeze-dried rat he has stuck to the top of his head. He clearly believes it's extremely life-like, and although you still see a few of these yokes in places like Drumshambo and Cootehill in Cavan, this is my first in the Big Apple, so I'm laughing out loud when he says, 'Would ya mind explainin' please, what's so goddamn funny?'

'It's just, well, this bar is exactly like one I used to drink in on my holidays in Skibereen in West Cork, it's quite uncanny really, that's all. No offence meant.'

'None taken,' he says. 'None at all.' In fact he seems very happy with the explanation, I've clearly made his day. He says, 'beer?' with a caterpillar eyebrow up, so I wink at him as if he were tele-fuckin-pathic. He brings me one straight from the tap, 'There ya go buddy, get that inta ya.' And in the filthy dirty mirror the guy looking back may not be beautiful but he is interesting, possibly even charismatic, plus he has the best part of 600 bucks in his arse-pocket, he is feeling quite inspired, *Yep, you're dead right there Trevor, it's always nice to get one over on a complete and utter asshole, now isn't it?*

The beer tastes like more. I lift up my glass and he nods. 'Right you are, friend.'

Jesus, this guy is so fake it's flabbergasting.

I'm waiting for my heart to return to normal when in she comes, her big wool bag swinging in time to her hips. She lifts her red head up slowly, like the snake in that D.H. Lawrence poem—you know the one that's set in some really hot oasis country.

She says, 'Oh hi,' and puts her head back down, debating, before the bag starts swinging again.

What a strut. She's one of those people could put a pile of hardback books on her head and go water-skiing if she wanted. And do you remember at the start when I asked do you ever look at people and wonder what sort of animal they'd be? Well, another excellent thing to do is grant them a little soundtrack of their own, and I don't even have to think about it, right away she gets that Hendrix number, *'Tyre marks across your back, baby. I can see you've had your fun.'* Still, I decide not to be judgmental, just to be friendly and open, then to see what happens.

'Ya wanna buy a girl a beer?'

I look around in a real exaggerated way, bit like Little Bo Peep.

'To be honest, I don't see any girls. But I've no objections to buying an experienced woman like yourself a cold one.'

'Whatever. Whiskey-sour, Mike!'

Every tiny transaction with these people is a scam, and *buy me a beer* means *buy me a whiskey-sour* and it may seem like a small thing to you but I find it hugely annoying on top of which she lights herself a Camel without offering, and I seem to have left mine behind in the rush so I have to ask, 'May I?'

She just nods and slides the pack over a little as she blows smoke out both nostrils, which isn't very attractive, in fact it makes her look like a Welsh fuckin' dragon.

She collects her drink from Pal Mikey who started mixing it the minute she walked in. He brings me another beer without asking, this time with a paper mat attached. *Gee, thanks Mike.* Then he takes a pen from behind his cauliflower ear, he puts two little ticks on my frilly mat, none on fuckin' hers.

She says, 'Here's mud in your eye, kid,' which I haven't heard for a while, not since I watched a Bogart movie and I say, 'Cheers,' but at the same time I'm thinking, *Slow down now, Clever. You've already had two with Ellie, one and a half in Studio 54 and two here, plus there's another one in front of you and you pumped out quite an amount of adrenaline; it's still pretty early in the day, so don't lose the run of yourself completely, OK?*

She wants to know what I woulda done if she hadn't stepped up when she did, so I say I don't really know but I would've thought of something, and she says, 'Like what, be pacific.' I'm tempted to correct her pronunciation, or at least to do an impersonation of an ocean, but I just say, 'Well, basically it boils down to a case of fight or flight and I've got extremely long legs.'

'That so, huh?' Then she blows smoke without looking at me, for effect. 'Pete has a button under the bar, it locks all the doors and windows automatic. Plus, ya oughta know Gordy is a real piece of work, used to be a vice cop, always has somethin' tucked up in his boot, ya really should be more careful. Ya know, this ain't Ireland, things ain't settled with fists and sticks no more.'

'How do you know I'm Irish?'

'I seen *The Quiet Man*, OK?'

Her eyes are a strange cabbage green like seaweed after the tide has gone out and I'm wondering is she just trying to freak me out? If she is, she's doing an excellent job: all I can see is this little white button being depressed, locks whirring internally and welloiled bolts sliding across, *click*. And I suppose one of my Achilles' heels is that I can't see the *Danger! High Voltage* sign until it's way too late, and my stomach is in a terrible tea-towel knot, it won't go away especially when she puts her warm hand on my arm and pulls the red hairs, softly.

'Where'd ya learn to arm wrestle? Ya don't have to tell me if ya don't want.'

'It's OK, I don't mind.'

She exhales, only this time she doesn't narrow her eyes, her way of pretending to be interested.

'I was working in Stuttgart for a while, in a car factory, Mercedes-Benz. There was this old Turkish dude beside me on the assembly line who took a bit of a shine to me.'

'I can see that happenin'.'

'He used to be in a circus, he was the strongest man I ever met, I mean, the guy could actually bend pig iron. It was him who basically showed me how.'

'Yeah?'

'Yeah. He said I already had the hands, but that what I really needed to acquire was the *grey matter* and he used to tap the side of my head like this, *tap-tap*. Then he'd say all I had to do was close my eyes and picture their bones turning to chalk dust.'

'Jesus.'

'Yeah. It really is that simple. Will power. Mind over matter.'

What I don't tell her is, the same guy sometimes used to shout, 'Russian tank, Russian tank,' then point his polished head and run at the brick wall of this *bier keller* on Königstrasse. And sometimes what we don't reveal is more important than what we do, like food labels in a supermarket.

She's considering things, you can see she's one of those people that has to break it down then put it all back together again in little boxes inside her smoky brain, which means she's probably used to being lied to.

Finally, she says, 'Weird fuckin' thing ta teach someone.'

She takes a greedy sip of her drink, you can see thick liquid moving up the straw, and for some reason I'm thinking of liposuction in Hollywood, plus I don't like the way she leans forward and pulls her hair back with one hand—it reminds me of this curled-up earthworm of a woman at the Clinic who had sick in her hair at the Christmas party but still had the nerve to suggest a blow job. And some of them really were relentless, seriously, seduction for them was a form of attrition, trying to wear you down every day, *Why not Trevor, don't you like me, just try kissing me, my lips are normal, see what that feels like first, come on no one will ever know.*

'Maybe you're the kinda kid people teach weird shit to.'

More of a statement than a question, which kind of kills the conversation for a while. We sip and smoke in silence until she shouts, 'Hey Mike, anyone been in askin' for me?'

And did you ever notice how incredibly rude Americans are, the way they leave you out of the loop? It's like when you're out on a date and the girl meets some ancient fuckin' school-friend and it's all that *Jesus, do you remember the time we did this*, and *Oh-my-god* hands flying up to their geisha faces and *Tell us, whatever happened to so and so . . .*

I tap her elbow and enquire, 'Would you like to accompany me to Chinatown for something nice to eat?'

Rat Head vanishes.

She looks straight at me without blinking and you can see this big book inside her head, it's a red ledger with Debit and Credit accounts, and she's slowly weighing up the odds.

Then she says, 'Sure, I like you plenty, why not?' She puts her drink down and with her cigarette still in her hand she rubs my head roughly then she leans in a little to kiss me, her lips parting like those red corduroy ropes they place outside night clubs.

It's an underwater feeling probably because of the seaweed in her eyes and it lasts about nineteen seconds. I'm pretty accurate about time due to the fact that when I was on the school swimming team my Jesuit coach used to count out loud the time that elapsed between me touching the cold silver bar and the next guy: *Two, one thousand, three, one thousand, four, one thousand.* He had this real snotty sneer in his voice, *sonorous*, you can imagine how popular that made me in the dressing-room there was always some fucker staring, you'd swear winning a tacky little gold medal at sixteen was a matter of life and fuckin' death. Then again, for guys whose fathers were waiting just inside the door with hazelrods and switches, maybe it was.

Her mouth is much wider than mine, her lips are amazingly soft, her lipstick tastes sweet, and it's one of those kisses that when you open your eyes you're quite surprised to find yourself in a bar, in daylight, in America.

She says, 'That was nice. But before we eat there's something we should take care of, less a'course you don't find me attractive?'

'No. I find you extremely attractive.'

Which isn't strictly true, but it was a very good kiss; not greedy, but not too lazy either, bit like a pike tugging on the bait but being real careful not to swallow the hook.

'So. You a lover as well as a fighter?'

'Maybe.'

'You're not sure, huh?'

'I'm sure.'

'Yeah?'

'Yeah. Say the word.'

'Fuck. Now you say it.'

'Fuck.'

'Slower.'

'*Fu-uck.*'

'Harder.'

'I get the picture.'

'Good. 'Cause some guys don't. I like someone I can talk to when I'm doin' it. It's more grown-up that way, don't ya think?'

'I suppose so, yeah.'

'We can leave now if ya want.'

'Maybe we should get to know each other a bit better?'

'We will, don' worry. An' afterwards ya can go on your merry way an' ya never have to concern yourself 'bout calling me or any of that shit, OK? Maybe if you've been a real stud Ma will fix breakfast, I might even bring it in on a tray with a flower, what do ya say?'

'Sounds truly wonderful, but do me a favour?'

'That depends.'

'Drop the Ma stuff. It's kind of unsettling.'

She laughs, and it's a surprisingly soft sound, even if there are too many *Boogie Nights* and tangled sheets in it. When we stand up she goes, 'Ooh very nice, I must say,' in this bad Eliza Doolittle voice as I put her coat on.

Out in the street she can do that wolf-whistle thing. I know it's childish but I've always wanted to be able to do it so now I'm looking at her thinking, *I dunno, you tell me, is she kinda cool or just a walking cliché?*

Too late for debate, we're sitting in a yellow cab heading uptown, less and less white faces. Amazing how an un emptied trash can or two hooded guys leaning against a corner changes the landscape goes from doorman to dingy in a set of crookedly hanging traffic lights.

Outside her building there's a delay when we go to pay, I'm thinking, *No fuckin' way, she can stump up this time, I coughed up for all the drinks, plus she rang up twenty smokes on top.* She mutters under her breath as she fishes out a crumpled note. 'Cheapskate fuckin' Mick.' The inside of her handbag is a complete and utter mess.

There's a reinforced door she needs her shoulder to open, then it's up the stairs behind her, thinking, yep, *definitely* the type who would've had her name on the side of a B-52, put there by a some lantern-jawed jock who comes home to a 'Hero's Welcome' except he's no longer able to get it up five flights of stairs, after which there are an awful lot of locks and bolts. At one stage she looks back over her shoulder and smiles, except I can't think of a single thing to say, I mean absolutely nothing springs to mind as I watch her hands move up and down the door frame I feel it in my spine, like a xylophone.

Finally we're inside, it's much cleaner and brighter than you would've thought. 'Home sweet home,' she says and throws her bag on an overstuffed chair. She's more relaxed now that she's let go of the Barbara Stanwyck impersonation, although she still makes a production out of lighting a smoke and putting it between my lips. Then she kicks off her shoes and disappears in the kitchen, I can hear a bottletop hit the floor, like brief applause.

When she comes back she takes a long drag from my cigarette. The smoke goes curling into her eyes as she pours my beer but she just closes both of them and doesn't spill a single drop.

'Got everything ya need?'

'I think so. Thank you.'

'You're welcome.'

She leaves the bathroom door open as she cold-creams some of the war paint off she calls out, 'G'head, snoop around, put on some music why don't ya flick through a book or somethin'?' There's lousy taste on her shelves, apart from some Carl Hiassen and Elmore Leonard it's all shite on how to improve this, how to transform . . . that's when she reappears.

Minus her blouse.

Her body at least from the waist up is even better than you would've imagined. She stands there in her skirt and black bra which has little serrated flowers around the edges, and the titles that appear below her amazing breasts say: *Extremely hot in the sack, play your cards right and this could be something to write to Dalek and The Captain about.*

'What? I remind you of somebody?'

'No. It's just, you look . . . '

'*Younga* than ya thought?'

'Yeah.'

'That's 'cause I am.'

She steps out of her skirt like Lucille Ball she has black stockings and suspenders, the whole shebang, and I'm a sucker for all that old-fashioned stuff, I'm getting hard. 'Say somethin'.' 'You look lovely.' 'Lovely?'

'Yes.'

She turns sideways and puts one surprisingly long leg out in front, like a can-can dancer.

'Ya like my legs?'

'Yes. They're long and lean. Like a racehorse.'

'That's nice. Nobody ever said that before. What else do ya like?'

'I like your breasts.'

'Tell me more.'

Which is a line from *Grease*, isn't it?

'They're full and round and very inviting.'

'Ya wanna feel them?'

'Yes please.'

She repeats *yes please* like a fat kid who has just been asked *Do you want more chocolate-chip ice cream?* or maybe it was me that sounded like that the first time, I don't know.

Then she walks over to me, slowly. At the risk of repeating myself it really is first-rate, I mean she could be on a ramp in Paris with all that jutting hip, pouting lip stuff going on.

She takes my hands and she places them on her damp soft face, then in her hair which has sticky gel in it, not that I care. She's telling me not to be afraid, which I'm not, then she takes my hands again, she places them over her breasts, which sort of vanish underneath. That's when she whispers, 'Jeez, poor Gordy' and I'd completely forgotten about him, but at this stage who gives a shite? She's on the verge of unhooking her bra, however, I can't wait.

'Don't move.'

'Ya gonna take a leak?'

'Yeah.'

She kneels down suddenly she starts to unbuckle my belt all the while staring up like Linda fuckin' Lovelace. She slides the belt out of its loops, lets me know it can have other uses if I want it to, and, in terms of communicating with eyes and eyebrows, she's definitely an exception to the rule.

I step out of my combats, I still have my sneakers and socks on. I realise this isn't a particularly good look, but she doesn't seem to mind since she's suddenly all folded out on the floor, like yesterday's news.

Her perfect breasts are cupped in her thin, white fingers, but I have to go, I mean, I *really* have no choice, except she catches me looking in the direction of the bathroom so she moves one hand down to her crotch; see the white spider crawl across her hard belly and down.

'Do it.'

'What?'

'Rain on me, baby. Not in my mouth though.'

'I don't think so. No.'

'Don't be such a square. I like it.'

'I dunno . . . '

'Come on, baby. You'll like it too.'

'How do you know?'

'You don't want to make me happy? I'll make you happy after and . . . '

I don't care if we're going to shower together, then fuck and suck like demented Duracell bunnies. I don't care if she is going to tie me up and do it 'til the cows come home wagging their tails behind them. The truth is, I'm sick and tired of every-body in this kip putting themselves first. Anyway, I've got so much beer sloshing around inside I'd probably drown the wagon, plus there are an awful lot of gaps in her floorboards and you never know who might live below, knowing my luck one of those survivalist fuckers with a big beard and a Bowie knife stuck 'tween his teeth.

'I'm going to leave now, OK?'

'G'head, ya might miss choir practice at Saint Patrick's.'

She's telling me I'm an asshole, and a fag, as I step back into my combats I'm searching around for Alan White and she's back on the sofa, fiddling with her bra. She lights a cig-arette, takes a huge drag, releases hardly any smoke and says, 'You're a total loser, what's worse, you're a lousy fuckin' kissah.'

Apart from the magical moment in the Chase Manhattan, I've been restraining myself all day so I tell her a few home truths, including my theory as to why she wants to be pissed on, because 'that's what you do to everyone you meet, in fact your vocation, your fuckin' calling in life, is to urinate all over people's hopes and dreams, and by the way your hair smells of piss and your apartment smells of piss, while I'm at it your whole fuckin' life smells of piss.'

She says, 'Yeah whatever, shut the goddamn door behind ya, jerk-off.'

'Right, I will.'

And I nearly take the thing off its hinges, except halfway down her stairs I realize it can't wait a second longer, *shite*, there's no way I'm doing it outside in an alleyway, not in this part of town—never know who the fuck might decide to appear just when you have your dick in your hands. No, I'm going to have to go back up, knock on her door, push past and say, *Hey, I need to use the jacks so shut the fuck up and go back to imitating a Welsh fuckin' dragon, alright?*

Music is coming from inside. P.J. Harvey's 'Tales of the City' which I quite like.

I'm knocking with my knuckles, now the palms of both hands, plus my sneaker, but Polly Jean is screaming her lungs out about how badly she wants a pistol and Rain on Me Baby can't hear; or maybe she can and she's just sitting there releasing dragon smoke, going, *Fuck him.*

So I do it against her door, not in her mouth, and I'm laughing so hard I can hardly maintain a flow and I have to keep moving out of the way of the stream, then river.

The noise on her door is like a monsoon, then all of a sudden there is no liquid left inside I feel empty and very weird altogether as I'm walking back down the stairs I'm thinking, *the stupid cow looked like the Crazy King's wife in* Chitty-Chitty*, lying there cupping her thrupenny bits, fumbling with her brillo-pad.*

And out on the screaming street I'm doing my best not to get shouldered by the loose-limbed brothers who've all gathered to gawk; it's like a scene from a Spike-Lee joint, just before everything implodes.

And what I'd like to know is, what made Rain on Me Baby think I'd want to do something like that in the first place?

If you *really* want some free advice, when you feel like this you should avoid looking in shop windows and restaurant fronts, when you feel like this your reflection is always blurred, and wavy, like Ed's handwriting you are unformed, you are unfinished, you may have the body and hands and other bits and pieces of a man but you have the blank face of a novice or wimpled nun, you have the twirling mind of a fool at an amusement park you are neither one thing nor the other, you are confusing reality with fantasy, you are not in control, not in possession of your faculties.

You can do nothing.

Except . . . *Keep walking. And avoid the waving madly mirrors.*

When things start to get all Lon Chaney and hairy, when the ticker goes into overtime, when strobe lights register doubt and flickering uncertainty behind your eyes you should visualize the surface of the sea.

You can let it be quite angry at the start, but gradually you should fight to make it calm. And steady. Atlantic to Baltic.

After *the episode* behind the school shed when the two whispering rich kids—the type that think nothing will ever go wrong in their gift-wrapped lives—tried to trip me up and one knelt slyly behind while the other tried pushing me over, but they didn't quite get the timing right and something snapped inside, that was when I had to change schools and the family felt it best to move *lock, stock and barrel.* It was a bit lonely at the start but the best thing about moving to Wicklow was the sea, especially in winter, when in between the white waves crashing you had this awesome moment of respite; the harder you listened, the longer that interlude seemed to endure.

I like it when you can get lost in Time—you know, when you're doing something you really like, say gluing together an air-fix as a kid and you look up at the kitchen clock and go, *Jesus, I better do my eccker,* or you're floating on the sea after an exhausting race out to Lambay Island and endorphins kick in with a surge you're thinking, *Fuck, it doesn't get much better than this.* Or you're lying on the bed talking to your Ma, and you realize you're hungry, and you stand up and stretch as you look out the window of the bedroom you realize the sun has gone down slowly, the sky has gone black, or even better, it's turned an inky purple which exactly matches the easy rhythm of your breathing.

That's better. In through the nose, out slowly through the mouth.

A gypsy cab slows down like a hearse in a gangster movie it takes a long look and as the driver winds down the window I say 'Astoria?' with a black question mark in the air.

He just shakes his head slowly. 'No,' he says. 'I don't go out over the bridge no mores.'

I thank him for nothing and walk on, except he hugs the kerb beside me, he says, 'Hey, you walking way too fast man, you drawing all *kindsa* tension to yourself.' For ten dollars he offers to take me *somewheres* more safe, so I say that would be very nice indeed.

The seat is hot and sticky, like tar on a rooftop in summer, I'm hoping someone spilt soda, not spunk. In the rear view he says, 'I seen you before. You that Polish dude on TV, rescue all the old peoples in that building. You up for getting' that *science-tastin'* thing from the Mayor, right?'

I say, 'No, I'm afraid you're mixing me up with somebody else,' and he says, 'Nothin' to be 'fraid about, maybe you jus' got one of those faces.'

And now it's my turn to mutter under my breath, *'Maybe you just got one of those faces, what the fuck does that mean? And for your information Mr Smelly Cab the word is citation, citation.'* And, if you want, you can put an echo on it all the way home—*citation*—up the stairs—*citation*—and it's still there when I open the fridge and peer in to see one of her poxy yellow post-its attached to a litre of nice cold milk: 'Don't even think about it. Buy your own!'

Citation.

Fuck her.

I drink as much as I can then I carry the carton into my room. In the middle of the night the cardboard pops back out, it makes a small sound like when you put your tongue up against the roof of your mouth to imitate a horse, *clop.* Except when you're drifting in and out of a drunken stupor this is the sort of tiny sound that makes you think someone with a hand-gun and silencer has slipped in, *fuck,* maybe the sexually frustrated cow you share with has finally flipped her lid.

No. You are not dead. You have not been shot. You are wideawake; you can hear her walking around with the cordless, she is hissing like a rattlesnake.

'I left a note, but he just went ahead and drank the whole fucking thing, he's obviously trying to freak me out, he obviously wants the apartment to himself . . . No, you *have* to help me, you're going to have to come here and talk to him . . . I don't care if he's the size of a fucking mountain, you have to help me get him out, you hear? Jesus Christ!'

When I open the door of my room to the hall, she looks like a cornered rat. She holds the phone to her tits, then her slack jaw opens a degree but she just makes this trapped animal groan, *Oooh.* And that's when I say, 'Hey, it's OK, I'm leaving so you can have your mental fucking breakdown all on your own, alright?'

She hangs up, badly. I hear the line go dead, over and over. She starts to cry, I mean really fuckin' cry, what with hot snot coming out of her surgically-enhanced nose, and sobbing shoulders going up and down, like pistons. And I have no choice, I have to hug her for a while I keep saying, 'I'm sorry OK. I'm really fuckin' sorry.' Except, we're both in our underwear and it starts to feel uncomfortable, 'specially when the temperature of our skin starts to climb, and things become a little hard and clammy.

It's been quite a while since I've held a woman in my arms. But to be perfectly honest, hugging someone you weren't even sure you liked is better than hugging no one at all.

Nothing happens for a while, just the sound of the fridge humming and the phone line thrumming in the background. And all the while I'm rocking her gently from side to side, 'I'm sorry. I'm really, really sorry.'

And it's weird, it's as if I'm apologizing for the all things I've done, and all the things I haven't dreamt of doing.

And out over the looming metal bridge and the deep dark water swirling, out across the vaulting cathedrals and fake fountains foaming I feel him. I close my eyes and lay my huge hands upon her gently this time she sighs and falls into me, her body a book abandoned on a never-ending summer's day.

She is giving herself to me wordlessly now all I can do is remain standing, breathing and quivering inside I am thinking of what will happen tonight in her room, then tomorrow in his, I am thinking of what will happen when it is my turn.

When I will be called upon to quietly make the sacrifice.

5.

There's a disturbingly beautiful creature sitting on Ed's bed when I come to work, all riddled with remorse feeling like an overseas container with the wrong address stamped on. It's like the time I came home from the Clinic to find my ex-girlfriend the actress upstairs with Ma, the two of them eating grapes, spitting pips and laughing the way women who know things about you always do.

She's one of those people that's incredibly alive: Her hair is the colour of a copper beech in September, no mucky fuckin' products in it, her skin is alabaster and her eyes are steely and determined, like the actress who once played Carrie—*Spacek, Sissy.* Only without the freckles or bucket of blood on her head, obviously.

She is petite, but you can see she does a serious workout; in fact she's the sort that would last a lot longer than most if this city really were under attack and everyone had to live on rations. I can feel it already, in my balls, an invasion of detrimental tadpoles. With her chiselled cheekbones, perfectly proportioned shoulders, and tiny scooped-in waist, she makes me feel like a Golem. Still, I know enough not to say anything until she does, except she doesn't; she just stands up silently and proffers her hand.

It is cool, with delicate, long, tapered fingers. I put my hand over hers and make no effort to squeeze.

'It's OK. I won't break.'

Her voice is molasses and honey. The sound of the South hidden deep down in it.

'And when it rains you won't melt, right?'

'Right.'

She smiles, and I'm not saying my knees go weak, but something akin to a butter churn turning over is going on inside. Then she takes her other hand, places it carefully on top, and with her two resting there she starts moving the pile up and down. I'm like a puppet on a string.

'Dana.'

'Trevor.'

'The new guy?'

'Yeah.'

'I'm Ed's physical therapist. I want to go through some of his routine with you,

'OK?'

She lets go and asks what I'm laughing at, so I tell her the word *routine* makes him sound like a member of a synchronized swimming team.

'You know, Esther Williams and all that?'

She doesn't know. And she doesn't find it all that amusing; in fact she looks away and says she's sure Ed will be along any second now. And that's when my stomach rumbles like a storm gathering, so I say, 'Sorry, skipped breakfast, didn't want to be late. You know, first day and all that.'

She arches one of her perfect eyebrows and says it's OK, she nearly always eats when she's over here too, no big deal, no need to feel awkward; except she leaves a little pause before the word *awkward* and I'm thinking, *Red alert, red alert! She's reading your thoughts, she's a fuckin' witch. Make your mind a total blank.* Which I do and then I can't think of anything intelligent to say, obviously, so I just come out with, '*Eh*, she's an amazing cook, isn't she?

'Ellie? Yes. But you be careful there, Trevor is it?'

'Why?'

'Because she'll eat you up, that's why.'

She nods her head in an exaggerated way, she lets me know I can stop being afraid of her, then she moves to the door which is slightly ajar and checks to see if the coast is clear, craning her neck and standing on her tippy toes, bit like Alice in Wonderland, except I don't think Alice'd be wearing a thong.

She sits back on his bed, folds one leg under and pats the duvet the way his mother did, only this time it's different.

I cross over and sit down, carefully. It's a relief he has an expensive mattress which doesn't sink too deep.

'This isn't as easy as you might think.'

'Who said I thought it was easy?'

'Hey, Big Guy. I'm on your side. OK?'

'OK.'

'What I'm trying to say is, Ed is very weak, very sick.'

'I gathered as much.'

She bites her bottom lip. 'Can I ask you a question, Trevor?'

'Yes you can. Dana.'

'Have you ever worked with sick or dying people before?'

'Uh-huh.'

'You wanna tell me about it?'

I worked for nearly a year at the Central Remedial Clinic in Dublin.'

'OK. Good.'

'Plus, I nursed my mother right up until the end.'

'Oh. I'm sorry.'

'That's OK. You had no way of knowing.'

A pause. She shifts her body towards me. 'Do you know what "skin hunger" is, Trevor?'

'Uh-huh.'

'Well?'

'It's when sick people like Ed yearn for what we call "nonclinical contact." But back home, we used to refer to it as plain old-fashioned loneliness.'

She smiles as if to say, *Ya got me there buddy,* but I don't smile back. I'm feeling quite sad actually I'm remembering the time the chalk scraped the blackboard and Dalek started screaming—the way he was jumping around in his chair you'd swear his little kiddie-pants were on fire. I found out afterwards that a wasp had flown into his shirt, and after they'd all gone home I dabbed his stumpy pigeon chest with vinegar and cotton wool. That's when these huge, slow tears began coursing down his hard little face, the sort of injured mask you find on street-kids in Belfast, or Baghdad, or etched on pale victims of clerical sexual abuse. And I could hear my ventriloquist voice saying, over and over, 'Hey, it's OK, it's over now, it's OK,' but it wasn't because of the wasp that Dalek was crying, it was because no one had touched him lovingly in years.

I really want to tell her this story, I really want to show her I'm not some total fuckin' chancer who just walked in off the street but sometimes the more we want to say something the harder it becomes.

Before I left for Dublin Airport my father stood on the steps of our house, his mouth opened like a greyhound trap. Words refused to spring forth. There was just the acrid odour of his undigested breakfast. Then the longest-ever pause. During which he retreated up two steps.

'Goodbye Trevor.'

'Bye Dad. I'm sorry.'

'So am I, son.'

Dana smoothes the duvet by my leg, she says she is sorry if she was, *like, in any way patronizing.* Then she gives me this really genuine smile, except James Mason is saying, *My dear boy, exercise caution since it's entirely feasible she's one of those disconcerting individuals, like Andy Garcia, who can do that instant empathy thing with their eyes, alright?*

'You need to understand something, Trevor.'

'OK.'

'Ed has no friends. He has no future. He has no idea of what he can and cannot say to people.'

'I see.'

But all I can see is her collapsing naked on my chest after making love my cock still inside her, *Jesus*, wouldn't it be amazing to drift off to sleep like that?

(Yes.)

'Most guys last about a week.'

'Sorry?'

'With Ed.'

'Oh. Right.'

'Less, if you have any kind of ego. Or you can't handle insults.'

'I'm Irish. Historically, we're used to being insulted.'

'I'm serious here. You work in this house, you leave normal rules of society outside that door. Your companionship is being bought, you understand? You will never be friends with him. Probably, you will never want to be. He's a cruel and shallow young man and he has an anger inside him that no matter how hard you try to justify, it doesn't allow for him to . . . Look, what I'm trying to say here is, Ed's not really a very nice person.'

I'm thinking, *It's probably best if I make up my own mind*, but I just nod and say, 'OK, thanks.'

There's a long pause as she stretches her legs out in front— you'd swear she was on a little swing bench on a porch in Georgia.

'Have you met his mother?'

'I've had the pleasure, yes.'

You can see her trying not to smile.

'What's the jackanory with her?'

'Excuse me?'

'What's the story, what's wrong with her?'

'Technically, jack shit. She broke her leg in a skiing accident upstate about ten years ago. Then she just took to the bed.'

'Jesus. Her husband must've been over the fuckin' moon.'

'You've met the Judge?'

'Yes.'

'And?'

'I dunno. I think his bark is worse than his bite.'

'Did he talk money with you?'

'It's OK. Ellie already briefed me.'

She's talking suddenly about how much wealth they have, and about this *amazing* place they own in Saratoga, 'you should *see* it.'

But all I can see are the tiny places in the corners of her rosebud mouth where there is no gloss shining. And I'm thinking of those excellent scenes in old black and whites where the hero grabs the girl and starts tongue-sandwiching her and little fists come up to beat him on his big broad chest, *You beast, you beast*, then she just gives in*, Aaah.*

'You listening to me?'

'Your lips are moving. But I switched the sound off a while ago.' I was actually saying to myself, *Self, this has to be one of the most amazing women you've ever seen.*

'Jesus. Another fruit cake.'

'What are you doing later?'

'What?'

'This evening. What are you doing?'

'I'm having dinner with my . . . fiancé.'

'You remind me of a mermaid, do you know that?'

'A mermaid.'

'Yeah, I really love your hair. Can I touch it?'

'No.'

'OK, relax. What about dinner?'

'I told you already, I'm meeting someone.'

'I was hoping you were going to say "I'm washing my hair," because I'd really love to wash it for you. In fact, I'd pay you.'

She smiles, despite herself. 'Seriously, how does twenty bucks sound?' She's giving me the *how-could-someone-like-me-be-interested-in-a-whacko-like-you* look, but I just reach out and touch the silk on her head, and she's laughing at the audacity of it now she pushes me away, so I push her back, then she pushes me again, trying to get me to go sideways on the bed.

Dana is very strong for her size; she is made of rock, she definitely will not break. I push her hard this time she rolls over and her foot comes up so I grab it and give it a sharp tug, then she starts kicking and laughing. We are ten years old and I have to say, it feels very nice. Her hair is cascading back on the starched white duvet, she really is astonishing.

That's when Ed rolls in like Jack fuckin' Nicholson with this fake grin planted on his mush, like a plastic yellow sunflower. As his smile melts his elongated face becomes disfigured, like the Wicked Witch in *The Wizard of Oz* and it isn't funny anymore, so we sit up.

She rises slowly she fixes her hair solemnly, and walks over to him. I'm trying hard not to look at her perfect Kylie Minogue little ass, thinking, *Fuck I'm off to a disastrous start.*

I hate when that happens, don't you?

Ed points the wheels of his chair at me, like the captain of a doomed nuclear sub.

Dana stands behind him, her fingers resting on his skeletal shoulders, her morse code eyes flashing: *Remember, he is shallow and cruel, he has no friends.* When I look into his watery, weak ones, they are giving me daggers, and a volcano inside me wants to erupt. *What's your fuckin' problem, pal? Is no one sup-*

posed to laugh or have fun in your presence? And tell us, where's the Scottish fucker? And how many people applied for the job, Ed? How many mature, responsible English-speaking people with genuine experience are standing outside the fuckin' door? Well?

But of course I say nothing, just try to make my big potato face a blank, a canvas he can project and paint on, a clown at a rich kid's party.

Ed stares at his pedals as if he's just been told that, on top of having six months to live, he has to give all his money to Fidel Castro. He'd like me to step outside for a while I can hear him talking with Dana all low, slow, and serious.

I'm called back in. Dana says she'd like to see me lift Ed from his chair, *please.* Then place him on the bed, *gently.*

I can't stand when people use schoolteacher voices to underline things that are patently obvious; I mean, it's not like I'm going to pick the little prick up and toss him across the room, though come to think of it . . .

I bend down slowly. I slide my hands under his thighs, put my arm around his emaciated shoulders and when I stand up straight it's like holding a really skinny young dog. Dana says, 'Jesus, you're strong.'

I say nothing, just step carefully towards the bed. Ed looks up. The whites of his eyes are yellowed, as if someone was religiously dropping iodine down in there while he slept. He is so helpless it's impossible to remain angry, so I wink and let him know I'm here to protect him, not to do him harm.

He exhales, it is hot and foul, but I feel him relax a little, so I spin round like a housewife with a bundle of laundry who hears a love song on the radio that she used to dance to years and years ago.

Dana says, 'Whoa, take it easy, please be careful,' but he just laughs and a little piece of his lank hair sticks out in the playground wind he says, 'It's. OK. I feel. Safe.'

And that word is like a code, it's magic and all of a sudden you can see pettiness slink out of the room, its tail between its legs, its pointy ears pinned back completely.

I put Ed on the bed, like a package at Christmas.

Dana explains how his bones retract during the day, she shows me how to bend them back without hurting him but I've done all this before at the Clinic especially when we went on this long drive to the Cliffs of Moher and they all wanted to get as close to the edge as they could to scream obscenities into the howling wind that swallowed their words, and some of their cares as well.

Afterwards we all went to the pub to get locked, except a lot of them had severe pains in their necks so I had to rub them and they were like children looking for chair-o-planes at a party—*me too, me too, me too*—all except Dalek who was too busy doing his demented grin at a table full of tourists; that little fucker had evil enough in his eyes to make fat people leave hot food behind on a very cold day.

Dana can see I know what I'm doing, more importantly she can see I could never hurt anything so pitiful and small. As she backs away she smiles at him and says, 'Looks like the big Irish guy might know a thing or two, Ed. Maybe we got lucky this time, huh?'

He smiles and closes his eyes as I lift him under his shoulders to raise him up on his pillows my fingers establish that his ribs are the same size as worn-out pencil nubs, just as easy to snap.

Despite everything she said Dana genuinely seems to like Ed but maybe it's just pity she feels, not that there's anything wrong with that, some people these days can't even muster up that much.

Without saying anything she leaves us alone and there is no pause, none whatsoever, he says, 'Sorry. Man.'

I nod, fluff his pillows and try not to breathe in as he breathes out.

'It's OK, Ed. No biggie.'

'No. I need. This. To. Work.'

'So do I, Ed.' Which is true.

'I was. Being a. Dick.'

'It's OK. I know what you were thinking.'

'You. Do?'

'She's very beautiful.'

'Yeah.'

'Like a Princess. In a fairy tale.'

He smiles. The gums are bloodless.

'I think. She. Might. Like you.'

'I don't know. I'd be a bit afraid.'

'Of. Hurting. Her?'

'No, Ed. Of being hurt.'

This is the best thing I could've said, he blinks twice like a man in solitary exposed to a sudden bright light then he says 'I know. What you. Mean,' but how could he? Ed is sick and small, he's never been used by someone who conveniently (for them) confused physical strength with the emotional kind. And Ed has never watched someone on a windswept beach whisper, *I'm sorry, I'm really, really sorry*, then walk away without looking back, not even fuckin' once.

Ed says Dana is the only one apart from his mother that has stuck with him. Then he closes his eyes; he is dead to the world, with his waxy candle skin I wish he wouldn't do this.

Eventually he speaks: 'I dream. Of dying in her. Arms. That's my fucking. Fairy. Tale.'

It's OK. I'm used to melodrama from people in chairs so I say nothing, just wait until he opens his eyes again. Then I smile patiently and say I can think of much worse ways of buying it, 'How about Ellie lying bollock naked on top of you, eating a giant pepperoni pizza, watching a really long, subtitled French fuckin' movie?'

He laughs, a bit of single-barrel snot escapes and the thing with this job is you can't make a big deal of little domestic accidents, so I take a tissue, trap it like an insect, then throw it in the paper basket. It's a nice shot, right in without touching; isn't it funny how a pointless thing like that can make you feel good again?

'All I ask Ed, is that you make an effort, OK?'

And it's weird because that's exactly what my old fella used to say, *All I ask is that you make a bit of an effort, Trevor*— except of course that wasn't all he asked, as a matter of fact in the end all he asked was that I *steer well clear* and stop asking questions, the answers to which I was not emotionally equipped to deal with.

Nice mellow mood in the room now it's time to go out to the hall and fetch Alan White; he opens one eye to watch me leave.

Low moans and elongated groans down the corridor the mother's door is closed, inside her voice there's a terrible nasal whine: 'That's too much, stop I said, didn't you hear me, Jesus Christ, don't you understand plain English?'

I'm wondering, is Il Judgo-Perverto bent over in there with some hot wax dripping, or maybe a blow torch stuttering blue flame with a Zorro mask on when I hear Dana's patient voice: 'Relax, please. Breathe out on the effort, that's right, once again, up two-three, gently, down two-three.'

See sweat gather in the grooves of those grey elephant knees, see Dana use surgical gloves and palmfuls of talcum to get a purchase on the hanging folds of flesh.

See Dana walking, alone.

See Dana at home. She is standing with hot water hitting her head, hard, it's running down her face, fast, and with all the steam rising in the cabin it's impossible to tell if she is crying.

Then again maybe Dana's the sort of bird, like Carrie in *Sex and the City,* who strolls home after a hard day's work thinking,

Mmm, I wonder what kind of clutch bag would go best with my new Jimmy Choos?

He still has just one eye open when I return, 'What. Is. It?'

I'm thinking, *Well, it's not the Book of fuckin' Kells?* But I just tell him it's a record I bought from some guy in the street, but at the same time I'm wondering, *Why the hell am I leaving out the word 'black'?*

He shifts his shoulders like a woman moving an invisible bra strap. He gets his arms ready to hold the LP and when I tell him Alan White used to be the drummer with Yes, he is completely lost for words.

His nose twitches like Hazel the Rabbit from *Watership Down*, so I scratch it, very lightly.

'Thanks, Trevor.'

'No problemo, Ed.'

He asks 'How much was it' and I say 'It's a present' and the poor fucker lies there grasping it as if it were a Matisse, then he looks up, smiles and darts his doe eyes the direction of the sound system. 'Over there. Please.'

I take the record from him and place it on the turntable carefully; I can feel him boring holes in my back, which is tight and tired from all the politeness and performing.

I sit on his bed. He nods and closes his eyes. We are both hoping the music will work some kind of spell.

Fair play to Squatting Man, the record really is in nice nick, the needle stays lovely and steady except it feels like we're waiting for Yaweh or Charlton Heston to talk to us through the speakers you can hear this crackling coming, then at last it starts up, and it's not bad actually it has quite a bit of life in it and an excellent chorus in one song, *'Don't you know you're a radio, when you get a good reception, you begin to glow.'*

Ed opens his eyes slowly, he swallows as he looks at me,

guilty as hell, so I smile back as if to say, *It's OK man, you've given me a very good reception, can't you see me glowing away?*

But he's not the type to beat himself up for very long. Then again Ed doesn't have much time to waste on regret or human pomp and ceremony.

We listen to one whole side without a word which is good since there'll be an awful lot of downtime in this room.

I stand up. I'm halfway across the room when he whispers, bit like Don Corleone, 'It's. OK.'

'You sure?' I turn. He nods.

'I'd like to. Keep. The. Other. Side. Till later.'

A grey, brave little smile, those cardboard teeth rotting in his head, my feet moving, my hand extending . . .

Now the needle lifting . . .

BOOK TWO

The hail shall sweep away the refuge of lies,
and the waters shall overflow the hiding place.

ISAIAH, 28:17

1.

June/July/August

Days slide by, wisps of cloud scudding across the windows of darkly mirrored 'scrapers.

Ed reversing the electric chair left, and right, showing me where everything is; his *Simpsons'* tapes stacked in order of preference; his voice-activated pocket recorder into which he intends to dictate the story of his ebbing life, which he never will; his VHS and DVD movies arranged by mood, not title; his alphabeticallyarranged albums and CDs; his pills and prescriptions, his atomizers, dehumidifiers, vaporizers and decongestants.

His bedpan, his bendy straw.

His porno mags.

How to recharge the batteries for the chair, how to operate the breathing-machine, how to sterilize it and the mask attached *pro-per-ly*, how to zip-lock the plastic curtain round his bed into the floor so the area gets turned into an emergency oxygen tent.

How to entertain him. How to keep him alive.

His voice, in time to the motor of the chair, 'Cut my. Food. In. To. Smaller. Pieces. *Whirr.* Bend the. Straw. Towards me. *Whirr.* Please hold the. Pla-stic beaker. Steady. Help me. *Whirr.* In. And out of the bath. It's import-ant for you to. Stand out. Sssside. The door. You know. People can drown. In. Less than. Four inches.'

While he bathes he keeps calling out my name, like a lamb at Passover. But I'm always there like a sentry I am always waiting to wrap him in the wonderful white towels that arrive, as if by magic, every single morning.

Ed says the Scottish guy used to just walk away and watch TV. More than once the water went stone cold. Have I any idea how useless and completely powerless he felt, just sitting there, like a plastic fucking duck?

When I tell him I would never do that, never, he just nods his chin towards his concave, completely hairless chest. It will be some time before he believes in me.

2

I'm still on four days a week, which is ideal. In fact, it's the way the whole wide world should operate because people would have more time for families, funerals, friends (if they had any), pets, hobbies, exercise, sketching, diary-writing, poems, springcleaning and rooting through skips on Madison marvelling at what bored, rich white people hire Puerto Ricans to toss out.

Behind white dusk masks they glare, envying my hazy, lazy days.

I'm generally just strolling around the whirling city, picking things up in shops and putting them carefully back down again, like a good tourist should, when I get this thick Bronx voice in my head telling me to visit St Patrick's, probably because Rain on Me Baby suggested it in her own inimitable way. And like an advertising jingle for a discount electrical store the notion gets stuck in my head and it won't go away, so *fuck it*.

There's this priest there. He's pretty good looking and let's face it most of them are desperate-looking yokes with red scaly skin and white crystallized dandruff on their collars, and if they weren't priests what would they—or could they—be?

Grifters? Pyramid salesmen? Con artists?

Anyway, he seems pretty popular in that a lot of people are hovering around him all listening and nodding intently. Then he calls them his children and gives them a group blessing, which I have to say I find kind of offhand and lazy.

He sees me staring. He smiles and I nod.

'Welcome, my son.'

Which is a line from a Pink Floyd song, isn't it? *'Welcome my son, welcome, to . . . the Machine.'*

'Thanks, Father.' Then I look away.

'I'll be hearing confession now, if you like?'

'I think I'll just say a few prayers, thanks all the same.'

'No sins?'

'None worth wasting your time with, Father.'

'You're Irish?'

'Uhuh'

'You probably have some ancient sins on your soul, you sure you don't want a quick fix?'

'Pretty sure, thanks all the same.'

'Would you prefer to just sit and talk?' Which you have to admit is a pretty clever question, I mean I've already told the bloke I'd prefer to just say a few prayers, but priests are fishers of men and clearly I'm not going to be the big one that got away.

'Yeah. OK.'

Turns out this guy is a Jesuit, which is definitely the best kind of priest, very philosophical and normally able to look at things from unusual, maybe even skewed perspectives. He's a good conversationalist, and a good listener also, and in America it's rare to find both qualities available in the one person so I'm no longer in such a hurry to depart the scene.

We start to chew the fat about God, Death, Fate and Pre-Destination and he tells me he finds me a very unusual, intelligent and well-read young man, which is probably over-egging it. Anyway, we get to talking about intelligence. I explain to him how I believe there are several specific and unrelated types.

There's *academic intelligence,* which really isn't worth a whole hill of fuckin' beans, and I tell him for proof all you have to do is look at my family, and he says, 'What do you mean?'

'Well, Father, I guess I mean that any one of us can start up their own dusty little library and fill their head with pithy quotes and witty *bon-mots* and Wildean epigrams but, like, what's the point if you have shite taste in clothes and music and no friends that you'd want to be seen out in public with?'

He nods diplomatically and says for me to continue, so I do.

I tell him there's *emotional intelligence*, the kind that allows you to keep love alive and be aware of the needs of others and to take into consideration duties and responsibilities that go beyond the norm, whatever the norm is. I mean, to be honest, sometimes after a hard day at the Clinic particularly when Dalek and The Captain were acting up I didn't always feel like marching up to my mother's room to listen with intent, or to change her sheets that used to get rightly soaked from night sweats and the sideeffects of the cocktail of drugs she was on, or to hand wash and hang out her nighties and knickers.

But you see, I knew it was the sort of daily detail my old man and my sisters would neglect, and let's face it when you're dying you shouldn't have to worry about the fuckin' laundry now should you?

I tell him all this, and he seems genuinely interested, so I explain to him how emotional intelligence allows us to subjugate ego and he smiles and nods and inside his head he's probably saying something to himself in Latin. Then I say that emotional intelligence is the most valuable kind because it enables us to make sacrifices and all of a sudden he's nodding enthusiastically the way priests do when you even mention the word *sacrifice,* because basically they like to remind the rest of us that their whole life has been one big, long one.

Then I pause and say, 'Of course Father, there's also *criminal intelligence* which really shouldn't be underrated either.' And I tell him that people who spend a lot of time figuring out how to rob insurance companies and bypass security systems in vaults and release non-toxic sleeping gas through air vents in banks are also pretty fuckin' resourceful, like George Clooney and Brad Pitt in *Ocean's Eleven* (not *Twelve*, which was a bag of shite).

He nods. And this time he doesn't tell me to continue, so we sit there for quite a while.

He tries to do the staring into your soul thing, really peering into my eyes so I close them and wait. Eventually it's his go.

He explains that intelligence is like a mirror. The first reflection we see is that of ourselves; then, with maturity and a degree of self-sacrifice we see how others might perceive us. And finally, with His grace, we see how God sees us. And that moment is a revelation, that moment is an epiphany because we see our soul rising; it is our moment of passing and our moment of becoming, and we enter the Light and are assimilated into God's infinite wisdom and understanding.

I've got this weird thing about mirrors, I can't help it. I start laughing and it's the high-pitched one I told you about earlier. He looks hurt for a second like a dog that's been shouted at for bringing muddy paws into the dining room. He asks why am I laughing? I tell him I'm trying to imagine what my family back home might see when they peer into the proverbial looking-glass. He asks me what I believe they see, and I tell him I haven't the fuckin' foggiest so he asks me how I 'envision' them and that's the way he talked and you shouldn't hold it against him, a lot of Jesuits spend too much time with their blackhead noses stuck in out-of-print books.

'Well Father, they're like this awful, pseudo-intellectual circus act with spontaneous bursts of applause for clever little quips in Latin, or sharp inhalations of breath, *oooh*, if someone scales new heights in analysing the way, say, Beckett's time as a beret-wearing member of the French Resistance helped to inform his assault on the conservative forces that dominated European theatre.'

'I'm a fan of Sam. I must admit I'd never considered it like that before.'

'No, Father. Don't go down that road. It's all bolloxology.'

'I see. Go on. Your family is a circus act?'

'Well, all families are circus acts when you think about it, but yes mine in particular seems to fit the bill. My father is the ringmaster and my sisters are these little performing ponies, you know those miniature brown ones with yellow manes?'

'Shetlands.'

'Yeah. So my sisters, the Shetlands, they're leaping through these little circles of conceit or deceit with poodles on their backs. *Hey hoopla, hey hoopla! Look how clever we are!'*

Now he's smiling and nodding, and maybe I had a little, tiny toke of Ellie's grass before I left my room and I'm on a bit of a roll.

'And at night when they go to brush their manes in the mirror, they don't see how ridiculous they are, all they see is their red rosettes and silver cups and stupid square hats.'

'*Mortarboards.'*

'Whatever, and their endless poxy degrees and diplomas, and the ringmaster standing there waxing his moustaches in his demented red coat and it's all pointless, it's all . . . '

'Bolloxology.'

'Nice one, Father.'

And apart from the deliberately loud whisperings of the zealots and the quiet, determined sobbing of a lone fireman whom the priest hadn't had the heart to approach, the only sound you can hear is coins falling solidly into the slots where ancient Irish people are lighting candles.

'See, it never dawns on them, Father, not for one single second that there's no one watching except for maybe God and me and Ma. And that we don't actually find them all that clever, especially Ma who told me she was worried sick that they'd never meet any men, and she'd never get them out from under her feet. I mean, they never even went into town and, *Jesus,* you should've seen the heads on their friends. 'Specially the blokes.'

'What was wrong with them?'

'What was right with them, Father? Do you know people who've no idea about cars or clothes or modern music or the latest films or what was on the telly the night before?'

'I must confess that as regards popular culture, I . . . '

'No. No. The sort of people, and yes I know I'm generalizing here, Father, but I'm the one who opened the door to them and shook their flaky little pastry hands and watched the way they went all red when the dog stuck his nose in their odourless crotches, the sort who think sex and tongues and pornothoughts and dizzying arsey smells are, well, a bit mucky, sort of yucky and *aren't we much better off having separate beds* and *do you feel like reading dear, or shall I switch off the light?* Sorry, Father.'

He says, no, no, it's OK to talk to him in this vein—it's actually quite instructive.

'Anyway, you know the type. The sort of women who answer surveys and say they prefer a good hug to making love which you would too if you saw their husbands with their curly black teeth and coke bottle glasses and brown shoes with blue trousers.'

He's trying not to laugh but you can see the capable, green eyes dancing. You can see he really loves being talked to as a nonpriest. It's like when your world has shrunk and the only humans you encounter are worn-thin frazzled teachers, the guys in class who give you a wide berth after lessons, your swimming coach, your decrepit relatives on your father's side, and your sisters. And they all have this frozen set image of you, this rigid fuckin' script, and then you meet someone new or you have the opportunity, maybe through a new job, to step outside the prison of their perception. And you get to become someone different, maybe even the person you always dreamed of being.

And suddenly you find yourself looking forward to meeting that new individual, to talking to them at length, and after you meet them things always speed up a little, new ideas, new possibilities, and your dreams are more vivid and . . .

'I take it your sisters' boyfriends weren't exactly your cup of tea?'

'Well, in my dealings with other people, Father, I try not to be judgmental. But I have to be honest: they were just so terrifically, soporifically boring.'

'Well, boring is never good.'

'No. And if one of them was even half alive, why he'd be officially declared a card, a character, a ticket, and he'd smoke cheap cigars and wear outrageous bow-ties and go all weird if you brought him upstairs and put on some Jim Morrison and maybe smoked some skunk, or a tiny smidgen of sensamalion.' I need to be careful—I'm nearly confessing.

'And he'd sit there, his face changing colours like a baboon's arse in heat, and he'd go, "I say, do you know something, Trevor? I'm not nearly as jolly as everyone presumes." And you're thinking, "Hey man, neither am I, but I don't go around telling perfect fuckin' strangers." No offence, Father.'

'It's OK, son. Go on.'

'And he keeps sighing like a big bellows. "Phew, I say, what is this stuff ?" as his big boneless face goes from purple to red to green, to a kind of deathly pale. And Jim Morrison is singing his guts out, *Break on through to the other side.*"—Oh, and I should have said, Father, that it's Christmas and my mother isn't very well at all, and that my sisters wanted to book us into a poxy, atmosphere-less hotel in Dublin to avoid all the fuss and bother of cooking which my mother actually enjoyed 'cause it used to take her mind off pills and pain. And they're pretending that they're thinking of her when really they're just thinking of themselves which is what people do best, isn't it Father? And they haven't bothered buying me any presents, they've just given me money in a plain white envelope, as per fuckin' usual.'

There's a bit of a silence and he asks was it possible that I went out of my way to upset my sisters, or indeed their friends? And I say, 'Mmm, maybe once or twice, Father.'

And he says it's OK. We all had transgressions that could be blamed on our youth, I could tell him, so I do.

'Well Father, it's like this: Barry, the guy with the bow-tie, just wouldn't leave me the hell alone. Sat too close on the couch and kept pressing his jelly-baby leg against mine and if I got up, even to rub the dog or to throw a briquette on the fire, so did he. He was like a shadow, but a shorter, thicker one. Anyway, I know it was dumb but I put something into his drink and well how was I supposed to know that people like that get all panicky when the walls of their mental estates come tumbling down and all the turrets and tent-poles of their beliefs start to slip and slide? Do you know what I mean?'

'No.'

'You know when you actually see someone's house of cards collapsing. The scaffolding falling away, *aaaaaaagh*, conviction and certainty and maybe even sanity melting, like in that painting by Salvador Dali.'

'The melting clock?'

'Now you have it.'

The priest, who now that I think of it was called Emmet, asks me what I did next. And I remember at the time that if you listened really, really hard in the kitchen of my father's house you could hear Kylie Minogue singing on the radio. '*Everybody's doing this brand new dance now . . . So come on, come on, do the locomotion with me.*' And it was like when you hear your thoughts being broadcast over the radio in a taxi. And yer man, Mr Outrageous Bow-Tie, he's on his arachno-back and his legs are pumping the air as if he's on this invisible unicycle, almost in perfect time to the music. And I had this overwhelming desire inside to get up and boogie on down. But it's OK, I didn't, I mean, there are limits, right?

'So what happened. To Barry?'

'Well, Father, the local doctor—who knew me well because I was accident-prone until I was about fifteen—comes around huffing and puffing and holding up his little leather valise as if it held the answer to the riddle of fuckin' existence.'

He's smiling again which is good because previously he was doing that therapist thing. You know when they just look at you and say nothing but with their furrowed eyebrows they're actually saying quite a lot and isn't it weird the way none of us can stop our minds leaping to conclusions even when we don't know half the fuckin' facts?

'Anyway Father, this doctor, he asks is it possible the guy with the tie has had access to anything other than brandy and cigars and they all look up at me *shock horror* like these really bad actors on a murder mystery weekend. I say yes, it was maybe slightly possible Barry might have *eh* inadvertently taken one of my Ma's painkillers which had fallen on the ground and been trampled on by a high heel and then somehow got confused with the hundreds and thousands, you know, the little dressing-dots on top of the Christmas cake he'd been wolfing down from the moment he arrived.'

'And was this poor man OK afterwards?'

'He was grand. He gave up drink and probably saved a fortune, lost weight and avoided getting gout and a big purple fuckin' nose. He even came out of the closet—something my ugly sister should have been extremely grateful about but which she always kind of held against me, which you have to admit is not exactly rational now is it?'

He pauses and considers what I have told him. 'What else do you remember about Christmas, my son?'

'I remember wishing I belonged to a different family.'

'Why?'

'Because mine were so contrived and controlled and no one laughed out loud at *Willy Wonka & the Chocolate Factory* and there was no sense of wonder left inside them, and therefore no sense of loss when she finally died. It was just business as usual. The inevitable had happened.'

'I'm sorry for your loss, son. Do you miss your mother?'

'Sorely.'

'And since her departure?'

'It wasn't a flight, Father. No disrespect.'

'Since her passing, what do you feel now about religion? And God?'

'I'm still very religious in my own way. The first school I went to had us all write AMDG in the margins.'

'*Ad Majorem Dei Gloriam.*'

'For the greater honour and glory of God, yeah, and I believe that's what I try to do with my life's work.'

'What is it that you do, my son?'

'I'm a companion to a boy with Muscular Dystrophy.'

'I too have worked with the sick. So you know about sacrifice?'

'I know about sacrifice and toil and sickness and doubt and sitting in a stuffy room all day long with nothing happening except time passing slowly and Death filing his fingernails in the corner.'

'I see.'

Go on tell him.

Almost as if he hears it too he says, 'Go on, my son, tell me what else you feel.'

'I sometimes feel these voices questioning the reasons why I do it, Father, and some of the voices are sort of cynical and uppercrust English, and they say, *You're not really making a sacrifice, Trevor. You're just trying to draw attention to yourself, trying to prove to God that you are good so he can move on to the next candidate and leave you the hell alone.*'

'God bothers you?'

'My conscience does.'

'Many theologians would contest that conscience and God are one and the same.'

'I've heard that alright, Father, yeah.'

Emmet seems to have forgotten that I was Jesuit-educated which is annoying because I've kind of presumed this, in fact I've based my entire conversational riff around it.

'In what way does your conscience bother you?'

'It niggles me. Undermines me.'

'How?'

'It gets at me at night. It says, *Trevor, you're performing in a bizarre little theatre of the absurd. You're play-acting and the script is destined to get weirder. And the Director is going to ask you to do something to make the play's dramatic purpose clear. Something ritualistic and sacrificial. Something strange yet familiar, just as the lights are slowly dimming and . . .* '

I'm totally losing it and he's looking at me the way they all do, trying to find a way out. *Oh look. There's someone I know. I really must rush. Toodle-pip, old bean.* And it's not nice to feel you were opening up only to find the other person takes a look at what's inside and turns their nose up like a housewife in a fishmonger's being shown yesterday's catch, up close.

But no, I'm wrong, he's not retreating, he's just gathering his thoughts.

'Listen to me now. I believe you are making a *genuine* sacrifice. I believe that for a young man to devote his time, and his energy, and his love, in order to assist a dying person is a wonderful, life-affirming deed.'

'Maybe.'

'There's no maybe about it.'

And that's the problem with priests and psychiatrists and people in general isn't it? You open up, you disclose, you try your utmost to be completely honest then afterwards they say emphatic shit like, *No, I think what you are doing is right, I don't see how it can be any other way.* When the whole bloody point is that you're supposed to see it the other way, you're supposed to try and see that even ugly sordid barbaric truth has a right to exist. I mean, you don't have to necessarily agree but at least you see the possibilities. At least you acknowledge the grey areas, *swirling*.

Shit, maybe American Jesuits aren't as well trained as Irish ones.

And I don't tell him about the keyhole, or how ritual and sacrifice are linked and repeated, repeated and linked—that's how primitive tribes lived. And that none of us are half as fuckin' civilized as we like to think.

And I don't tell him how some nights when Ed's head is resting on the starched pillow it looks like he's already dead, or how my hands feel on his scratchy, eczema-coated flesh, or how some days the need to scream rises up inside like oppressive opera music. I don't tell him how small I feel under the exaggerated skyline, how insignificant I am, how the job is the *only fuckin' thing* that gives me power, the only thing that allows me some small degree of control even if I have to do my breathing exercises three times a day in the hall, the only thing that permits me to feel vaguely God-like when I brush his thinning hair last thing at night, before I stretch him out. And his feet are wrapped up in a hot white towel, and he is smiling down. Beatifically.

And I don't tell him my theory about how we all attempt to be God-like at some point in our lives, how maybe we don't even know we're doing it. Perhaps it's a broken person too dedicated to their dead-end job, a perfectionist computer programmer with no outside life who works on into the night and forgets to eat, or sleep, or think; a grim-faced, granite-jawed street urchin in Rio practising with a football until his feet go numb; the boy-Achilles attacking shadows with his wooden sword; perhaps it's a woman who gets slowly confused and starts to tidy her house obsessively ironing tea towels; a vaguely angry man firing a handgun at a black target every morning before taking the crowded subway to work; a fat lonely child whose parents have divorced and who watches a *Barney* video, over and over again, until he knows every frame, every beat, and can therefore enter it, become part of it. Control it.

I tell him none of this. Instead, when he asks me what's wrong, I just tell him that the odd time I can get, well, a bit isolated, a little bit down.

'I'm always here.'

'Hardly. I mean you don't live here, Father.'

'No. But God is always here.'

'Is he, though?'

'We have to believe, son.'

'Why? Because if we don't, there's no point in trying to be good?'

'No, because if we don't it makes a mockery of His sacrifice and His love, and too many people in the world today are already making that their vocation.'

There's a trace of anger in his voice, which is OK, because in the newspaper today there was a story about fundamentalists invoking God's name moments before they blew apart some mothers and smiling toddlers outside a primary school.

'We need to balance the equation, is that right, Father?'

'That's right, son.' He does something incredible now: he tilts my chin up, the way my swimming coach used to. 'Believe in yourself, son. Believe in the goodness you hold within. Believe in God's grace which is limitless and which He bestows upon us daily. Look at me now.'

I do. It's as if he's hypnotizing me.

'I want you to believe in the sacrifice you are making. I want you to make it for Him. Believe in your own power now and recognize it as His. Recognize it as His love flowing. Recognize the forces at work in your own heart. Understand that they are

His. Understand that you are His instrument, His channel, that through you His eternal goodness flows.'

He blesses me with his eyes closed, touches me softly on the forehead and the chest and mutters '*Ego te absolve*' which are my three favourite words in Latin, and probably any other language to boot. I feel Grace descend like dust upon my shoulders and I when I stand up, he opens his eyes, smiles and nods as if to say, *It's OK now.* It's the first time in quite a while that I remember how big and strong I am.

'Thanks, Father. I'll probably see you in here again—soon I hope.'

And before I walk out I stop and touch the fireman on his broad back, softly. He places his hand over mine without turning and says, 'Thanks big guy, 'preciate the gesture.'

And it has been returned, it has been rendered unto Caesar, *the ability.*

As I walk through the massive doors out under the Gothic archway down the steps, *I am a giant. A gentle giant. There is no shadow of badness, no mark of doubt upon me, no danger within.*

And what I spied through the keyhole shook me to my core, burned and lowered me, but did not knock me over, did not cause me to crumble and fall.

3

S ome of the smells, certain aspects of the daily chores, I'm not going to get into. Why? Because it's just not that fuckin' pretty, OK?

It's like when the bloke I used to buy LPs from in this dank, second hand store in Greystones started keeping stuff behind the counter for me, telling me out loud in front of the whole fuckin' shop that he'd been waiting all week to play something special for me. And one afternoon in October I suggested a pint and the child-part of me really believed we were going to become fast and firm friends, even if he did have coated, yellow teeth and a cracked leather waistcoat with an Old Holborn tobacco pouch protruding.

Except it turned out he was one of those whackos has to tell you everything about his last sexual encounter right down to the squishing, farting noises, and whether or not he did it from behind with a fuckin' Spiderman costume on.

I remember the sinking, panicked feeling as the head of my pint went slowly mildewed and old while he talked about his simple country girlfriend, the awful finger things he made her do.

Say nothing.

I wash his hair and say nothing when it comes out in clumps that clog the drain, I say nothing when he tells me to place a porno rag on the plastic shelf in front of him in the shallow bath, I say nothing when his eyes tell mine to move his dead white hands into position; and afterwards, as I lift him from the tepid water, I say nothing.

Just watch grey tadpoles swim towards my disposable rubber gloves.

Breathe in, breathe out . . .

With his lashless eyes locked on mine he deliberately slides his lukewarm, leftover food off his tray, down onto the carpet. And as I bend to scoop up the soggy mess I can hear Dana's whispered warning: *Most guys last a week, less if you have any kind of ego.* It pays sometimes to put an echo on—*ego, ego, ego.* To pretend I'm out strolling in the Swiss Alps. And that the air up there is so rare I can actually break into a smile. It works, the odd time. But mostly when he does something like this to test me I excuse myself politely and walk abruptly from the room, face flushed, heart sinking like a stone.

Sometimes you'll find me doing breathing exercises, *in and out*, in the hall. At night you might hear me playing Nirvana or Queens of the Stone Age, screaming, laughing at the glorious release.

And if you happened by Madison and 57th of an evening you might just see me squeeze my head out the little window, a gargoyle brought suddenly to life, sucking down the first real breath of the day. And the air up there really is so amazing that I have to shout out comes Barney, out from under his awning, yep, the cap is coming off . . . there he is staring up . . . see him scratch the hair on his stupid Beckett head.

If I'm going to ask Dana out on a date, what I need to understand is: 'When she come out of that sick bitch's room, she always gonna have that *don't-come-near-me-now* face on. What you need to do is work on your timing. What you need to do is quit looking at her like a lovesick puppy. You way too huge to be gittin' away with that kinda shit, *a'wight?*'

'OK.'

'You axe me, that skinny little white girl is way too weak to be pulling that Moby-Dick bitch 'round in the first place. Shit, that woman should be on Wrestlemania in a one-piece, twirling people over her ugly supersize head. You pay per view then. Yeah, you laughing now and it feel real good, right?

'Uh-huh.'

'You forget all about Mr Ed, his turkey head, his fucked-up inner organs.'

'Jesus!'

"Cause that what that bad breath be, baby.'

'I'm eating here.'

'You always eatin'.'

'Whose fault is that?'

'You wan' me to stop cookin' and bakin' for you?'

'No.'

'Look, Clever. Just 'member to make her laugh. Dana got just as much shit to forget end of every day as you, OK?'

'OK.'

'Shit, didn't your Mama teach you nothin'? She musta whisper it one time?'

'Whispered what?'

'Think real hard now. Can't you hear her?' She's leaning in, her incredible purple lips almost brushing my ear. 'Hey baby Trevor, it's your Mama. Don't get sore now, but you ain't never gonna git with the ladies on looks alone, not with that big old TV set up top your neck pretendin' like it's a regular head. You gonna need a lotta money, you gonna need to be seriously funny, you gonna need to be talking that bad-ass terrorist-shit all the time.'

I'm really laughing now, but a lot of it has to do with how weird it feels to have her hot breath entering my ear.

'Shit, you one of the ugliest white people I ever did see. You uglier than Jay Leno, an' nurses, they just throw they hands up and run out the *dee-livery* room when they see his big TV set poppin' out.'

'Nice pie. Not as nice as yesterday's, though. I think the pastry was a little soggy.'

'Yeah, that why you ate up every bit. So you want me to git her number?'

'Would you?'

'Maybe.'

'What do you mean *maybe*?'

'I mean maybe you stop comin' in my kitchen with that long face on, maybe you stop staring out the window saying nothin'. Shit, maybe you start being funny again.'

Some days Ellie has her own stuff to contend with and the kitchen is quieter than a boathouse in winter.

Ed's mother wants Italian meatballs; then, at the very last minute, she demands Irish stew. She keeps ringing up asking, 'Where is it? Where is it? Do I have to come in there and make it my goddamn self ?'

And there is only so much of that kind of crap Ellie will take. With her see-through bag of weed laid out on the kitchen table she is going to put her Walkman on with the volume all the way up, then she'll just park and smoke and listen to the Mills Brothers crooning '*Lazy River*' or '*You always Hurt the One You Love.*'

That's when the little phone rings right off the fuckin' hook.

And the door of the Judge's office swings wide—I'll tell you one thing, he'd surprise you with the depth of his roar.

I've watched her more than once putting twigs, stems and bits of her stash in on top of the mother's food—the odd time too a big slow dollop of spit, liquid-hate, falling like sinews from her purple, whispering lips.

Dana's schedule changes from week to week so there's no

point trying to figure out what days she's on or what days she's off; if you do that you end up stopping like a de-programmed robot in the corridor before you walk into the kitchen. And you're always making sure your voice is low and gentle when you say, 'Hello, stranger.' And you sound way too fuckin' practised and you're hoping she won't notice your eyes as she looks up from her ginger and lemon tea. But to be honest she usually just says, 'Hey Big Guy. What's up?'

Then she moves her chair around so you can sit next to her, which is nice.

'How's Ed?'

'Tired. And emotional.'

'Oh. OK. And how are you coping?'

'I'm alright.'

'You sure?'

'Yeah. Thanks.'

'If you need anything, just let me know, OK?'

'*I need you to love me.*'

It's alright, relax. I didn't say that last bit.

I pass the Judge in the corridor sometimes when I'm emptying Ed's bedpan he nods and tries to smile but it's hard for him to face up to reality; he always waits until we're busy doing something like eating, stretching, watching a DVD or a TV show then his caterpillar head pokes round the door, 'Oh I'm disturbing you guys, why don't I drop by later?'

He never does, however.

And that's when Ed requests his headphones, hanging like a black noose in the corner of the room. Then he closes his eyes, retreats into the world of Alan White, Peter Gabriel, Rick Wakeman, Steve Hackett or *The Lamb Lies Down on Broadway*, all four sides without so much as a word I drain the pipes on the breathing machine, I rinse them thoroughly, check the levels in the oxygen tanks, refill both inhalers, re-examine the *best before* dates on all the decongestants, phone the pharmacy, check the atomizers and vaporizers as well as the tiny sprays he uses to ease his vocal chords. And all the time I'm hoping he will ask to be wheeled in to his mother.

Please God, please let me be alone. For just five fuckin' minutes.

I did say that last bit. Almost every other day.

In the sanctified time he is gone I can use the Dustbuster under his bed, I can shake the curtains clean, open the windows wide, breathe in and stretch a new rubber sheet on his mattress. I can rub down his chair with anti-bacterial wipes. *Fuck it*, I can lift the bloody thing right up.

See, I can hold it there for as long as my arms and shoulders will allow.

It is not a crime to be strong. It is not a crime to stand tall.

It is not a crime to be me.

It is a crime to let resentment grow, like damp rising on the wall of the 92nd Street Y.

A faded sign says:

Please consider others.

Please wipe down all surfaces after use.

Please confine your time to 20 minutes at peak periods.

The cross-trainer asks me my weight, my age, how long I'd like the session to last. *Choose from 1-60 minutes.* I key in sixty.

After all, it's my job to be considerate, and I'm finished working for the day.

Sitting alone in the sauna, two of his flawless white towels wrapped around me, thinking about the sea and my dog when the door with the cracked pane opens and two black guys enter. They are arguing softly about some bloke called Delroy.

One is saying, 'Nah, he definitely said he mighta broke his tibia,' and the other says, 'Nope, fibia,' and on it goes. 'Fibia,' 'Tibia,' 'Fibia,' 'Tibia,' until the older one with the slightly highpitched voice says, 'Well, whatever he broke, we ain't worth shit 'less we find another guard by Saturday.'

That's when I lift the towel from my half-baked head and say, 'Hey.'

They both look at me. The older one smiles and says, 'What's up bro?' But the younger one, whites of whose eyes are bloodshot and angry, leaves all conversation-making to his friend.

'You play?'

'A little. I was on the school team.'

'Where?'

'Dublin.'

'Shit. They play over there?'

'Yes they do.'

'How tall are you, man?'

'Tall as you. Maybe taller.'

'What you doing now?'

'Part from talking to you, and being stared at by your side-kick, nothing much. Why?'

He's laughing now, elbowing the other guy, telling him to quit messin' around. Then he asks is there any way I could get dressed again, maybe play a bit, just so they can see for they-selves?

There's nothing worse than putting back on clothes you've been dripping sweat in—no, that's bollocks, there are much worse things in this world. And I'm tired of being all fuckin' deep and heavy in the evening it's amazing how completely silent a court can be in a busy city like this, *zing*, I hear a ball bounce in the corridor then the younger one explodes the doors open and his red eyes say, *Gonna mess you up, white boy.*

His gentle friend comes in, he says, 'Thanks for doing this for us.' He motions me to stand under one of the hoops, 'Stop the young blood scoring.'

Which turns out to be impossible.

The older guy smiles, 'Step aside.' He starts showing me how to do it properly, 'Make like you the man's shadow, but with your arms up and around like this, see. You should be breathing down his neck like so, always let him know you watching the ball, not the man. All the time let him 'preciate you not going to fall for stupid old tricks of the head, shit, see the way his body go one way an' the ball go the other, I got you, see the way I punked him. Look how I do it, see? If he turn, I turn, if his shoe squeak, then you jus' know my shoe gonna squeak. *Gottit?*'

They stop like pieces of a clock at the same time the younger one says, 'Your turn.'

It's more serious and silent now when he tries a jump shot I slap the ball right out of his hands. He picks it up, he comes right at me, his teeth are bared, his mouth melting into . . .

A magnificent smile.

'You learn fast.'

'For a white guy?'

'Nah. You just learn fast. Man, you got some big hands. Strong too. What they feed you?'

'For breakfast, we usually consumed a lightly salted English child.'

They're laughing now. It feels good again my cares are lifting the ball off the ground with one hand he says they're going to 'step up y'alls education, so to speak.' They start passing it over my head, Piggy in the Middle.

'What's your name?'

'Trevor.'

'JD. That out-of-breath old man, his name Charles. Let's play!'

They show me what will happen in a real game, how some 'fast little mothafuckas'll stand on your foot, elbow you in the ribs and under the chin as they pass they might say some shit you might not be too happy to hear if the ref 'ree has his back to you gots to be real careful 'bout who you messing with, team we playin' Saturday, they got two guys from Bed-Stuy, that's where 'Iron Mike' comes from. Those *niggahs* got some serious 'tude. Last time out, they threw the ball right up in Charles' face, caught it an' jus' laughed they asses off. One of them has all that gangsta shit in his mouth, look like that real ugly moth-afucka from that James Bond movie.'

'Jaws?'

'No, man. *Jaws* be a film about a great white shark.'

'Actually, I think you'll find Jaws is the name of the charac-ter in the Bond film you . . . '

'Whatever. Watch this shit!'

And I will never have their hand-to-eye coordination—their lightness through the air, the way they hang by invisible threads. But with their stick-insect legs, they'll never be rooted to the ground the way I am like an oak: after ten minutes they stop trying to go through me, instead they start to go around, except now I have arms that whirl and twirl, like windmills.

We take turns playing JD, and he starts laughing when I stand on his foot and pretend to elbow him in the ribs.

Afterwards, Charles presents his black-and-gold-embossed card; it says he is a 'roof-repair specialist,' but JD winks and says, 'Only thing Charles specialize in is making lonely old ladies think they house 'bout to fall down.'

Charles laughs and says he'll pick me up outside my build-ing at eleven a.m.

'Don't be late.'

'I won't.'

'An' don't go celebratin' Saturday on a Friday night, alright?'

'Alright.'

JD says bring some money, they go out if they win some-times they drive to the track, they might have some lunch, might drink some fine wine.

Then Charles nods his grizzled head and says, 'Yeah, could

be an all-day-out affair. Don't worry, you won't be the only white guy,' and JD adds, 'making an ass of his-self.'

They start talking very fast, it's exactly like the way they play: 'Listen up, yeah pay attention, dress nice, true, you gonna need to look sharp, ya never know who you might hook up with, only don't let Charles introduce you to none of his sisters, don't be listening to him, he only date coyote-ugly women, on second thoughts, don't let Charles introduce you to none of his female relative, neither, they get pregnant a brother so much as smiles in they direction.'

When we shake hands JD smiles at the size of his hand in mine, then he says it must be 'somethin' in the evolution of Irish people, maybes the fact they worked on railways an' sub-ways for so long, yeah that's probably the deal'.

And as they walk out bouncing the ball down the corridor I hear Charles say, 'Man, how the hell you know the guy wasn't a surgeon? Shit, not every Irish guy you meet's a motherfuck-in' housepainter.' And then JD says, 'Shit, surgeons be manual workers too—what you think, they operate with they feet? Anyways, me and him, we reached an understanding.' And Charles laughs and says, 'Yeah, you understood he could crush you like a cockroach.'

JD is laughing now. He says out loud, as if he knows I am listening, 'Nah, dude might be strong, but he have bitch's eyes. An' he was never on no school team neither.'

My gym bag feels extraordinarily light in my head I am free to pass The Subway Inn without being tempted, and when you're happy like that it spreads like gentle flame it fans all kinds of encounters along the way a big fat seated guy I some-times buy Ed's porno mags from looks up and winks.

'Hey. Look who it is. Mister Big. What's up, bro?'

'Same ol' same ol'. You know, keeping the wolf from the door, pullin' the *divil* by the tail.'

He laughs his big white socks off and waves me away as if one more moment of my outrageous, infectious hilarity will kill him stone dead. And of course it's overdone, of course it's more than a little stage *Oirish*, but it's much better than walking home slowly with the other voices bidding at the auction in your head.

And in the Irish diner on the corner the ancient waitress grins her crooked grin as she shows me to the 'best seat in the house' she tells the cook I'm back, in fact she says out loud, 'He was lost but now he's found,' which is exactly how I feel.

And I can see myself fitting in like a coin into a silver slot and I'm thinking, *This is the real me, this is who I am, not the morose one in the sealed-off room, no, I am someone easy to be with, someone people really like.*

You can see it in the way the waitress touches my shoulder as she leans in, like an angle-poise, to pour.

4

I'm getting very fit and as an antidote to Ed—it very nearly works.

I've been out running, pounding pavements, racing 'round the walls of Central Park. When I get back, Jerome the black kid who does doorman at night is there, and my heart sinks a little because Jerome believes I'm friends with Barney the racist pig who always greets me way too warmly when Jerome is putting on his blazer he never looks into my eyes, he just says, 'Whatup.'

Then he starts waxing the lobby, or rearranging things that don't need to be arranged on his tiny, tilted desk.

It's important to clear up things like this, so I just come straight out with it: I tell him I don't want him thinking I'm anything like bloody Barney, that just because we hail from the same corner of the globe doesn't mean we share the same, you know, *perspective*.

He nods without looking at me and says, 'Whatever.'

There's a very long pause. He stretches and sighs. Then all of a sudden he starts moon-walking and body-popping, he's doing all these excellent old skool moves.

Then, just as suddenly, he stops, pops, smiles and says: 'What music you hear in that oversize head?'

I tell him I hear disco music—Sister Sledge, you know, '*Halsten, Gucci, Fiorucci.*'—and he says, 'Yeah, I can get with that.' Then the two of us start dancing around in the dark and he's laughing now at the way I'm moving to the beat in my head, he says next Saturday he'll maybe bring me uptown to this place he knows, 'put you in the middle with white shoes on like John Travolta in *Saturday Night Fever*. All the peoples'll gather round to look at the crazy way your sneaker feet move, man, they be like albino alligators sliding 'cross the dance-floor.'

When he laughs you can hear the marijuana-wheeze in his chest, like bagpipes.

Feels nice to be dancing, even if there is no actual music.

When I open my eyes Jerome is leaning on the massive mop. He says it's a pity I'm stuck upstairs with 'the Munsters' when we all could be down here, having us a blast.

Then when the elevator doors are closing he snarls: 'You know that Irish motherfucker make me leave my radio home, just so the night last longer.'

I don't know why he had to end it on that note, do you?

Barney has a message. He says it's personal and I should come down and see him.

'Some, *ah*, black guy dropped by this morning. Said some-one called Elroy or Delroy was OK. He was sorry, he'd see you at the Y.'

The message hurts only half as much as the way his mouth curls in on itself and hisses, like plastic in a fire.

5

Dana has a new job at a Jewish hospital called Mount Sinai so she spends less time with us now, in fact she's hardly ever in the kitchen with Ellie all she ever says is 'gotta run.'

I know by the way she avoids me that she has met a much older guy who doesn't live in a servant room at the corner of the corridor; he has distinguished salt 'n pepper hair, steady surgeon's hands, the sort of privileged fuck who grew up confident that when he finally got married, when he finally grew tired of shagging buxom, groaning Puerto-Rican nurses, it'd be to settle down with someone who had alabaster skin, incredibly clear eyes.

And hair that burned the air around it, like a halo.

When I tell Ellie this, all she does is shake her head and roll her eyes, 'You needs to get some action elsewhere, baby. If you don't, you going to feel mighty sore and silly on the plane goin' home. You know she ain't the only fish in the sea, Clever. *Chrissakes*, this is New *Yawk* City, they got more single wimmins here than you can shake your Jonson at.'

I'm beginning to believe they can smell the loneliness like a lotion on my skin at night when they turn to me after I've said, 'Hi, how's it going?' their nostrils are already flared, they are already searching the bar air for some trace of God know's what.

Perhaps it's dying Ed they sniff.

'Get lost, loser.'

I haven't said this before but sometimes his smell clings to me, like a cloak, it is a cloying stink, it makes it difficult to think of anything on your night off.

Except Death. And Alcohol.

It's easy for banana-bunches of jocks and stockbrokers to make a move, to break the ice; they have the safety-net of friends to fall back on. But if you get shot down on your own, even just the once, you feel like giving up and moving on. Except, when you elbow your way back out onto the street the summer air starts to needle with sarcastic questions: *What's the point pal, you're not exactly a player, now are you?*

And all of a sudden the prospect of going on to some other fashionable joint where no one knows your name doesn't exactly fill you full of hope, and if you stop and wait for Inspiration in the dead air, if you hang on for some *sign*, say some gorgeous mixedrace couple walking past who just happen to mention the name of a club where there are cocktails, soft leather couches and chilledout sounds, I swear to Christ just as the gorgeous girl says, *Hey, let's go to such and such's*, then the screeching brakes of a subway, or the coyote-scream of the half-naked man who runs past (with a fuckin' shower cap on!) will suck the words right out of her awesome Asian gob. And all remaining Hope out of your soul.

And you're back in your goldfish bowl, and the water needs to be changed, and before you know it your feet beat a retreat to The Subway Inn; at least they look up when you walk in, at least the barman knows what you drink, *fuck it* sometimes he even shares one of his fifty-year-old Jackie Gleason jokes. And as your shoulders move up and down in fake laughter at least you remember what it felt like.

Vaguely.

One of the regulars, this sixty-something Mayo man with cracked workman's boots and a fine layer of grey dust on his face that makes him look like a statue come alive in the amber glow of the jukebox, puts on 'Where the Streets Have No Name.'

Without saying a word he leaves a shot of Jameson at my elbow, then from a distance he raises his own shot glass up, holds it there in the smoke-filled air and begins to stare without blinking. *What the fuck is he trying to say?* Not 'cheers' or '*slainte*' or 'good luck, me bucko.'

No, I believe under the grey moustache his lips are saying; *Don't do what I did, son. Don't stay here all your life, this kip is not your home, nor never will be, these people are not your people, I'm telling you these selfish bastards care for nothing or no-one only the Almighty Fucking Dollar. Do ya hear me now?*

I hear you. But where am I supposed to go?

I tossed and turned all night my stomach burned, the whiskey rose up like a revolution inside its battle cry lay a familiar cold refrain: *Why, why are you doing this to yourself, why don't you just pack it in and fuck off home?*

When I finally drifted off, I dreamt I was at a swimming gala back in Dublin. Way up high on an Art Deco balcony I could see Ed in his chair. Then Jackie Gleason made a tannoy-announcement with a cheapo jibe aimed at Ed; he said, *Ladies and Gentlemen, Roll up, Roll up for the Main Event.*

I could feel everyone staring including Squatting Guy and the black dude in the glass booth and even Mabel smiled as Ed's mother was lowered into the water on the same contraption they use to lift cattle onto boats heading for the Aran Islands. Her bottom half was wrapped in bedclothes and, when the blankets fell aside, the spectators gasped in awe.

She had a huge whale tail.

Then the Judge appeared in his robes, and softly in my ear he whispered that it was my duty to be *considerate and kind*. He blew his whistle; when I dived in the water was too hot and way too heavy, like damp wool. And every time she kicked or flicked her tail I rose up and out of the pool, almost completely. Black and white people were laughing, pointing and whispering that I was a *fool to try and change things.*

I had no choice. I had no choice but to turn into a silver-speckled fish with cold, slow blood and a small steady heart at the bottom on the white smooth tiles, and I knew if I waited it out—*one, one thousand, two, one thousand*—if I watched the shadow of her huge tail rising, that in between its great, slow spreading I would find an interlude just like the ones in between the waves pitching and breaking at home.

Finally I was able to dart forward, finally I could rest, and bob behind the cold steel bar.

It was Dana who lifted me up, Dana who kissed me in the light, Dana who told the crowd out loud that I was beautiful in the water—no, I *really* was something to behold. She placed me carefully on a podium. She stepped away, and all applauded as she stood there and watched me, gasping.

When I looked up through my one dying fish eye, I could see Ed crying, in his hands a black boomerang wilting, like a stem.

With lungs on fire I awoke and threw the little window open. I could hear the city whisper and accuse, *We don't care what happens to the likes of you or poor pathetic Ed. And by the way, it's all in your addled head, the stuff with Dana.*

Down below in the silent street, a man my size was sifting through trashcans.

6.

The Judge walks in when Ed is mid-seizure. It's a real sinister fit of shudder this time an electric eel from the Sargasso Sea is scuttling down his spine is the branch of a tree, someone is shaking it ferociously—*Come on ya bastard, drop*—Jesus Christ, *stop*, I mean, what the fuck am I supposed to do when his eyes flop like a Barbie doll tossed casually aside?

See the egg-white eyes roll right 'round in his stuttering head his accordeon player hands rap the sides of his chair, *fuck*, he says inside his twirling mind, *where is this, shock, treat-ment coming from, Trevor where is my father gone?*

Out the door a fox sliding into a hole in the side of the night.

The Judge doesn't have the ability, which is American for he doesn't have the inclination or the interest or the time will come when he takes an expensively framed photo of his dead son up off his antique desk.

That's when he will be forced to ask himself over and over, like a broken record playing way too late in the day: *Why? Why didn't I try harder when he was alive?*

Sometimes at the Clinic, the day patients, the ones who didn't live in the leaking little wooden chalets, would be sitting outside in their chairs waiting for family cars to pull up with excuses and mobiles ringing, *Sorry pet, traffic was absolute chaos.*

Once, one of the mothers—all ski-blonde hair, robin-red-breast tits and Gucci sunglasses in November—asked me how much I would charge, roughly speaking, to take her son for an extra hour or two in the evening. 'Maybe you could see a movie, have a nice Chinese meal. He speaks so highly of you. My husband is really looking forward to meeting you; in point of fact, he has several *furry* interesting business propositions he'd like to . . . ' *put the cigarette in your mouth and say nothing, Trevor, just watch yourself exhaling in her naff fuckin' sunglasses, OK?*

And then the best bit, or maybe it's the worst bit: the guy in the reflection chair ramming the side of her silver Mercedes screaming, 'Could you not even fuckin' pretend you liked me? Jesus, could you not even do that much?'

Those were the days I'd head straight home to my mother's room, I'd lie beside her on the bed with my feet sticking out over the end and she'd ask, 'What's wrong son, come on' and I'd say, 'Nothing.'

Or maybe after a while I'd say, 'This is purely a rhetorical question Ma, alright? But what the fuck is wrong with people? I mean, do you have to practise to become that selfish or does it just come naturally to some? Well?'

And she would sigh and say, 'You expect too much from this world Trevor, you take the whole thing far too personally. What you need to do now is put on a pair of runners and take the dog down the beach, get some sea air into your lungs. Go on, do as I say please feel the wind in your hair, go on, and when you're running along at full tilt pretend you can you hear that *Rocky* theme song—you know, the one where he races up and down those granite steps with his little wool hat on? Tell us son, does he have a small dog with him in that scene?'

'I don't think so, Ma.'

And she'd always quote Kurt Vonnegut: 'how the sea can calm the ripples at the edge of the mind' and I'd come back wet with sweat and happy again. And she'd have struggled up and *put her face on* and we'd install ourselves by the fire where I'd prise open a bottle of my old fella's most expensive wine, *fuck him*. And I'd slowly pour three heavy Waterford crystal glasses full for me, one small glass with both blue-veined hands wrapped around for her.

She'd get me to tell her again of the field trips, and the Cliffs of Moher, and the time this famous non-able-bodied poet with a wand on his head came to visit in his chair with his blond willowy Eastern European carer, how Dalek started staring the moment they walked in, how from down the back of the class The Captain started hurling instant abuse: 'Sure yer man is a well-known fuckin' fake, a charlatan, a chancer, t'is common fuckin' knowledge his sister writes all his egg-head fuckin' poems.'

How Dalek's whirring chair was suddenly smack in front of the famous poet, how both black wands on their clouded heads lifted up slowly like blow-pipes by the banks of the Amazon; man, you should have seen the way they stared. And all the while The Captain continued his tirade. 'At least I'd be able to write about sex from experience, not the pie-in-the-sky intercourse you wank on about, Jesus Christ above, I've more talent in my fuckin' toe.'

How I had to light a smoke and try to stick it in The Captain's gob, except he kept twisting his handsome head still roaring abuse, how my hands were shaking so much from the laughing I nearly missed his motor-mouth.

'Shut up ya fuckin' lunatic, or you'll have me lynched. Now call that evil gremlin off, ya hear?'

Ma would laugh, then get all serious and lean in to whisper I was doing great work, 'No, you're making a real contribution, this is important, Trevor listen: you should hold your head up high when your sisters' friends come round demanding to know why you abandoned your studies at film school you should look them straight in the eye and say, "I'm doing something much more valuable now, something someone with a cold stone of a heart like you could never, ever do." Alright?'

'Alright, Ma. Thanks.'

Whenever I slide the log of my hours under the Judge's door that same day a cheque gets left out on a varnished table in the hall. When I go to the bank sometimes Mabel smiles; on one occasion she put her hand under the glass, like a talon, then she tapped it in time to what she was saying, 'The work you're carrying out is God's work . . . I can understand how ya might sometimes get vexed with outside people . . . What I'm saying is, you're alright, OK?'

'OK. Thanks, Mabel.' Then as I counted out the money in front of her she smiled and said, 'Make sure you treat yourself to something nice now, ya hear?'

You have to admit New Yorkers are weird the way they veer from one extreme to the next; it's as if all the passing through, all the strangers coming and going, makes it impossible to be just one steady continuous thing all the time.

Hooked up to the mask and the breathing-machine in the corner he sucks the energy right out of the room. Maybe it's a gift he inherited from his father I don't know, but he just sits there in his chair, polluting.

And sorry Mabel, but this is not God's work: this is God's fuckin' cock-up.

And I'm sick and tired of being all magnanimous. Do you know what the little turncoat told me this morning? He said I was misshapen, he said I was ugly, and really clumsy, that I hurt him all the time with my stupid big hands, that I had no friends, no outside life, that I was a fucking *para-site*, I was living off him and his family, it was his money I wanted, it was clear there was no friendship, he could see it in my eyes how much I fuckin' hated him.

I tried hugging him, holding him, shushing him. That's when the little bastard sank his soft little teeth into my T-shirt. It felt like I was being attacked by a gummy vampire.

Then eventually he just leaned against me, sobbing.

I waited for a while I stroked his thinning hair, then I told him he had crossed the line. He could cross it once, and once only. If he was going to pull that kind of shit again he could shove his job up his hole and then he could stick his poxy fuckin' ad back in *The Village Voice*, alright?

'Alright. I'm. Sorry. Man.'

'I'm taking the rest of the day off, OK?'

'OK. It. Will. Never. Happen. Again. You're not. Ugly, you're not . . . '

'Whatever, Ed. Later.'

When I came back that night he'd made me a card, which must have taken hours because he can't really draw properly; his figures are all unformed and wavy, like in that famous painting *The Scream* by what's-his-face . . .

Munch, Edvard.

There was me with a big sad face and a square head the size of a TV set, then this crazy little bat creature sucking at my shoulder. The creature was suspended in mid-air. It had long hair.

And no chair.

In his madness Ed had forgotten who and what he was.

Inside the card he'd scrawled:

Please believe me. You ARE my friend. I am TRULY sorry.

Americans are really shite at apologizing; they think the mere fact they bring themselves to mouth the words absolves them. They're not interested in the rites of penance, in listening to precisely how they hurt you, in understanding how small it made you feel. They want to move on, they want *closure* which is American for wanting things to go swiftly back to the way they were before. *Inside their heads.* They cannot comprehend that because they don't really know what they did wrong, that because they don't really need to know, the rest of us find them truly terrifying.

7

I met an Australian girl in The Subway Inn last night. She wandered in looking for directions and the barman pointed her to my table.

She was looking for a faded restaurant called Arizona 206, a Tex-Mex place where I'd occasionally scored margaritas from yuppie couples in exchange for tabloid tales about Ed, the more horrific the better. People like to hear about his tepid baths, his wet porno rags, the breathing machine in the corner, the pervading smell of Death; it makes them feel wholesome, healthy and suddenly happy with their lot. I've seen couples start to hold hands and squeeze meaningfully as I talk about our monotonous daily grind. And when it comes time to settle up, the guy will always pat my back softly and say, 'No, let me.'

The Australian girl was not my type—she had tattoos on her biceps and a large spider's web etched upon her downy, peeling neck. Plus, her entire demeanour was one of passing through. She reeked of impermanence and her conversation centred 'round places she had been and I had not, around scores of *fascinating* characters she had *bumped into* on boats planes and trains, characters I would never ever sit beside. And yet after three or four beers I started to forgive the over-use of *fascinating,* the fact that she never even offered to buy me a glass, the presumption that somehow I'd be the one to stump up.

She talked and I listened intermittently; overblown descriptions of shrines in India where you could enjoy *fantastic veggie food*, wats in Thailand where blind people gave travellers *incredible* foot massages, vine-clad temples in the sweltering jungles of Laos where, at break of day, Buddhist priests in purple robes chanted mantras that *moved your very soul*.

I nodded and smiled and every now and then said, 'Wow.'

At five past eleven when I couldn't take it any more I walked over to the jukebox to play 'Ring of Fire' for the second time and that was when she quietly and almost sadly asked me could she crash at my pad, just for one night. *No strings attached*.

I thought about it, right in front of her, letting her see doubts mount behind my eyes then I heard a darker than normal voice say, *She's used you, feel free to use her—that's what everybody else here does*.

And that's exactly what I did: I used her, over and over again, until it was time to stop pretending to be asleep, time to get up and stretch Ed out and empty his bedpan and hold his quivering electric toothbrush and watch the gums leak and bleed and wash his thinning hair and bend the plastic straw towards his sad, cracked lips.

Suddenly in the middle of it all I began to miss her sorely, my clamouring Australian girl.

And I realized that I was closing myself up, that all my small love was going in the direction of a dying man, that I could be bigger, better.

That I could be less alone. That I had disliked her simply because she had retained her enthusiasm. In spades.

When I raced back to my room, she'd left ten dollars and a hastily scribbled note upon my neatly made-up bed: *Thanks for the beers Trevor, I thought I had no change last night but found this in the arse pocket of my jeans. This will sound weird— but here goes . . . There is no need for a guy like you to be so lonely, you have an awful lot to give (I don't mean it that way, well I do)*.

Then three 'x' marks, and a lipstick kiss to seal the bargain. Her name was Karen; she could have been my friend.

That evening when I came into the kitchen Dana was sitting alone, waiting. She said, 'I'm really glad you're here, Trevor.' Then she left a pause. 'I need you.' Pause. 'To stop me eating all of this,' and she brought my eyes down to the blueberry pie on the plate before her.

After she kissed the air beside my cheek and left I was going to use her fork, I mean I had it in my hand when I thought *Oh, come on man, that's really overdoing it.*

She's changed her makeup, she's using real dramatic eyeliner like Chrissie Hynde from The Pretenders or Elizabeth Taylor when she was playing Cleopatra. It draws you in; you've no choice but to admit defeat as you look into her unswerving, unnerving eyes you realize, *This is someone completely and utterly sure of who they are, someone who does not deal with doubt on a daily basis.*

I freely admit I'm frightened by really confident people especially when they're not that fuckin' bright: Do you remember earlier when I said she was a *disturbingly beautiful creature?*

Ellie is kneading pastry in the kitchen, shaking her head, laughing, 'When I start out here, that fat bitch expect me to save coupons an' redeem them at the check-out, as if I was on welfare, not Madison. White people. Rich people. Shit, rich white Jewish people.'

I'm not really listening. There is glistening in the air as she sprinkles castor sugar, I see my mother and I baking, making this excellent snowscape on top of our last Christmas cake.

The whole family is stranded. There are faithful huskies, sleds, the whole shebang. I am Roald Amudsen or maybe Scott of the Antarctic or Shackleton in my parka. An icy wind howls

as they beg me for *oranis, oranis*—they all have desperate
scurvy on their mouths—then one of the ugly sisters points
slowly to a badly built igloo. *Hell hymn, hell hymn.* My father
is inside shaking like a leaf with serious icicles in his beard he
can't even lift his frozen fuckin' head to say, *Thang od you
heah.*

I transport them home on my stout wooden ship, except
they lose half their acid tongues on the voyage, which means
they're not able to speak properly, just these Down Syndrome
nnnffffgg kind of sounds, which unfortunately means they
won't ever be able to interrupt me again. And I'm afraid the
old fella will no longer be able to puff on his pipe like a prick
and say, *And what precisely is your point, Trevor?*

Ma just laughs and points the rolling pin and says that I'm
headed straight for trouble or for jail. Then she joins in creating icing-sugar storms and impassable ridges as she scatters
tiny bananas and lemons plus the odd plastic orange she smiles
and says, 'There. Some vitamin C to cure them of their scurvy.'

Every Mother's Day, if she wasn't above in the bed, we'd
head into town and drink cheap Chilean wine, then a truckload
of Irish coffees which she always made them remake because
she absolutely hated if the cream didn't sit stiffly on top, like a
priest's collar. But other than that she was very easy-going.

We'd drink until we hadn't even got bus fare, then we'd
agree about everything under the sun, especially the fact that
she should've had an affair while she had the chance, and her
back was still up to it. And we'd agree that the rest of the family took themselves terribly seriously, that they may have had
bucket-loads of letters after their names but they were *boring
bitches*, really bad dressers. And we'd concur—that was our
code because that's what he'd say after someone made a point:
I concur—that our *Pater familias* was a dry old shite in love
with the sound of his own affected voice—*I concur*—and that

at the end of the day he was a pointy forehead bastard with not much of heart, little or no romance and a really stilted, wilted wig of an imagination, plus a tolerance level towards the less-educated, less-informed, less like *him* that bordered on non-existent.

She'd laugh and tell me I really was my mother's son, that I had *blacksmith blood,* that my *poor endangered-species father* had never fully recovered from the sheer bloody size of me when I'd been born, that my ugly sisters had been very worried about her having me because it was very late in her life and the labour had gone on and on for days and nights because I'd done my best to hide inside like Otto in *The Tin Drum*, that when the doctor finally pulled me out with his forceps and slapped me on the arse I'd fixed him with a look as if to say— *Try that again, pal and I'll bite your fuckin' ear off.*

Me and Ma, we'd get so loud in restaurants we were often asked to 'please think of the other diners,' which we'd always take as our cue to order another round of Irish coffees. And they'd say, 'Sorry, enough is enough' and we'd be asked to leave politely and end up not paying for half of what we'd swallowed.

Quite a few times, 'one or other of them,' as my Mother referred to my sisters, would have to drive all the way into town to pick us up because word had got round that my mother would sometimes up-chuck in the back seat and Dublin taxi drivers would generally refuse point-blank to ferry us. So, one of the ugly sisters would arrive and we'd be sitting on steps somewhere, maybe the Lord Mayor's Mansion or the Shelbourne Hotel, and you should've seen the puss on them in their boring, economical little cars—you'd swear they'd been mortally fuckin' wounded.

We'd just sit in the back seat laughing, holding hands, sometimes singing 'Fairytale of New York' even though it wasn't

Christmas: *'You scumbag, you maggot, you cheap lousy faggot, Happy Christmas my arse, I thank God it's our last. And the boys of the NYPD choir still singing "Galway Bay," and the bells are ringing out . . .'*

I think of her whenever I hear church bells pealing I think of her singing and staring Death straight in the face, laughing at the absurdity of it all. And I wonder where she found the courage and I hope I've inherited her gift for picking up the pieces of a shattered life, her gift of carrying on regardless, her tired head held high, her unstinting heart worn out on her sleeve.

She didn't have a great voice but that didn't stop her, not for one minute and sometimes she'd laugh so much she'd start to cry. Then I'd join in, I mean, what else are you supposed to do when you're sitting in the back of your sister's Toyota Starlet with someone you love who is fading away in front of you and you're drunk as a skunk but not quite drunk enough to say what you're really thinking?

Of course if you wanted to you could just continue driving as if nothing was happening, in fact you could stick a shaking, classical tape in the dash and not look in the rearview mirror once, which is exactly what my oldest sister did. And you should realize it wasn't exactly a quick jaunt to Wicklow, in fact before they put in motorways—and ripped the whole place apart—it used to take more than an hour to get there and if you just sat in the back listening to Ma humming with your eyes closed it was weird, because soon as you opened them you'd always see a dead hedgehog or a squished fox by the roadside, three or more carrion crows alighting.

Once when we were tumbling out of the car Ma fell over in the black ditch mud and lay there in white linen shrieking laughing, looking up at the stars. I lay down beside her while my oldest sister started ranting about the damp getting in on her mother's bones, pneumonia, fecklessness, duties and *responsibilities*.

I picked my moment carefully.

I grabbed her wrist, *hard*, and pulling her in and down where my mother could not hear I said, 'Don't fucking dare talk to me about responsibilities, you ugly bat. How about holding your dying mother's hand some night for more than twenty fuckin' seconds?'

And the force of it stunned her, forced her to step backwards with her mealy mouth hanging down, like a ripped cloth.

Then my father came shuffling out in his pipe and slippers and lifted Ma up in his arms, and that's when my sister bent over. And under a blanket of twinkle-twinkle stars she poured black poison into my ear, telling me I might have been my mother's son but I was not my father's, I was not of the same blood as any of them. But I just threw back my head onto the clay and said, 'Well, maybe that explains why I'm the one breaking his bollocks laughing and you're the one with a face like a melted fuckin' Wellington. Maybe that explains why I'm as big as a house and strong as an ox with everything tight and in the right proportion while the three of ye are stunted cunts whose arses hang down the back of your fat knees like cow's fuckin' udders.'

And it was as if the stars had formed a crown of silver thorns on her bitter twisted head she said, 'Speaking of stunted dear brother did you ever for a moment wonder why we're all so academically gifted and you're, well, something of an intellectual pygmy? Did you never think it incumbent upon yourself to find out what sort of creature your father actually was?'

Stars were near, her voice was miles away.

8

Twinkle stars. The poisoned question pricking my cold, damp flesh.

Of course I fuckin' thought about it; in fact there nearly always existed in my head the possibility that my mother had become so rigidly bored by my egghead father that she'd had a fling with a former IRA prisoner-cum-poet at a party in my father's poxy university, that the prisoner-poet may have had some issues around authority drugs and isolation, which would be perfectly fuckin' understandable. That maybe I inherited some stuff that my old man—and quite a few other people I've encountered along the way—didn't feel too comfortable with. And maybe my mother told the country doctor and maybe even the calm-voiced shrink, maybe that's why they called me a *counterrevolutionary* and treated me like a fish out of water and advised me to do breathing exercises as if I had fuckin' gills, not lungs. Maybe that's why they encouraged me to do the sifting thought thing, to keep a notebook, not to be afraid when exercise and meditation and breathing in and out slowly didn't work, not to feel defeated or deflated just because I needed a pill—but that *maybe* swallowing it in front of the mirror wasn't such a good idea, maybe I should just keep them in the fridge, like vitamins, take them with some juice or cereal. And to be careful not to construct a mountain out of a molehill—an unfortunate image because in my mind I was condemned forever to burrow up into the light.

Maybe is my least favourite word, though I admit it is unusually powerful. You can spend years and years on *maybe*.

By the way, as regards being an academic pygmy I got honours in English (A), Irish (A), Latin (A), Greek (A), German (A), French (B)—and that was only because I didn't bother with the stupid accent in the orals.

And when I applied to Dun Laoghaire Film School the interview board said my 22-minute short about my family was, without doubt, the funniest thing they'd ever seen, that the voiceover (me!) was very *Sunset Boulevard* meets *The Waltons*, that some of the drawing-room scenes where family and friends sat around drinking port having pretentious discussions about politics and philosophy ranked alongside such anti-family classics as *Sybil*. And then another one nodded and said, '*Five Easy Pieces*' and then another nodded and said, '*Crumb*,' and this last one was younger and sexy with spiked-up hair and she smiled at me as if she understood every frame, every reference. Still smiling, she put away her manila folder and she said my mother—who really played it up for the camera—must have been very beautiful when she was young.

'Yes. She was.'

And then I was told, and not for the first time in life, that the college had Great Expectations of me. And I said I'd do my best to fulfil them but already I felt weighed down by the dead, lead weight of their anticipation.

And outside the interview door, and all along the echoing corridors, everyone looked so shiny, new and dependable that I immediately was rendered unreliable and worn, and my socks were wet with sweat.

And there were so many snappy dressers and pert, efficient types with demanding part-time jobs in production houses and advertising agencies and you could see they were always going to manage, could see they were always going to cope calmly, thrusting forward in the marketplace, so purposeful and bold. And I could see them installed already in expensive restaurants being uppity with foreign staff, see them networking, watch them chinwagging, flirting and exchanging derivative screen-play ideas with Neil Jordan—*'Interesting, yeah, 'specially in view of the whole, you know, cross-dressing post-colonial thing'*—and Jim fuckin' Sheridan—*'Ah jay-zus that's fuckin' marvellous alto-gether, it re-moinds me of when I was a chisler in Sheriff Stree' an' we had this TV aerial on the roof of our tene-ment . . .'*

And by the time I got to the bus stop my palms were pan-icked and sticky, and my heart was racing. And that's when they all began to pass me in air-conditioned Walter De Silva-designed Alfa156s, astride their polished Piaggios and classic Vespas.

One of the young women that buzzed by in her private, dustfree air-stream had silky blonde hair flowing out on the breeze like a commercial.

And a backpack made to look like a fluffy sacrificial lamb.

I wanted to throw a rock at her helmet.

Her head.

And that was one of the few times my mother and I argued when I got home she pulled her hair—*please Ma, stop*—and she screamed that I was a *defeatist,* that I was writing myself into the role of a loser when the truth was I had more fire and imagination in my head, more passion in my soul than anyone she'd ever encountered and would I ever *cop on* and stop beat-ing myself up simply because I had to swallow a few *sirs*—and she always got the initials wrong—or occasionally visit a head-shrink, *for Christ's sake* did I not understand there were peo-ple out there *crippled by depression*, people unable to get up in the morning, people who couldn't run or swim or speak, or even formulate the most basic thoughts that were racing round their poor, unfortunate heads, people who literally couldn't *function as part of the community.* I needed to get some *bloody perspective*, I needed to see I was genuinely talented, and I was going to throw it away, *and for what?*

That was one of the few times she didn't let me speak or defend myself, one of the few times she said she was *sick to her back teeth of listening to my self-pitying rigmarole*, one of the few times she just asked me to please close the door behind me, please think of her, please try to grant her a little bit of peace. Because the truth was she was *at the end of her tether worrying* and she wanted, no she *needed* to know that before she died I was going to be even vaguely happy and settled and working at something I was good at, entertaining people, making them laugh. Not making them sick with worry and everlasting doubt.

'I'm sorry, Ma. Please look at me.'

My hand upon the door handle, clumsy. Paw.

Most of the time however Ma did have this way about her; seriously, she could weave a spell around you, transforming, taking one feeling and turning it with gentle questions and advice, into another feeling altogether.

Small, everyday miracles, the softly whispered work of mothers sick and strong.

But others manage it, too: I remember right after the episode on the beach where the actress I really liked walked away, saying, 'This just isn't going to work, sorry.' She was carrying a little plastic bottle of Ballygowan, the green label began to glow and fade the way the Tardis does in *Dr Who* and I know it sounds stupid but I felt she'd lifted something *vital* from my insides and that's when I stopped going into college for a time.

And I don't know why but I'd stopped running with the dog, I used to just walk slowly on my own trying to figure the whole thing out, and everything appeared tattered, worn.

And one morning in November there was this ghost of a fog

hanging from branches of trees in the park and I felt I was disappearing, and that no one would notice. And then suddenly the warden appeared in his blue uniform, his little stick raised.

He touched me lightly on the shoulder, as if it were a wand.

'Ah. There ya are, me old *segocha*. Larger than life and well able to take on the *wor-uld* and his aunt, wha'?'

And maybe it was delusional, but I could feel it lifting from me, like a snake shedding its skin. And I'm standing there marvelling at this minor Medjugore miracle—I mean, this particular bout had had me completely down and out—when suddenly I'm laughing again because off in the distance was the sound of him impersonating Tom Jones, badly: '*Why, why, why, De-li-a-lah?*'

And here's another rhetorical question: aren't people like him, people like my mother, people like Ellie, the real poets and painters of this world? And isn't it amazing how they can colour in a whole new season behind your head which, when you stop to think about it, is no longer revolving like a dish in a microwave with the same dull thoughts going round and round and round all fuckin' day?

Sometimes I'd talk to her quietly about the doubts and the low voices murmuring. And whenever I did Ma was always patting my hand saying shit like, 'But you never hear them when you're out running or swimming or laughing, now do you?' And I'd say, 'No, Ma, I don't.' But I'd be thinking—*I never fuckin' feel them when I'm punching someone in the head or the ribs lifting them clean off the ground, I never hear them when I explode into action.*

And sometimes if we were out drinking on Mother's Day, I'd tell her that the voices really and truly unnerved me. And that's when she'd smile across and say, 'But that's the miracle of you, Trevor, that's what separates you from all the little people milling around pointlessly avoiding reality and truth, do you not understand that's the artist, the poet inside you, that's what makes you totally unique'—and I would want to tell her that unique doesn't require any adjective—and, 'Think Trevor, think what a dull, uniform place this weary world would be if we were all the same, if our minds all operated the same way, like . . . like bloody *tollbridges.*' But you see, I wouldn't have minded operating in a different way, wouldn't have minded if my toll-bridge lifted and lowered and let things in and out and under and over, and didn't get stuck, and didn't require massive leaps of faith to get from one part of the day to the next.

And she'd still be smiling over at me, waving her hand around the restaurant drunkenly, 'We're not designed to be the same as the next guy or the next; for God's sake Trevor, look at the state of these people,' and we'd laugh aloud. Except sometimes I wondered if we hadn't become stuck like two middle-aged men in golf clothes, cigar laughter drowning the sound of a world that has passed them by completely.

Sometimes I really did think of the other diners.

And sometimes, especially towards the very end, when we were stuck in the house and she was too tired to listen, she'd just sigh and say, 'Well son, to thine own self be true.'

But you see, it's not that easy to know yourself. You might think you've cracked it when you're standing up there in front of the class and they're all grinning and you're glowing with pride and you feel that you're genuinely helping them to let loose, that you've turned the tide in their favour, and you can see in their crooked grins misty eyes and bulging foreheads that they're suddenly more alive.

Then inside your heart and your head you get this snide voice chiding: *None of this is for their benefit, all of this is mere ego gratification, this is about control Trevor, yours over them. This is about the fact that you are nothing without an audience. It's clear that what you are doing is trying, rather desperately, to substitute lack of control in your own life for total control in the classroom . . .*

And on it goes, on and on, coldly, and you feel heat and the joy evaporate, like spilled petrol on a hot day. And you're not sure why you're holding the sticky snooker cue for one of them in the smoky pub after work as they grunt and slide it forward clumsily with their pimply forehead; you're not sure why you're holding your mother's hand in the morning; not sure why you're bending crooked, meat-hook Ed back into shape at night you're full of doubt about your purpose, you begin to question your performance, you're afraid that it's true, it's all about Control and the reason you answered the ad in the first instance is because you knew, you knew in your heart normal rules would not apply.

It ate away at her spine, it turned discs and vertebrae to dust until in the end she couldn't get out of bed or even hold her neck up properly, and the light in her eyes was dimming like a torch with a wet weak battery. I remember she was holding my hand and there was no squeeze left, none whatsoever. Then we were laughing one last time when she said, 'I'm all shrivelled up like an old Egyptian mummy,' and I said, 'No, Ma, you're all shrivelled up like an old Irish one.'

She told me to try and meet a woman with the same sense of humour, if such a woman existed. Then she explained she had put a bit aside for me and that's when she held me tight, well, as tight as she could manage, and I leaned in so as she could kiss my eyes and forehead. Then she put her lips to my ear, she whispered, 'Would you be good enough now to send your father in, that's the fellow. And remember Trevor, always try to turn the moment round, alright?'

'Alright, Ma.'

9

Through the keyhole he kissed her long and hard, his hands were shaking when their lips parted, hers were so dry they stuck to his, like wallpaper you're scraping in a really old house.

She was looking up at him, there was this terrific light in her face like a saint in one of those old religious paintings—*frescoes*—then he put the pillow over her face and began to recite some poem I didn't recognize, it must've been a poem he'd written for her when they were young and I could hear her voice all muffled behind the pillow saying the same thing as him, like a prayer.

They call it 'assisted suicide' and in this case it really was, because her hands came around like wings they descended on his, and pressed the pillow in.

And there and then I knew that I understood nothing about my parents, nothing about how the world worked and everything she'd said—no, everything *I'd* said and she'd agreed with—was a fat lie. She'd just been building me up, but really she should've said it was me that was the *amadán* because when you build someone up like that, when foundations are flawed, it all has to tumble.

Brick by brick. Stone by fuckin' stone.

When someone you love dies, air in front and around you becomes thick and slow and heavy, and cutting through it costs more effort than it's worth. Ignorant, blonde children in the back seats of massive MPVs stare and you're forced to look away from inside the black stretch Mercedes coming back from the graveyard all posters, all advertisements, all concert and circus hoardings are outrageous. And when the butcher starts laughing in the kitchen it *is* personal and your head hurts, and your soul aches, and their mouths move crookedly to form spaghetti sentences that tumble out when they approach. And all you want is your hand back, *please*.

To be fair, the odd time you can see one of them actually does understand because they too have felt the world shift beneath them. But the way I see it people live in neatly appointed, self-contained places where there's no room to turn around and care, where there's just enough space for their own feelings, their own little suitcase of hurt, a suitcase they hide under the bed and slide out only on special occasions.

And yes, I know time heals all wounds, but that doesn't mean you can't feel it still behind your eyes.

And there is some little part, a child that was lowered alongside, some part of your heart that quietly gave up the ghost the day the beloved passed away.

And that feeling of sluggishness tugging at your coattails is Morpheus, or perhaps his twin brother Phantases, calling *Hello, anybody home?*

And he just wants you to give him some time alone in a room is all.

And when your ear is his, you realize he's not trying to seduce you or entice you to smoke or drink or think yourself to death, in fact he's not half as bad as grief-stricken people often make out.

He's simply saying: *If you want, you can always visit here, just don't stay too long, OK?*

10

I still see my mother, mostly when I leave Ed and his sighs and smells behind and open the door to my tiny, servant room.

I see her in the Lazee-Boy recliner I reclaimed from a skip on Madison; she's sitting there patiently her eyes asking, *Are you OK, son? Are you eating properly? Getting plenty of fresh air? Are you making sure you get lots of exercise and get it all out of your system?*

After she died I didn't really feel like talking for a while, leastways not to anyone in my family who were so fake it was fuckin' frightening, knocking on the door of my bedroom all of a sudden tip-toeing in with toast and tea at all hours, patient smiles on pale faces. So I got back in touch with the shrink I'd seen before, except this time we didn't speak about kicking guys on the ground screaming swimming coaches ticking away repressed rage, all sliding out of control.

We spoke about my mother. And one Tuesday he suggested I speak to her myself and I was like, 'Eh, hello, she's dead, remember?' Except he shook his distinguished polar-bear head and said, 'No, what I want you to do is visualize her in the chair opposite. I would like you to *see* her there. I would like you to tell her all the things you've told me.'

I'm still not sure that was the best strategy for someone like me, I mean it only took two seconds for her to materialize like Captain Kirk coming in through the transporter room. I started to tell her how much I missed her, and I literally couldn't stop crying. And his secretary had to come in and hold me for at least three-quarters of an hour there was a hole that got opened up in my soul I could feel vast emptiness pouring in; I swear to God it was depth of the deepest, coldest ocean.

The secretary had this white uniform on and I blubbered so much all over the front that she could have entered a wet uniform contest but she just smiled throughout and at the end when I literally ran out of tears she held my face in her speckled brown hands and with her amazing, calming voice said, 'You are a brave young man, but like the doctor says, it is time for you to go out into the world.'

And he was sitting there, nodding away with this really encouraging smile.

And I suppose that's when I decided to fly to New York, although looking back on it now maybe I shouldn't have been in such a hurry.

And maybe neither should they.

Before I left for America the doctor told me I needed to realize there were several dozen random thoughts arriving, uninvited, into our heads every moment of every day. They were being relayed through our systems by memory and mayhem, by plasma and blood, by electrolytes and neurotransmitters; what I needed to do was close my eyes and sift through them much the way, say, a baker sifts through flour. Yes, I needed to let it all fall through my fingers, I needed to decide which particular thoughts and impulses to conduct, which ones to dispel.

It was quite good the first time we did it: we took half a dozen destructive thoughts and negative impulses about fear and loneliness and as we breathed them away, as they exited my electrical system like steam from a subway vent, I began to smile.

I could picture myself in a brighter future with people curious to know me, I was this experienced older guy and as they stood around in a semi-circle listening to my tales of derring-do they were nodding and smiling quietly in agreement. In the background with her shoes kicked off was this striking-looking woman with a black polo-neck and white-blonde hair, the sort Hitchcock might have cast in *The Birds*, the sort who doesn't need a fat rich bald bloke to take care of her, who even at sixty would smile each time you took her hand when you set out walking with your Weimaraner hunting dogs while behind you in the lit-up architect-designed house the party for your fortieth anniversary was twirling, like a majorette's baton tossed high in the sky of endless possibilities.

You know what I mean: the Disney dream.

The foolish, childish hope you carry. High up in your heart.

Imagine you're an oak, Trevor, an Irish oak; imagine your roots delving down into the dark Irish soil, becoming embedded there, finding a home; imagine them growing down and out, thickening, strengthening. Finding water and essential minerals. Now, imagine the branches up above, your branches, responding with newfound confidence, opening out, reaching for the Sun.

This was one of the Looney Tunes exercises the head-shrink used to get me to do. I'd sit there in the leather chair with my eyes closed thinking, *Maybe I'll study psychiatry instead of the priesthood, I mean this guy has a pretty handy number, probably doing the fuckin' crossword while I've my eyes shut.* Then I'd feel it, my rootlessness, and I'd panic a little and remember what he had said the week before, how this exercise was designed to counter the fact I had too many distractions, was too easily swayed, spurned, turned into something we weren't altogether happy with, now were we?

'No.'

I breathed in through my nose and felt my roots sink into the ground. Then it was all speeded up, shoots and roots flashed into damp black soil, and down, penetrating, pushing past igneous rock into the volcanic core where straggling fibres flared photowhite, and bridal.

Oak to ash.

When I opened my eyes he smiled and said, 'How did that feel?' And I lied and said, 'Actually, that's pretty good Doc, I'll definitely give that a lash next time I feel confused, next time I get into one of those, you know, situations.'

And all the while I'm sitting there smiling over at him, making him feel better because he couldn't make me feel better.

And I'm thinking the only time I ever felt fuckin' *rooted* was when I looked through the keyhole and felt the world beneath my feet catch fire, when I felt *understanding* being burned into me, when I felt I was being branded.

'Breathe in now, Trevor. Close your eyes and hold on to the memory of what we've achieved here today, hold on to the feeling—good, that's it. Now breathe slowly out. Good. Excellent. So, same time next Tuesday, it doesn't clash with your swimming practice or anything does it?'

I'd already told him twice I no longer swam competitively.

'No, Doc. It doesn't clash with anything at all.'

Maybe Rain on Me Baby hit the nail on the head.

Maybe you're the kind of kid people teach weird shit to.

Maybe I've been teaching myself a lesson or two in the dark, maybe I've stopped at the point where brittle bones settle back into place, maybe I've wanted to keep going.

Maybe I'm tired.

Of making the sacrifice.

Maybe I just want to go home, or on a date with someone nice, or on a long, hot holiday where people smile and fetch things for me for a change.

But for the moment I'm stuck. For the moment there is no escape.

11.

There never was a trip to India, no bus lurching, no baby crying, no bracelets jangling, no silk rope, no Socket eyes, no ululations—just too much time alone on my bed and in my head the thumping need to venture somewhere else when my mother died I couldn't cope with the grey world swirling.

Then closing in.

And I've never been to Stuttgart, never worked in Mercedes Benz nor listened to a soothing voice underground, nor knocked back apfel-schnapps on Konigstrasse with a shaven-headed Turk; by the indented shore I invented him between waves crashing. I often designed alternative lives, often saw another Trevor walking away in another, neater body, in another sweeter family, in another less chaotic schoolyard. And in another mirror I saw myself a house-painter on Mykonos, a tour guide in Athens, a circus strongman in Rome, a perfectionist pizza-maker in the redroofed, over-restored city of Dubrovnik.

But always I've had to come home. Always I've had to face the organ-grinder's music.

Don't know where I learned to arm-wrestle. Some things just come naturally.

The pills I gave to Barry that overturned, turkey-burned Christmas were mine, not Ma's. And they weren't sprinkled on the cake, all three were slipped into his drink sinking slowly I wanted someone else to feel like me for a while.

And it wasn't Kylie on the radio, it was Bob Dylan, and Bob

was nasally asking, '*How does it feel?*' And a new calm voice was saying, *Feels weird, Mister Zimmerman, now that Barry is down there on the Persian rug having a fuckin' existential crisis and I'm the one floating free, watching the scapegoat flailing from on high.*

And they're not called sirs Ma, they're called SSRIs— they're selective serotonin reuptake inhibitors—and yes, they're light years beyond the aggressive tri-cyclicals, but they're not perfect because, believe me, in the pharmaceutical world one size does *not* fit all.

Off them, you hear crackled things stuttered on the radio after it's been switched off in the morning you can't pass bus stops in the rain because sheltering people whisper your demise beneath black mushrooms twirling slowly the rhythm of casual conversation eludes you along echoing corridors in college. At crashed parties you go to fetch a cold beer for a girl who seems really nice, except, when you come back to where she said she'd be, there's nothing, just black space, white time and music you can't dance to.

Techno. Tangible tension. And laughter.

Moments don't turn round, they go on forever groaning children twist their rubber necks impossibly in the back seats of massive MPVs and you're forced to look away from people in the street who can see clearly now that all you have is your physical strength, seeping. And all you know for sure is that somehow memory is trapped in bone and marrow and muscle, and that the pain is contained in the stone of your heart, sinking.

And thinking too much about the same things always you fear relapse, reversal.

Remain indoors therefore, stay underwater breathing. Float on the back of the passive-aggressive sea. Talk to people paid to listen, indolently. Choose the most deserted times of day and night to walk the faithful slow dog. Wave at the butcher on the shore. Nod at the doctor at the crossroads. Try hard to think of something light to say to the overweight girl at the super-market check-out, then watch as she takes her 'Till Closed' sign and places it in front of your basket, like a dam.

Go for a drink with the man who sells second hand albums and watch your healthy pint go yellow as his mustard-gas breath, and his ugliness, seep in.

Feel yourself on a conveyor belt moving from bed to bus to concrete lecture hall. Feel knocked down because it won't be long now, won't be long before you will no longer garden with her, cook with her, chop for her, slice, dice.

Sacrifice. And Ritual. Fading.

No longer able to hold her hand. No longer able to lie beside her.

Laugh with her.

Lie to her.

Go out running in new trainers. See it up ahead, perceive it as a haze, tell yourself you can run through it, you know you can beat it—yes you can—you know you can beat it in your heart you know you can—

Never really beat it. Now that she is gone.

'We're upping your medication, Trevor. Don't be too sur-prised if your breath arrives slightly sour in the morning' and your mouth is sticky and sometimes you wake up after twelve hours kip completely exhausted with caked white shit on your lips and your piss is nearly as yellow as Ed's some days you can't stand up too quickly or you'll get dizzy and nearly, very nearly, spin back to the slanted, kneeling point at which it all began.

But you see, after a while, they work. After a while you are not so easily undone. Things cannot take root. You forget some days to feel afraid with strangers. You strike up conversation the way you strike a match on a windless day.

First-time. Fuss-free.

You fit in easily, even though you need a pill to do so. Who cares? Half the western world self-medicates on a daily fuckin' basis. The rest get high on Power, Money, Illusion.

Sooner, much sooner than you thought, you find people turn and smile when you say the locked-up thing that was hastily scribbled on your mind sometimes they even laugh out loud, and it's beautiful in your ear reverberating, and you can hear her laughter echoing down there too, and she's with you, always.

And you regularly experience what could very easily pass for pure, unadulterated joy coursing through chest and shoulders; alone at the cinema laughing, in the gym straining, training your mind in the morning not to be undone by the first thought that enters, feeling it being replaced gently with something new and hopeful in the corridor with his OJ balancing, bathing him, watching over him, feeding him, forgiving him, loving him, helping him to live.

And die.

Then you realize, *shit*, this joy is not yours, it is borrowed. And like all things borrowed you will have to give it back.

No. I'll hold on to this fleeting feeling, I will own it. I'll cling to it even after the moment is gone, I'll hold on to the memory of happiness, don't ask me how, and in the process you start to get stuck again. In the past.

And so, you learn to live in two places at the same time.

Open up.

Disclose to others what's *really* going on inside, kiss and tell, show them your past catching up, reveal the mist swirling round the wheel turning slowly, and they'll happily, merrily inform you that you're wrong. *Oh yes, my son, you're wrong. About yourself.*

People don't like truth. It's ugly, damp and old and it has a hacking cough that won't go away. It keeps them awake at night they run away from it, *Gee, is there really a cemetery there? I always thought we just had the mountains and the sea.*

Women construct ingenious careers avoiding truth. They mother lies, they nurture compromise.

Men refuse to acknowledge it, then are reduced to tears in book-lined offices by truth standing there in short trousers.

Judges have their heads turned by it. Nurses inject it.

And children? Children stop playing when they hear the truth whispered on the wind, bells stop ringing in the cathedral votive candles flicker, and die.

And in the confessional the priest's astonished mouth opens, and shuts slowly, when he hears the truth.

For fuck's sake. Look at the lies my mother told me.

Look at them, casually overflowing.

You're right, I have been holding back, I have been lying, by omission. But you see, I know from past experience that if you open up wide and say *aaah* too quickly, if you reveal too much of yourself too soon then people will see you're a timber wolf who's been out in the forest too long, you've been licking your wounds too much, the only taste you know now is regret.

Better to emerge slowly, to shake the snow and the past from your pelt, better to come into the light after breakfast when they've eaten and their semi-civilized stomachs are full, and they're not immediately, keenly suspicious.

Better to learn to walk slowly, to hang your massive head low, better to keep your startled eyes averted.

Cats know the deal. They pretend to be sophisticated, domesticated. They sit all day cleaning, preening and purring when, really, they're just waiting for night to fall. Cats see in the dark. But what they see is *themselves*, the way they saw it in their daydreams, descending,

You haven't a fuckin' clue what I'm banging on about, do you?

Who do you know that tells the truth? No one does, not in this city.

Here, everybody lies. The taller the building, the greater the lie that built it. Monuments to deception. Cathedrals to delusion and denial.

The uniformed doorman lies when he smiles as you enter, the uniformed priest lies when he touches your forehead.

Ego te absolve.

How, Father, where's your magic wand?

The President lies on TV. The Prime Minister lies beside him. Everybody does it. Ice-skaters are we, sticking to safe areas on the rink where it's possible to think without panic, to pirouette and perform. But as we leap about we know we are busily distracting all eyes from the thin, exposed areas of ourselves where we will always fear to tread, especially as we collapse into our Lazee-Boy recliners.

And reach for the remote control: just that *moment*, when the TV briefly ignores the thumb depressing.

We lie, mostly to ourselves.

The Judge manages it by staying out of Ed's room. By picking up the little phone to his wife instead of walking down the corridor to be confronted by the grotesque reality of how lies twist and grow.

Ellie lies to herself by getting lightly stoned each day, by asking me needle-questions about my life, my direction, my folks back home. What about *her* life? Where are her kids? Where's her husband, where have her dreams of a soul-food kitchen gone?

Up in smoke.

And Ed?

He lies when he says he won't hit the panic button unnecessarily. Then, when he wakes me up for the fourth time, he says he can't help being afraid, he says he's really fuckin' sorry man but it really felt like someone was there, breathing, staring, standing over him again.

Ed lies when he says he won't buzz me too early in the morning, or when I'm in the shower, or on a break sipping nice cold milk. He says he won't disturb me, he knows I've earned it, he realizes it all gets to me too, he sees I need my sleep, my space, my own company for a while.

So tell me, who's that on the phone?

Ed?

Or Tony fuckin' Soprano?

I lie to myself naturally I also lie to you.

I skate, and jump, and land with a thump on my huge feet I'm forced to stick to very thick ice; if I go out farther, if I venture out beyond, even a little, I'll be forced to watch the surface crack and run. Then, so will you.

You'll see it spreading. You'll start checking around for your car keys—yes you will—you'll discreetly tap your coat pocket thinking that I won't notice, you'll steal a glance at your watch or your mobile phone then you'll start to walk away. Maybe you'll turn around, maybe you'll give me one of those brave little smiles, maybe you'll say, *I'm sorry. I didn't think it would turn out this way.*

Or the perennial, the old reliable: *You know Trevor, I thought it was going to work out different.*

Newsflash: So did fuckin' I.

In The Subway Inn, every time I buy a beer the barman makes a big fuss of buying me one in return, even though it's not his fuckin' money. At the end of the night he knocks back three shots of cheap malt whisky, says he needs it for the subway. 'Helps deal with all *doze* animals.'

I do the three shots with him, even though I can't stand the paraffin taste when my head tilts back I'm thinking, *Why the hell am I doing so many things I really don't enjoy?*

I have the power to make people feel safe but I also have the power to make them feel afraid.

Sometimes I knock back the malt, then after The Subway Inn gets shuttered up for the night, I stand on the pavement like a totem.

I am a rock. They must divide and swim around me, even couples holding hands must be rent asunder. Dyed blondes in cheap denim jerk their stoned boyfriends into place, 'Don't say nothin'. He's twice your fuckin' size.'

Sometimes I walk the bitter barman down to the tracks and wait with him, and I don't avert my eyes. I stand and stare, I dare the animals to keep looking and I'm secretly hoping one of them will say, 'What's your fuckin' problem, pal?'

Sometimes who you stand waiting with says an awful lot about you.

12.

It's weird, with all the working out, with all the protein Ellie packs into me on a daily basis, this is the strongest I've ever been, I mean some evenings I amaze myself at the way the weights keep stacking up; I can see it in the steady way the black and white body-builders hold my gaze and nod, almost respectfully.

But I'm not feeling all that *mentally* strong. It might be the fact that these days Ed's mood swings are extremely erratic, might be that my hours are quite chaotic, might be something really simple like the fact that I'm attempting to give up smokes and steer clear of The Subway Inn, which isn't easy. Because at the end of a long shift I really need to forget him.

Maybe it's the Greek-heat of this city, it really is unbearable. It makes it impossible to strike up conversation—*if* there actually was anyone to talk to. Because, after half past five, streets are already sullen, and absolutely empty. And you feel it's the end of the world, that everyone else is at an amazing party out in the Hamptons, that they're all getting laid, gymnastically, between 300-thread Egyptian cotton sheets and afterwards they're sipping Long Island iced-teas or delicately salted margaritas. And The Dynamic Duo—which is pathetic Ed, and even more pathetic you—are the only fools who didn't get invited.

RSVP.

Ed has no stories to tell, none whatsoever.

But neither would you if you never had sisters, never sat in a dwarf-sized desk at school and relentlessly flicked the fruit-bat ears of the teacher's pet in front, never jabbed a compass up his spongy ass if he so much as threatened to complain. And you'd have no stories to tell if all you'd ever had was a private tutor, and you'd never let loose a hundred white mice down long polished corridors, or never made kung-fu stars in metal-work class and thrown them into the steaming, bovine crowd at rugby matches, waiting for the scream. Or tied fishing wire to a neighbour's door knocker and kept her awake all night. You'd have no tales to tell if you never had a dog that ran beside you and chased down pale hares, and you'd never lived by a beach and searched among twisted driftwood for bottles with notes in them, or you'd never had a boomerang, or been the Star Performer on a swimming team, or been to college, even briefly, or enjoyed hash days off from yourself, or floated on the sea, like a cork, after winning a race. Or been caressed by an actress with a perfect body, Charlotte Rampling cheek-bones and a sexy Anglo-Irish accent. Or if you'd never stood up in front of a class of people in chairs with no arms and screwed-on-sideways heads and felt yourself, reinvented.

And you'd have no tales to tell if you never sang songs with your laughing mother coming back from the red painted town.

And it doesn't matter if your old fella is rich as Croesus, or if you once had a private recording studio in your bedroom that had to be flogged off to make way for all the machinery needed to keep you barely alive; it's all fuckin' pointless. Because the truth is, you're dying. And not the way everyone else is dying, day by day; no, you're expiring by the hour, the second, and each foetid breath you exhale takes you closer to the moment, and you're not noble and all that *shite* in *The Tibetan Book of Living and Dying* because you never really lived, you simply were born then began to die, *post-haste*.

And some days you're so angry you can literally hiss and spit, especially at incredibly healthy fuckers like me who've never been physically sick, not one single solitary day.

And you want to lash out, you want to be cruel, and callous, to injure and inflict as much as your mean little spirit will allow.

And maybe the only joy you know is the peace that comes after an argument, the feeling of things being washed away by coarse, salty tears.

And you wish you could bleed to death heroically, not just leak like a stain into the carpet.

There are days when I don't assist, when I don't react to his tirades, his name-calling, his incessant, childish yammering for attention. Days when I just smooth the cold pillow for his dying face, days when I look down at the carpet and let him shake, and jolt, when I literally watch him sweat.

See pores open, see poison pouring out.

I hear conflicting voices then: *Go to him, please hold him*, followed by: *Nah, just watch the little prick shiver an' hopefully shrivel and die.*

This will always have been precipitated by him being unusually cruel; I told Ed far too much at the beginning I laid myself bare, made myself weak in order to make him feel big and strong.

It was a mistake.

I'll never make it again, because when you make yourself small and worthless, and when you finally rise up, the shadow you cast on the wall when the house is fast asleep may not be the shadow you expected to see at all.

13

Unlike Ed, I have plenty of stories to tell. This one's about Control:

The first time I *really* felt it slide, like ice inside glass, was when my mother called me in and told me that she wouldn't be going into town on Mother's Day, that it had come back again, there was no point pretending.

I tried to be strong, I stood there really tall and she told me I looked *amazing,* I was getting a real Olympic-swimmer's silhouette, 'like yer man Mark Spitz, do ya remember him Stretch? No, you were probably just a kid.'

But the truth is, standing there I might have looked like a man but really I was still a child inside and I felt incredibly weak and dizzy, as if I'd just smoked grass someone had mixed with horse tranquillizer.

I didn't sleep for three days, not properly, even though Ma gave me a few of her sleeping tablets, but they didn't work and my head was groggy, and there was no point going to college so I'd stayed on the train past Dun Laoghaire, on into the dirty, lowslung city. And now I was sitting alone in a bar called The Harp, raising a dead pint to my lips when I heard this calming voice telling me to *call it a day*, to *head on home.*

I picked up my crombie and moved slowly to the door. My back was stiff, my feet trudged, my laces were undone and seemed too far away to be worth the effort. There were spots in front of my eyes, I don't think I'd eaten anything solid in twenty-four hours.

I was pale and shaking. I couldn't seem to get the fucking coat to fit over my hoodie.

One of the bouncers—and I think it was because earlier I didn't get out of his way when he was walking to the gents and I didn't seem suitably terrified by his pale eyes—decided he'd have a bit of fun with me. He starts helping me into my coat, and I know what he's going to do, he's going to wait until my hands are half in, and he does, then he starts to tie me up in the fabric, he gives me a few little slaps, 'Oops-a-daisy, sorry about that pal, oops, silly me, there I go again.'

His hands are fast, and light. But they're the size of a ten-year-old girl's.

The other bouncers, these beer-bellied red-faced fuckers at the door, they think this is hilarious. They clearly believe he's the new Peter Sellers, *ho-ho-ho*, so he ups the ante, he starts to slap me on the back of the head saying all the while he's hitting me gently, 'You big overgrown dose, you big, clumsy, stupid dose ya.'

He stops, dusts me down, looks over at his eternally appreciative audience.

When he looks back, his pale blue eyes are smiling, perhaps expecting me to nod and laugh.

I don't laugh. Instead, I stand up very straight, which hurts. Then I stoop down quickly like a bird I cleave his crinkly forehead with the top of my head.

Rock. Paper. Blood.

He falls to his knees. Worshipping.

With my left fist, because my right is still inside the coat, I break his nose, right down on the bridge, the soft spot.

They really went to work on me and I couldn't get up no matter how hard I tried and I couldn't think and it wasn't all slow anymore, it was really quite fast and blurred especially when Ol' Blue Eyes re-entered the fray and the black boots and white fists took on a more urgent, disco rhythm.

Then all I remember is being punched and bundled out into a wet lane, black boots and shoes raining.

And finally, an empty Guinness barrel being dropped from an impossible height.

Because there was no way, no way these round little men could suddenly be so tall.

It took a long time for someone to come along, and I lay there, oozing like a goldfish flicked from the bowl by a cat.

The first thought that came into my head was straight out of a Sam Peckinpah Western: *I will never, ever go down again, I don't care how many of them there are.*

The second thought was of my poor mother.

I was nine days in Cappagh Hospital. They broke my nose, three fingers on my right hand, the little finger and index on my left. They dislocated my jaw, damaged my spleen and ruptured something in my inner ear, which means I have a balance issue that comes and goes, like a ghost, without warning. It hurts to fly. And I can't dive, though I can snorkel, which I love.

But the main thing is, they took something away. Despite my size, I was never the type of guy who swaggered or shaped down city streets, but up until then I had also never, ever looked away from other men.

Now I do.

And I hope when I look down it is going to be enough, that whoever is staring and daring me will allow this acquiescence to suffice.

And only someone who has been knocked and kicked and screamed at, only someone who has felt the blows move across his body like rain on an already watery bog, only someone who has had something taken from the clay will fathom.

I will never go down again.

The worst part was sitting in his study conspiring to lie to her, inventing a story he would tacitly back up, of slippery tiles, concussion, cold compresses, concerned nurses.

He barely nodded.

The worst part was taking the awkward story up the stairs with her tray, and flowers plucked from her garden, painfully.

The worst part was listening to myself: 'Ah it wasn't that serious Ma, really I stayed there because at the end of the day it was more convenient, you see there was a real need for them to assess the hand injury on an almost daily basis because of the threat to, you know, my swimming career . . . ' And how they had to show me special physio exercises . . . 'And how was the dog while I was gone Ma, had the lunatic with the lawnmower been around again, had the butcher kept scraps, I wonder will I move that rhododendron bush Ma, what do you think, would it be better off getting a bit more shade, jesus how the devil are you Ma, come on, how are things, any small sign of improvement, your hair looks shinier?'

She smiled and lied back just as proficiently, 'Everything's fine, son, just fine.' Then she said she'd missed me, she'd been very worried, she would like to have visited but it was deemed out of the question by you-know-who. The doctor, too, had ruled against it. The legs. The back. The bloody balance gone.

'Must be a family trait, Ma. Mine's terrible too, though the tiles *were* very slippy.'

She smiled and held her hand out, feebly. My heart was racing at the pace of our dishonesty. I could see in her worn-out eyes that she knew I'd lost it again, knew from the bruises, from my voice, and from the way I was fidgeting and sitting down and standing up too quickly, and letting go of her dried-out hand, and stopping too far from the bed, and talking, talking far too much. She knew. That it was something in my head that had snapped, not just the bones in my hands.

'I tried to break my fall and failed, Ma. The orthopaedic surgeon said I was lucky, it was quite a weight that impacted on the bones, lucky I didn't snap the wrists completely, lucky too the bench I hit my head off was made of soft wood, not steel or concrete.'

Talking pure tarmac. Rolling it out in hot waves sticking to my tongue, the roof of my mouth, my furiously blinking eyes.

'It's good to have you back, son. But why don't you lie down for a while? You're pale as a sheet and you have the black rims back. It was probably hard to sleep in a public ward, was it?'

'Yes Ma, it was a bit.'

We lie to protect. We lie to inure. To keep on going we have to lie.

14.

Naturally, there was a big palaver made and my old man had to call in all kinds of fuckin' favours from news-paper *proprietors* to keep the story out.

And he reminded me that we had 'already had to move house once because of a similar *escapade* when two small boys had been hospitalized with broken ribs and smashed hands because I'd leapt up and down on them like, like . . . '

And I'm thinking, *Like Donald bloody Sutherland in* Day of the Locust.

By Nathanael West.

And he's droning on in his incredibly world-weary voice that it was in my nature to disappoint and to *disport* myself– did ya ever hear the like?—on the streets of the Capitol as a *savage*, a *thugee*, a *throwback*. He's banging on about *the half-man, half-beast* thing again, and how a leopard cannot change its spots and it was unlike him to mix his metaphors and I was thinking, *Well, which am I? Half-man, half-beast, leopard with spots, leopard without?* And maybe that's the moment I decided to see people as animals, because clearly that's how my father saw me.

Actually, sometimes I don't see them as animals, I see them as monsters. And once, when I went to a Francis Bacon exhibition in Dublin I started running from painting to painting pulse racing, it was as if he'd been inside my head: there they were, all of them, my sisters with their twisted mouths bragging and dragging the evening on, and on; my father sideways and half hidden in the scribbled corner, silently criticizing; my

Jesuit swimming-coach counting down the seconds; my demented next-door neighbour with the lawnmower, screaming. There was even a Steven-Berkoff-type bouncer with a shaved head, I swear to fuck I didn't know where to look. And you know when MTV reporters ask celebs who they'd like to meet, well I'd like to meet Mr Bacon, I don't care if his father caught him dressing up in his mother's clothes. In fact, I'd like to have sat for one of his paintings; I'd like to have had acknowledged, formally, the monster deep inside.

For the record, I'd also like to meet Jesus, Judas, Lucifer, Dante, Leonardo, Michelangelo, Caravaggio, Shakespeare, Milton, Mary Wollstonecraft Godwin Shelley, Conrad, M.P. Sheil, Jung, Preston Sturgess, Frank Capra, Johnny Weissmuller, Ma, Gene Rodenberry, Charles Bukowski—though I think we'd have ended up fighting—and Laurie Lee. Bruce too.

Anyway, when it came to court the old judge with the ludicrously theatrical voice said the doormen had behaved like animals, my considerable physical presence *notwithstanding,* and that the beating they'd administered was cowardly and low. I had the right to defend myself, of course, but it was possible that in my anger I had 'o'er stepped the mark' and he waited for me to nod in agreement, but I didn't, *fuck him.*

I said I had just wanted to go home.

At the back of the courtroom someone in a shiny shellsuit laughed, probably because one of the bouncers was modelling a steel triangle on his flattened nose, he looked a little bit like Hannibal.

Lecter, not the guy who crossed the Alps, obviously.

These days I don't really feel up to sitting in the kitchen listening to another of Ellie's *Sermons on the Mount,* so I spend a lot of time in my tiny room, alone.

She seems to know I'm a little bit low so she nearly always leaves a freshly baked pie or a hero sandwich under a starched white cloth, plus a funny little note: *All work-outs and no play makes Clever a dull boy* or *The way to a white man's heart is thru his gettin' bigger belly* or *Hot pie, when you gonna ask me out on a hot date?*

Sometimes, I'm sitting there enjoying the sweetness of berries, the bitterness of cloves and the childish calmness of milk and I'm thinking, *I wish my head were just a little bit emptier, a little less busy*, when I hear Dana's steady footfall along the hall.

I close my eyes, all the better to see her.

Her back arches a bit because her perfect ass is held so proud and high, she also has a strange habit of clenching her fists loosely as she walks towards his mother's room—she's like a little warrior preparing to do battle.

I'm rarely if ever easy in myself, but the days that Dana is around I feel like a fraud changing my T-shirt three times, putting on more aftershave.

What difference will it make? She hardly knows you exist anymore.

15

I should exit the sweltering city for a while I should bob and float on the sea, I used to love that feeling of suspension, of being held like a gift, a white and green offering to the blue sky, smiling.

I'll ask Ed for a day off. He'll say yes, partly because he's so low himself, partly because he knows I need the time, partly because we've nothing left to say to each other these days we just sit like stones in air-conditioned silence.

Out here in Coney Island the slack oily water looks like it would suck you down and hold you under, like a crazy lover who will never let go. The boardwalk groans under the strain of impossible dreams: *Instant Romance; New Beginnings; The Past Being Left Behind.*

We lie back to view the photo-exhibition being curated behind our knock-off sunglasses: on top are rows of kitsch fifties photos of people laughing, swimming and holding hands. These are titled: *What We Expect on Our Days Off.*

Underneath lie garish, Parr-ish images of overflowing garbage pails; fat kids with crumpled stomachs licking runny ice-cream on uncomfortable, bumpy towels; an harassed traffic cop waiting to let loose on a loudmouth Italian wearing a *Playboy* baseball cap; see him hanging down and out of an incredibly red Camero; a snow-white woman with a prancing-stallion tattoo on her veinless arm, drinking from a bottle; see her suck smoke in, then warmly wash it down with an inherited, male grimace.

These images are captioned: *The Reality of What Unfolds*.

Everywhere the eye is under day-glo attack. Everywhere the ear is assaulted by the din of other people's portable rap. Fifty Cent boys smoke huge, cartoonish spliffs while their heavily pregnant girlfriends ease into the viscous water. As one of them drips back up the beach towards her smoking crew she stops the sun from shining on me, and when I look up as if to say, *Please move*, she announces for all the world to hear: 'The fuck you lookin' at, you ugly *mothafuckah*?'

Her male companions spring up in the sand like black and tan weasels sniffing the salt air for trouble.

I say nothing, do nothing. I put my sunglasses back on, try to look the other way. When I take off my shirt and start to rub sunscreen on, one by one the young punks stop staring. And when their screeching, Macy Gray girlfriend tells them to 'do somethin' 'bout the big white *mothafuckah* still starin',' one of their number shoves her down in the sand he spits, 'Shut the fuck up, bitch, he ain't the only mother starin', now put them watermelons away for the day!'

We are extras in a dreary, low-budget movie about nothing in particular; dreams fading, crude expectations leaking, like oil, from an accidentally overturned barrel. Director and cinematographer have moved on without telling us we are superfluous to the story. And so we are stuck staring, not at each other, because nobody really wants confrontation, but at the flat dull sea.

As a child I used to drive my parents to distraction on holidays I'd regularly refuse to leave the seaside. In my head I was convinced it was an amusement ride, that someone in the sky was going to pull the plug then the sea and its wonderful sound effects would shortly fade away.

I look around now, I'm thinking, *Wish someone would pull the fuckin' plug here*. It's like that scene in *Taxi Driver* where

Travis Bickle says, '*Some day, a red rain is gonna come an' wash the scum away.*'

All of a sudden a sweating, egg-shaped man selling hot dogs from a squeaking cart says in a fake-friendly voice, 'What'll it be buddy, the works?'

Egg Man starts squirting obscene amounts of mayo, mustard and ketchup in squiggly lines along a flaccid dog I have no intentions of eating the perspiration running down from his brow is soaking into the off-white tissue in his hand. I can't resist, I have to say, '*You talkin' to me, huh, you talkin' to me?*' Except I don't get the accent right, I don't sound one little bit like Bobby de Niro, I sound like a Chinese guy who's had too much to drink.

The hot-dog vendor picks up his cart and moves away, squeaking like a gigantic mouse he says he doesn't want no trouble, he's 'just trying to feed his family, is all.'

On the standing-room-only, rocking-horse train to the city, a prune of a black lady with horrific, dyed-blonde hair swings her plastic sack up on the worn hot seat beside her.

Without taking her red-brown eyes off me she opens her legs wide, pulls down her laddered tights and floods the seat, then the carriage floor.

Yellow despair, edging towards tired mothers and feral children in open-toed sandals.

16

L ast night at a downtown place called The Ear Inn they
had an open-mic night for poets.
I had my diary with me, I decided, *fuck it*, I'd have a go.
I read 'I Am a Companion to a Boy with Muscular Dystrophy':

Dis-distrophy sits
swelters, frets. Gets het-up in wheelchair heat
snarled feet tap-tapping metal pedals
like an inmate
rapping a tin plate at mealtimes,
at mealtimes I shovel fork-fulls of food into his
gob gobbling mouth.
Then we watch TV, at last we watch TV.
Sometimes his turkey-thin neck
and his tape, tapered thighs
hurt, hurtle
jerk, jerk, jerky spasms
down his spastic frame
sending fits of shudder
along spider-fine veins,
splintered waist,
wall-flower spine.
I observe these rat, rattlesnake contortions jolt him
Then wipe the spittle that gathers
at the elbow-edge
of his graveyard mouth.

Then we watch TV, at last we watch TV.

When I cross the corridor in the evening
I stand under the scalding shower to get rid
of the cling-clinging stink
And I think:
Why do I never tell him
how much I feel his pain?

Then I watch TV, at last I watch TV.

Tremendous silence afterwards you could hear the coffee machine percolating away in the corner this one black guy in a pinstripe waistcoat stood up and said, 'I could feel it too man, hey I could feel his Pain, I was there with you, brother.'

Which would have been perfect, except the fuckin' eejit overturned half a cup of cold coffee abandoned on the table behind him I could see dirty brown liquid running, like diarrhoea, towards the formica-edges.

The only slight relief was the silent, communal decision among the other poets to watch the Spanish waitress mop, not to watch me leave.

17

The Judge sat with us today perched like Miss Muffet on the edge of the bed. He asked Ed how he was feeling, then nodded and swallowed when Ed said he wasn't too strong these days. The Judge then said it was most likely the heat and tried to perk things up by asking what the hell we did all day, what sort of oddball music we listened to.

And that's when Ed said I should put on Alan White for his father.

The three of us sat there listening and to be fair to the Judge he joined in as best he could, tapping his foot and nodding his tiny head. Then he said, '*He-hem*, it's true, in the old days transistor radios really did glow.' And he told us a story about how, when he was our age, he sat listening to the President talking about war, and duty, how the very next day he signed up to fight, how he was awarded a medal for bravery, how proud his father was when he finally came sailing home.

He looked straight at Ed, he nodded his sad tortoise head, 'My father, however, could never have been as proud as I am every day because *no one* is as consistently brave as you Ed.' Then he looked at me, 'Yes indeed, the truth is, *he-hem*, Ed is the bravest soldier I have ever encountered.'

When he stood up—you could see he was thinking of giving Ed a salute before he walked out—he did the *he-hem* thing one last time.

I turned to Ed, I thought he would be delighted, but he just sighed, 'That. Happens. Once. Or. Twice. A year. He comes in. And. Talks about. Me. As if I. Was. Already dead.'

My father at my mother's funeral, fish out of water, shaking his head slightly as he listened to the priest droning on about Resurrection, Truth and Light.

The weight of his dismay.

How he looked up at me; how, in one split asunder second he made me question *everything*: the candles, the congregation, their intentions, all the invocations and inventions of religion.

I was the one who had to shake all the hands, *Sorry for your trouble, sorry for your trouble, wonderful woman, I remember she was always singing in the garden with Trevor doing the digging, good man Trevor, may God increase your strength.*

My father couldn't even bring himself to look at them, so they just touched his coat-sleeve, gingerly.

And I wished I could comfort him but my sisters had formed a half-circle around him, a membrane, and I couldn't penetrate his pain, and they never even came to the graveside, *the cunts.*

And later, when I returned to the house alone, I didn't argue when the oldest one informed me that the only reason my mother had been buried amid such pointless mumbo-jumbo, the only reason their distraught father had subjected himself to such a barbaric, philistine ritual, was so I could see her face in the casket.

So I would stop lying on her bed in the morning, talking to thin air.

So I could *fully appreciate and comprehend the reality of the fact that our mother was dead.* And would I stop going into her room at night, please? It was driving their father mad listening to me wailing like a banshee; if necessary, they'd bolt the door shut and hire a handyman to hammer the bloody thing tight, alright?

I didn't argue. I didn't even speak. I just began to squeeze her thin, long voice and her ugly mouth with one hand, *hard*. And I used my cold palm to cover the poison hole, and she couldn't breathe or make any animal sound, and it was a good thing for her, and a good thing for me too I suppose, that the bouncers had broken three fingers on my right hand because now I was using just my thumb and two other stiff fingers on my weaker left.

And I could feel her jaw-bone, *mandible,* its socket unhinging, and I could watch her eyes grow round and white, like tabletennis balls.

One, one thousand, two, one thousand, three, one thousand, four, one thousand, five, one thousand, six, one thousand, seven, one thousand, eight, one thousand, nine, one thousand, ten, one thousand, eleven, one thou-

She knocked over a vase cleverly, it smashed, loudly, it brought the other two running, they screamed for her and became winged creatures up on my back and in my hair, tugging. And then my small father came running.

And when I saw the look in his eyes, I let go.

I have never felt such shame, and I suppose that's why I cried so much on the plane, not just because of my mother, but because it had ended badly with my family, to put it fuckin' mildly. And you may think you can cut ties, you may think you can just pack a suitcase and walk through departures, *sayonara*— but it's not that simple.

Family stuff sticks. Family stuff whispers. Family stuff is where the Doubt begins. And never ends.

I sent her flowers through Interflora the day after I arrived and a long, long letter, trying to explain. Everything.

I wrote the word *sorry* at the end of every paragraph—I even cut out the letters, like a serial killer would, and stuck them on the last page. She never wrote back. But then I didn't provide a forwarding address, just a hotmail account. It's funny, isn't it, when you're receiving a list of messages you're back to being a child again? And before you open the little golden envelopes on screen you're full of hope, then your heart sinks. Because all you have to read, all you have to look forward to, is junk mail, info on cheap flights and a hastening school reunion.

Ed has the brave face on today, it reminds me of that Beatles song 'Eleanor Rigby'—wasn't she the one had a face in a jar by the door?

I haven't looked at him properly for weeks I've just been going through the motions, sleepwalking, swapping one *Simpsons* video for the next, one untouched tray for another.

His skin is seal-grey and oily, it's as if he is suffering from some untreated tropical disease. Believe me, you don't want to know how bad his breath is.

We have nothing to say to each other, even when we watch his favourite episode, the one where aliens run for President, *nothing*.

When it finishes he stares at the screen and while the video begins to automatically rewind, he says, 'Why. Don't you. Take the. Evening off ? Go shopping. I'm sick of. Looking. At you. Wearing the, same. Shit.'

He does this high false laugh, except it catches in his throat, then he kind of gives in for a while he says nothing, just stares down at the carpet.

A monumental pause after which he asks for his headphones.

I believe it will be easier in winter it will be normal to turn inwards, to be quiet and bare, like trees.

I never know what to buy in shops these days nothing ever seems to fit properly and when assistants say *ooh that looks really nice*, the insincere fuckin' smile on their face makes me think of jackals, or laughing hyenas.

Around Bleeker and Canal it's worst. The geeks who work

in vintage clothing stores think they've a God-given right to rip back the curtain, like Dorothy in *The Wizard of Oz* and sometimes you're only halfway through putting on the fluorescent blouse they've forced into your hand, then *whoosh,* they're standing there with their pupils, purple hair and snot-green shirts saying, 'If you want my opinion'—which I don't— 'you're the sort of guy could really pull off that whole *Midnight Cowboy* retro look.' And you are not sure if you've actually said it, not sure if the words have uncoiled from the corner of your mouth, *Hey, do us both a fuckin' favour—put your eyes back inside your head, pull the curtain, and get the fuck back behind that fake-antique cash-register, OK?*

Anger lies fallow just beneath the surface it could easily turn to rage.

Why am I so angry? Is it because I am growing old with Ed, is it because some essential part of me is expiring at exactly the same rate that he is slowly curling up? Is it because my hopes, my dreams, lie crumpled round his pedals?

Is it because I came to save him and realize now I cannot save myself?

Fight it.

I need to think of something positive: There was a nice black lady today in a travel agent's; she had a smile that lit up her eyes, I really can't stand it when people grin with just their teeth, it happens quite a lot in New York, especially in restaurants. And what I'd like to know is, why do they always prick up their little plucked ballerina eyebrow and ask *just one?* as if there's something wrong with you, I mean maybe my wife died in childbirth, maybe I've just woken up from a five-year coma and don't know where my buddies are, maybe I'm happy sitting on my own with my black diary and my iPod, OK?

Maybe I choose to be alone. I don't, but the possibility should be permitted, the way it is for the very rich, very beautiful and very vain who waltz through New York and through Life, without ever being accosted by some snotty, accusatory cow—*Just one?*

I best tell something nice and balanced about the old man. One white Christmas when he'd invited one of his professor friends over I'd gotten the two dweebie, bossy kids—who instantly assumed they were smarter than me—to have a snowball fight outside.

I placed hard smooth rocks inside the snowballs, took careful aim, missed once, then skulled the older of them, stretching him flat on the laughing snow. *See how smart you are now, Cedric.*

After they drove away, he called me into his study. He had this amazing sound system, speakers in every corner—*Bose* I think—and he puts on Bach's 'Cello Concerto.' We sit and listen. After a while it begins to open staked stuff inside my chest, reverberating down and along the echoing chambers, unlocking and slowly sliding open warped, medieval drawers. I can't stand it any longer, I start to cry. And I can only ever remember this happening once, he calls me over and hugs me gently he says he will always love me, *no matter what.* Then he tells me with tears in his smiling eyes that I am *a monster, a terrifying unruly, uncivilized beast, a halfman* and he asks me *What are you?* And I tell him *I am a monster, a terrifying unruly uncivilized beast, a half-man* and I add the word *satyr* to impress him, and we laugh.

Together. In the book-lined study with that magnificent music washing over us.

Next day, he winked at me over dinner when one of my sisters was banging on about how well she'd done in some school debating contest. But about a week after when one or other of them won a medal for reciting a poem about some dead Indian—'Hiawatha' by Longfellow, I think—he went back to not noticing me.

Old habits die hard. In parents. And in children.

18

At home buying shoes or sneakers was a real ordeal; there was this one shop on the quays in Dublin called Heathers and although they sometimes stocked my size, their styles were the kind favoured by lesbians with elephantiasis, thick-necked country priests and aromatic middle-aged hillwalkers who wore shorts in winter. In city sport stores I always felt like a freak, especially when some smart-ass sales assistant would shout *Does this come in a 15?* so as the whole shop would stop, and stare.

Here it isn't an issue, the sales-guy doesn't even blink when I state my size and squeeze down into the little chair.

There is something familiar about him as he smiles he opens the box, fluffs up the noisy pink paper, and asks, 'So, where you from?'

'Dublin.'

'Me too.'

'You haven't lost the accent.'

'No, thank God.'

'How long have you been out here?'

'Three years. I go home at Christmas though. For good.'

'Fair play.'

'How 'bout you?'

'I've been here a few months now. I'm nearly at the end of my contract.'

'You in construction?'

'Yeah.'

'I was thinking you looked *incredibly* strong. So, what will you do when the job's done?'

'I think I'll do some travelling. Head out west. Maybe buy a bike.'

'What kind?

'A hog.'

'A *what?*

'A Harley'.

'Wow. You could drive to California. Route 66 and all that.'

'Yeah, maybe'

'I go to San Francisco quite a bit myself.'

'Really. What's it like?'

'Oh, you'd love it, so you would. You'd really love it.'

I hate when people who don't know you tell you that you'd love something, just because they do. I'm trying to avoid his eagerbeaver eyes and the pink tissue paper in the cardboard box is the exact same colour as his perma-press tie which is dangling down in his, *jesuschrist,* he has my heel right up against his crotch, the little fucker is pretending to be tying up the laces but really he's massaging my foot against himself under the cover of pink, don't know how the hell I didn't notice, *fuck.*

And this black guy is shaking his massive Afro-head, *shit,* he thinks we're two butt-holers getting it on in public I really don't like when my head is all foggy like this so I tell the little bollox that he's made a major fuckin' mistake, except he says 'No, it's the right size, it's a perfect match, just like *Cinderella,*' and the way he says that word is just too much to bear.

I'm standing now with one new sneaker on and my sock is wet with sweat and everything is all undone; it's like the time I got on a roller coaster at Funderland in Dublin I could barely fit it into the little car, *definitely* going to topple, so I started shouting, I made them stop the whole thing after just one ter- rifying circuit. Cheap, chewing-gum mothers and leather- backed fathers were staring, *fuck them, I knew in my heart it was going to crash* and for days afterwards I scoured the papers to see if there were reports of any fatal injuries, but of course, there weren't.

Outside the sweating shop I do my breathing exercises then I start to laugh out loud: Jesus, I must have a sign on my forehead saying—*Try your luck.*

A summer-bum stumbles past like a runner in a relay race he picks up the sound-baton and begins to roar with thunderous, rolling laughter. He points his finger at me and nods, then puts the filthy finger to his mouth, *ssssh,* protecting our secret. Then just as suddenly he disappears.

I am alone again. That's when I hear a cold voice telling me to *face up to the fact that I am a dickhead, a dip-shit, a ditz, I am to be taken advantage of forever, I am the sort that people teach weird shit to, the type that gets asked to piss on total strangers. I am out of my depth, clutching at straws.*

Drowning, not waving.

Maybe.

But I'm alive and I'm strong and I still have some small sense of humour intact and a growing sense of what a ridiculous figure I must cut among the well-heeled, the powerful, the cruelly ambitious, the purposeful, the killers and conmen, the business types who've always known exactly where they're going. Exactly what it takes to get there.

I have no idea where I'm headed. I see little or no point in planning ahead. I embrace chaos.

I also don't feel like working for a while.

19

E d's mother wants to know what makes me think I have the right to just take whole days off *willy-nilly*, why yesterday Ed sat all day long in *soiled pyjamas* and I'm thinking, *Yeah—well he wasn't the only fuckin' one.*

Except the smell in her room is not piss, it is poison. It is the smell of burnt hope, the stench of extinguished dreams. It is a smell I cannot stand to see her lying there, beached whale, surrounded by all those sticky trays and caramel plates, it makes me sick to my stomach to see her squander Life so wantonly in her filthy fuckin' room.

And if you listen hard you can hear Him whispering to himself in corners you can see his manicured fingernails move delicately on an abacus he is calculating how long it will take for gristle to grow like white ivy round her bloated heart, how long it will take for the pump to fail in her ailing blood can you hear the silting cells scream—*That's too much stop, don't you understand plain English, STOP FUCKING EATING.*

Her foghorn voice is hailing from behind the door, again.

I tell myself remember, *this is his mother, be polite, be respectful, please be very very careful.*

No. I am not going to sit on the side of her bed, *tap tap.*

I am not going to fetch the négligée from her bureau; *Why thank you.*

I am not going to swap the TV sets around; *My, what animal strength you possess.*

I am not going to bring English tea from the kitchen, nor faded magazines from the hall, I am not going to help look for the remote control which is always hiding between the sheets.

Here's the deal, Miss Piggy: I didn't sign on as a companion to a woman with a broken leg.

Or a tenuous grip on reality.

When I tell Ellie the sort of things I've been imagining, manicured nails on an abacus and goateed, Louis-Cyphre types in corners peeling eggshells, she says, 'Shit, maybe Irish people can't handle sense, maybe it's like Red Indians and alcohol, maybe you should stick to The Subway Inn for a while.' Then she touches my hand and adds, 'I ain't always gonna be here baby, you know there's only so much of this shit a body can take at my age. For what it's worth, I don't think you're cut out for it neither.'

'What do you mean?

'All them tall-tales you told me from the Clinic always had lots of different peoples in them, what I'm saying is, maybe you need to be Companion to more than one person at a time. Maybe you could do somethin' else?'

'Such as?'

'I dunno, Clever. Shit, maybe you could teach kids to swim that might be nice for a change, you might meet some pretty mothers poolside.'

'Maybe.'

'Gots to be other jobs out there for someone like you, Clever.'

'Yeah.'

We both know there isn't.

She pops me a beer, I sit there peeling the label thinking, *This isn't the worst job in the world, not by a long shot.* Anyway, there's not much time left.

He is so weak I have to hold the phone to his skin-peeling ear, I can hear his mother planting her little sly seeds of doubt, *Who was it authorized this amount of overtime, whisper, whose idea was it, whisper, you know he sometimes stinks of drink, Barney says, whisper.*

Ed says 'No.'

Then he looks up at me, and tells her she needs to listen: 'The. Scottish. Guy. Left. Because of. You. In your. Room.' He flicks his hair, concentrates. 'The overtime. Bill. Is your. Fault. Too. You haven't. Bothered. To run Dad's. Ad. Again. You should be. Grate-ful. Trevor is. Pre-pared to. Do all this. Ex-tra. Work.'

This is excellent, he is standing up for me, but also for himself, which is inspiring. 'Here's another thing. Mom. I want the. Old mattress in his room. Thrown out. It is too soft for. Him. I. Want. A new. One brought in.'

He's on a roll, improvising. 'I've decided to. Up. Grade my. Sound-system. I want the. Old one wired. Up in. Trevor's. Room. It would be. Great. If you could. Organize that. OK?'

He's really mastered the American knack of asking questions that are really sly commands. And you can hear her, protesting down the line, *Why Ed, when did he suggest it, whisper, we have to be careful with people like him, whisper, we have to stick together Ed, remember blood is thicker than water, whisper.*

It takes him a while to get his breath back. Then he just says into the receiver, coldly, 'Could you. Respect. My dying. Wishes. Please?'

After he hangs up he laughs so hard I have to stand by with the inhaler, like a fireman. He takes three hits and without even thinking I take one too, this makes him choke and laugh all over again. It is not a nice sound, it is a hacking cackle that releases something old and black inside.

'Hey.'

THE COMPANION · 223

'What?'

'Quit. Looking so. Nervous. OK?'

'OK.'

'It's not. Like. I never said it. To her. Before.'

'OK Ed. Cool.'

But it's far from cool, it is very fuckin' dangerous. You see, I don't want him turning against his mother; if he does that then I am the only thing that stands between him and God knows what if I decide to walk out one night with a ticket in my pocket and my arm raised up, what if I sit into a yellow cab and say, *Can you take me to the airport please? I'm going to Montserrat, it's this island in the Lesser-Antilles, they say the sand is black there from volcanoes erupting all the time.*

'What's up. Trevor?'

'Nothing. I'm just a bit, you know, *distracted.*'

'Talk. To. Me.'

'I'm OK. It's just . . . '

'What?'

'Sometimes, well, it's all a bit much. You, me. This house.'

'I under-stand.'

'Do you Ed?'

He looks up, he does the brave little smile. Some of the gums are black now. Wine-gums.

'Tomorrow. Take another. Whole. Day off. OK?'

'You sure?'

'I'll be. Fine. There's a day. Service. We use. It. All the time. It's where we found. Dana.'

'Thanks Ed.'

'No. Problemo.'

When I pretend to look out the window I can see his reflection plain as day. Wisps of long dead hair are moving like weeds underwater, his neck is twisting, his cracked dry mouth with all the cold sores round the edges says, 'Hey, man. Look at. Me.'

I don't turn round. I can't. In his wheelchair lap his palms lie open, like a Minister in front of his congregation.

'I don't want. To. Lose you.'

'You won't. '

'OK. But. Make sure. You. Tell me what. You're. Thinking. OK?'

'OK, Ed. I will.'

Which is exactly what we say when we can't tell them what we're thinking.

Just inside the door of The Subway Inn there's this old-fashioned phonebooth, the kind gangsters used to get shot to death in movies in my head I often think of ringing Dana after a few scoops, but I'm glad I don't have her number yet, I mean, what the fuck would I say? *It's me, hi, oh nothing, I was just thinking about you for the fiftieth time today.* And I remind myself how I've been down that path before, getting all obsessional about a woman I don't really know.

Sometimes in the hall at night I catch her perfume hanging, like incense. I heard her one day telling Ellie it was *Issey Miyake.* She put on a Southern accent and said it was her *one li'l indulgence*, then the two of them started laughing like a pair of old crones and I knew they'd been getting stoned together and it was really hard for me to walk in over the threshold, I felt like a mailorder bride. It was the opposite at home I used to find it really difficult to *leave* the room when all the family gathered, and if I stopped outside to eavesdrop one of my sisters would always be muttering some sarcastic shit like, *Christ, how can one person take up so much space?* or *When in God's name is that galoot going to get another bloody job?*

You'll like this.

One of my sisters had this boyfriend called Josh, he was this real studious prick with ears, always agreeing with everything my father said *Oh I say, bravo* and all that mock-erudite shite. I caught him one night when he was supposed to be lighting the fire, my job because it involved going out into the real world for more than five seconds, and there he was, standing at the mantle waving his wet-fish hands about, practising what he was going to say. And, like I already said, I have a major fuckin' problem with people who practise shit before they say it, myself included. I shook the coal-bucket violently *Eh, hello, is this amateur hour?* and he leapt out of his baggy skin, seriously, you should have seen the way he went all red, like a tomato with legs, then deep purple like an aubergine.

You could see him all night waiting for his chance to make some crack at my expense. So, when my old fella made some ancient Julius Caesar pun—*Or, more aptly in your case, dear fellow, Vidi, vici, veni*—he, Josh, mutters something about the reference possibly going over my head, something about the gaps in my knowledge, *the lacunae*, not remotely aware that I had better Latin than any of them.

All of a sudden there's this excellent silence, even the dog pricks up its ears, and they all know he's skating on really thin ice, you know, trying to diss me with my own mother sitting there. So I get up slowly. I stretch out like a lion. I walk over to the fire, pick up the brass poker and they're all watching me now, weighing it in my hand. Then I start giving the fire a real going-over, *boom, bang* which they all hate since it sends soot and shit out into the room, but no one says anything, not a jot.

Through clotted sparks and curling smoke see fear increasing in my oldest sister's eyes.

Awful-early this morning I passed Ed's father still in his dressing gown and I stepped to the side, *Good Morning judge, how are you today?* but he just sailed past without acknowledging me and it's not like I'm easy to miss, especially in a narrow corridor where your silk dressing gown is swishing against the walls, and against my knees.

I really hate when people pretend you're invisible.

When I came into Ed's room he asked, 'Hey man, what's up?' which means either I'm getting worse at hiding things, or he's getting better at finding them.

When I tell him what happened in the hallway he says, 'I wouldn't. Take it. Personally. Guy's an. Ass-hole.'

'You're probably right.'

'I'm. Defin-itely. Right.

I tell him how I'd be coming down the stairs at home, and I'd say to myself, *Self, come on now, make an effort, he is your father after all* but he'd just look up and sigh when he saw me.

'What does he. Do. Your. Dad?'

'Most of the day he hides away in his study, no one knows what the fuck he actually does in there.'

'Tell. Me. About it.'

'In the evening, he comes out and changes his clothes as if he's been doing something physically demanding, then he sits in his leather armchair puffing away on his Meerschaum, or whatever you call those hand-carved Sherlock Holmes pipes, stroking his chin and saying shit like—"Of course Aristotle says that the essence of drama is catharsis, which is fascinating, because, at one point, catharis was actually the Greek word for menstrual flow."'

'Who. Else is. There?'

'Me. Ma. The Ugly Sisters.'

'What are they. Like?'

'I realize I'm not exactly an oil-painting . . .'

He laughs and it's odd isn't it, how, in a really close relationship when one person is down the other automatically goes up?

' . . . But compared to them I'm fuckin' George Clooney. I'm Brad Pitt exiting the casino with the fountain foaming in the moonlight. I'm Robert Redford in *Butch Cassidy and the Sundance Kid* astride my horse with the sun setting behind me, it's lending my hair a nice warm glow and granting my eyes a merry little twinkle and . . .'

'They're like. Totally. Ugly?'

'With a capital U, my friend. *Hounds of the Baskervilles*. One of them actually has a mole with two huge black hairs on it.'

'Gross.'

'I offered her fifty fuckin' quid once to let me get the tweezers at it which, considering the fact I wasn't even working, was quite a lot of money.'

'And their. Hus-bands?'

'They're like the intellectual version of the Seven Dwarfs. They nod at every single thing my old fella says, they go, "Mmm how interesting."'

'No. Way. José.'

'Yes way. I'm telling ya, Ed, it would make you want to to scream. Seriously, they'd spend half a century discussing the nuances of certain Greek words, and if you got up to pour yourself another glass of wine, you'd hear his voice, like a stuck-up cricket umpire, *That's number three, and by the by, that particular vintage is not exactly inexpensive.* For instance, and this is

him talking, so think a high, whiney, bagpipe kind of voice—
Were you aware . . . puff puff.'

'What's. That?'

'Well it's not a fuckin' train going past, is it? It's him. On the pipe.'

'Oh. Right.'

'*Were you aware . . .*'

'Puff. Puff.'

'*That the Greek word for love—Eros—is but a vowel away from the word for hostility—Eris. Asshole.*'

'Major. Ass-hole.'

'To be fair, sometimes he'd come out with the odd interesting one, so you sort of had to keep one ear open. Generally, I'd sit away from them by the fire, with Ma and the dog. We'd have a bottle of wine. They were cognac and whiskey people. One time, he looked over at me, which was an event in itself, and started to tell this story about the Viking word for adolescent or teenager, *zinderkund* which means fire-child, because teenagers in ancient Scandinavia used to just kip by the fire all day, the lazy bastards. But you see, back then not a whole lot was expected of you, you kinda had this transition year or two where you could just lie there, staring into the flame, seeing great battles and victories and no one was hassling you to clean your room or any of that shit. I talk too much.'

'No. I. Like. It. Go on.'

'Anyway, he could be reasonably diverting, but boy did the Husbands-to-Be lay it on with a trowel. I swear to God, one time one of them actually clapped and said "Oh, I say bravo!"'

'Je-sus.'

'Same asshole dissed me in front of my mother one time.'

There's a pause and he nods as if to let me know that despite what has gone down he still has no choice but to love her, and I'm right to be telling him a tale of filial love and duty. And a very important part of this job is drawing them out, reminding them of people they love and giving them reasons to live, and sometimes we have do that with ourselves, so it's not like we don't know how instinctively, alright?

Anyway, I tell him the tale of catching Josh when he was supposed to be lighting the fire, and the *lacunae,* and the poker and the dog and the excellent silence that ensued.

But Ed is expecting a much more dramatic tale of revenge, he wants much more than me staring at Josh brandishing a poker about, which is good, because it means I've never really threatened Ed with my eyes. He says, 'How. Did. You get. Him back?'

'OK. One fine day, Josh left his faggoty suede jacket on the banisters and I swiped the keys, popped the bonnet on his poxy little Nissan Micra and pulled the coils out, which meant it wouldn't spark. So, it's time to go, and he gets in and just sits there turning it over, until the idiot completely drains the battery. I told him there was a battery-charger in my old fella's shed, but he said he was *loathe to let someone like me start rummaging under his bonnet.* Fine. So I just walk away and he asks about the possibility of calling a taxi and I just laugh and say, "Here? Why surely you must be jesting, Josh," because, as you know, we lived way out in the sticks.'

'Wick-low.'

'Right. And here's where it gets funny. He says, "Fuck! Fuck! Fuck!" Three times. With his head going like . . . '

'John. Cleese, when he's. Beating. The. Car. *Fawlty. Towers.*'

'Nice one Ed! And he says he has never in his entire academic career once been late for class. So I ask him what he teaches and he looks at me as if I have two heads, and he says he is a Professor of Humanities which I thought was pretty fuckin' ironic because the little bastard hadn't a human bone in his body.'

'What. Hap-pened?'

'I offered to give him a lift into town on the back of my motorbike.'

'You have a. Bike?'

I don't, but Ed doesn't know that.

'Yes, a big, powerful mother. A Honda Blackbird. So, he gets on, and you can see he's real nervous so all the way into Dublin I fuckin' lash along, mirrors tipping and clipping parked cars on corners, his little corduroy knees colliding with the edges of bumpers and, once, when we swerved in behind a builder's truck, his pointy fuckin' forehead missing a big steel pole by the skin of ant's cock.'

'Ex. Cellent!'

'I can feel him, getting tenser and tenser. He tries twice to get me to slow down, but whenever he taps my back or bangs on my lid, I just drop a gear, *whannnnng*, open her up even harder. So, we get to Trinity . . . '

'*Matrix.* Trin-ity?'

'No. It's the college where he teaches. And he takes off the helmet, and underneath he's a sort of greeny-grey, like seagull shit, totally ready to void. And when he walks away, or tries to, he goes all crab-ways, first to one side, then another. That's when I call his name.'

'Hey. *Josh!*'

'Yeah. And he turns, and I do an excellent greener.'

'A what?'

'I gob, I spit. And it lands real close to his poxy Clark's commandos shoes, and I say, "You ever speak down to me in front of my mother again I'll set your poxy little Nissan on fire. Maybe with you and that cunt you married tied up in the front seats. *Capiche?*"'

'Tot-ally. Excellent. What. Did. He. Say ?'

'He tried to tell me that my sister had warned him about me, saying I was deranged, but with his tongue all undone like a fuckin' liquorice lace he couldn't speak properly and he ended up saying I was *drained* and I said, no, actually I was feeling pretty fucking good thanks, it was him who looked all drained, except of course for where he'd pissed his pants.'

'Had. He?'

'No, but I made him look, then I sang, "Made you look, made you stare, made the barber cut your hair." Bit childish, obviously, but like really playing up the demented whacko brother bit. For effect.'

'Yeah. Fuck him.'

'Fuck the lot of them.'

'Fuck. Your. Old. Fella.'

'Fuck yours!'

'Fuck your. Sisters.'

'Nah man, they're too ugly. Even for you. If you had a barrel full of mickeys, you still wouldn't give them a lash.'

His eyes are moist, he is all aglow inside, like Jesus with a lighted Sacred Heart, and it was Ed driving the big bike like a loon, it was Ed that spat on the ground right near the guy's boots, just like Clint after he chews a wad.

He is happy. To have escaped the room.

'Wanna. Watch. Some *Star Wars*?'

'One condition.'

'What?'

'You're not allowed to duck your fuckin' head during the light sabre fights as if you were Luke, OK?'

'Fuck. You.'

I put on my Darth Vader voice:

'No, fuck you, Luke Skywalker.'

I attack him, tickling and tapping, and I say, 'The Force is strong with this one,' and I fall on the floor, wriggling around, pretending he's sliced off my arm at the shoulder. And in our imaginations my blood is spurting everywhere, Picasso patterns are all over the walls, which have ears, but it's OK because all they can hear are his Fred Astaire feet tapping the pedals with sheer fuckin' delight.

Dana passed me in the corridor today, she smiled and said, 'Hey, Big Guy.' Then she slowed down to talk, except I was carrying Ed's stinking bedpan for the rest of the day all I could think was: *When she goes home, she will lie on her bed, she will put her hands behind her head, she will tell herself, 'Jesus christ he probably stinks of shit all the time, I'd never let him touch me now.'*

Down in the Village, near Tompkins Square, there's a guy with a cardboard cut-out of the President. This guy can take your photo in such a way it looks like the President is listening to you with a quizzical expression.

I put my arm round the Prez, then I assume these stupid voices mostly to amuse myself.

'Sir, I have to say, I think that quite a few things are wrong with your country.'

'I'm listening son. I genuinely respect the opinions of your generation.'

'Thank you, Sir. Well first of all, I think there's too much shit on TV. That stuff is like chewing-gum for the brain, it slows the populace down, makes people more and more stupid by the hour.'

'I agree whole heartedly, son. But the First Amendment states that . . . '

'Sir, with all due respect you need to make an amendment to the Amendment. You need to take Ricki Lake and Gerry Springer and all their ilk off the air, I'm serious here, Mr President, we're talking about the values and morals of future generations.'

'What should I put on instead, son?'

'Well, Mr President, I personally believe you should have more Discovery Channel type things, you know, nature documentaries, anything with dogs and cats, or a feel-good factor. People like animals, Sir. We can learn a lot by observing Nature at close quarters.'

'I see.'

'I don't mean animals tearing each other apart Mr President, but things like otters building dams, or how the flying squirrel gradually transformed itself into a bird. I think that by observing other species evolve, it might help us now, in our present, you know, predicament.'

'These are difficult times for Americans everywhere, son. What's your name?'

'Trevor, Sir.'

'You Irish, Trevor?'

'Yes I am, Sir.'

'I have Irish blood in me.'

'I know that Sir. I can see it in your eyes sometimes when you're on the telly late at night.'

'I don't think so, Son. I haven't touched a drop in years, I've got to go now Trevor, but I'll have my people look into all of these important issues. I want to thank you for bringing them to my attention. The Nation thanks you, Trevor, and all the other Trevors out there.'

And I was only messing, but half a dozen people have gathered round and Americans are so easily entertained, I mean they burst into applause if someone so much as farts, and now they're all clapping and the guy with the camera says, 'No charge buddy, ya should be on TV at least have your own radio show.' And then this other guy with a beer-can baseball cap and this huge pretzel in his fist says, 'Hell, I'd listen to you in the morning, no shit.' And this wizened old witch beside him says 'You didn't kiss that blarney stone, you goddam made love to it.'

They're all laughing now it's incredibly loud and false, they're slapping each other's fat backs and wobbling with delight and it's a bit overwhelming after being sealed off for so long I'm feeling like an alien, and I don't mean an illegal one, I'm thinking *It's probably best if I head back to the apartment, check on Ed, or maybe just hang out in the park instead.*

Have I mentioned I can nearly see his window from this one bench I like to sit on? It's near the entrance, just off the street, you're sort of in the park and outside it at the same time, which is nice.

At first I think he's pretending to sleep, then I hear this terrible catch in his chest, it's as if there's a wheezy old man trapped inside him which, when you think about it, is exactly what there is.

I sit by the side of the bed, I stroke his head, he opens one eye and smiles.

'Hey.'

'Hey yourself.'

'I thought. It was, your Day. Off.'

'I'm a glutton for punishment. You want me to hook up the machine for a little while?'

'You're. Becoming. Ob-sessed. Man. I need to. Rest.'

'OK.'

'Don't come. Back. Without buying. Something. Alright?'

'Alright dude. Later.'

He lifts a pale finger on the duvet, it stays up for a second, then collapses, like a blind-born bird lifting its featherless head.

I'm wearing new sunglasses in the park. I purchased them from an incredibly calm Korean who didn't speak a single word during the entire transaction even when I tried to haggle he just shrugged and pointed at his sign—*All glasses five dollar.*

I'm smiling now, remembering my mother years and years ago on a park bench in Dublin, feeding breadcrumbs to overweight pigeons, saying 'How do you do?' to old people and young. Taking off her silk scarf shaking out her still thick hair, raising her handsome face to the sun. Bathing in its heat, smiling down from behind Jackie O sunglasses: *Isn't it great to be alive, Stretch? Isn't it a zillion times better than being dead and buried?*

I like when she floats back into my head without bidding, they're usually the happy memories, the ones that arise naturally, whereas if you sit with a bottle and force yourself to remember at night you usually come up with stuff that's not exactly pleasant to look over; veins spreading, like cracks on a porcelain vase across her pulsing temple and forehead; the flesh tightening, as if Death had pressed a layer of cling-film over her exhausted face; her hair thinning, then breaking off at the roots, never to grow again; the light in her eyes fading, a leaking boat slipping out on the tide, *Decide which thoughts to conduct, which to dispel.*

I miss her which is normal, I mourn her which is natural, I talk to her at night which can occasionally be quite soothing. But sometimes I'm like a drunk priest down on his knees who realizes he has no Faith left, he's just talking into the vacuum, emptying his mouth and mind into the void: No one is listening, no one gives a shit. And if he wanted, this priest could lift his fist and shake it at the buffalo and bison water stains on the peeling ceiling above, but then he'd cut an even more ridiculous figure, now wouldn't he?

Two guys my age are playing frisbee, they think they're the greatest thing since the sliced pan; they have these big baggy shorts and naff tattoos like the guys from Red Hot Chilli Peppers they think they're really hard. They float the red disc nearer, it is coming lower and lower all the while they are laughing themselves silly, *Yo man, look at the great white hope. No man, look at the great white dope.*

They don't understand if it so much as grazes my outstretched arm, I will rise up, I will take their stupid beaded necks in my grandfather's hands, I will . . . *Nah.*

It's my day off. I will lie on the grass till the sun sets behind the darkly mirrored buildings. I will watch secretaries sip soda, and listen to them talk about J-Lo's latest flame. I will watch as a distracted father releases an expensive model boat on sluggish pond water. I will wait in the shade for wind to blow slow understanding towards his overweight child who knows now the boat wasn't bought for him.

It's a Kodak moment; it may define him for Eternity.

I'm no xenophobe alright, but why is it Americans have to advertise the fact they're having a really good time? I mean, what is it with these fuckin' people, why do they have to try so hard to tell you with their perfect teeth that their day off is better than your day off, *fuck it* their whole life is better than yours? I mean, here comes yet *another* waxed chest, John Kennedy Jr. lookalike with the latest in-line blades and a shit-eating perma grin straight out of an Orbit Sugarfree ad. On his helmet he has this little mirror, see how he checks out the babes as they zoom past. See how his Mayflower-eyes instruct me to get out of the . . . *No way pal,* today you move round me, 'Yeah stare all you like. I'm going nowhere.'

He flits past, fast, his air hitting mine. He wheels round, balletically. Bent over like a giant insect, his over-muscled legs crisscross as if they were made of rope, and it's weird because I feel I'm the one who is going backwards. And did you ever notice how on your day off you might be strolling in somewhere, say the Whitney Museum or the Algonquin Hotel, and everyone else is coming out, and the revolving doors spin a little too quickly for comfort, so you end up standing there for the longest time? And I've been meaning to tell you just how much it pisses me off when people bang on about how wonderful, ethnically diverse and supremely entertaining New York City is, because here's the realdeal.

When you know no one, you wind up on your day off

watching the sun sink behind a fake fuckin' castle in an over-populated park five minutes from where you live, *whoopee.*

A Puerto Rican girl on my favourite bench holds the answer: an ice in a little paper cup against which her lips are the most incredible colour, like coral. She has this cropped top on, with these tiny cut-off denims below and I'm thinking, *Jesus, she's much hotter than the worked-out wasps flying by.*

Miss Puerto Rico has a lazy kind of way of moving her fingers through her hair as I approach she holds her hand there, like a visor.

'You need somethin'?'

'I was wondering, where did you get the ice?

'This?'

'Yeah.'

'It's a really nice ice. Really fuckin' freshing.'

'Where did you get it?'

'From a guy.'

'What guy?'

'A guy with a little silver cart.'

'That's the guy I'm looking for.'

'He's gone.'

'Where?'

'Dunno. Maybe he went to some cold country to get more ice.'

'Alaska?'

'Yeah.'

'Or the Antarctic maybe?'

'You some kinda geography teacher?'

'No. I'm a gyna-fuckin'-cologist.'

'Yeah. And I'm a fuckin' weather girl. On TV.'

'I'd pay per view.'

She laughs and drops her hand.

'You would?'

'Yeah, definitely.'

'Dressed like this, an' leaning over the charts?'

'Dressed exactly like that. And leaning all over the charts'

'You can have the rest of this. Here.'

'You going?'

'No. I'm jus' being friendly. Take it.'

'Thank you.'

Her lipstick has blemished the ice; a ludicrous Latin priest voice inside says, it looks like my soul will look *when all of this is done.*

'You're blocking the sun. Why don't ya sit?'

'OK.'

'Man, your face is all red. Shit, you a fuckin' lobster.'

She touches my cheek and draws away, as if I am on fire. Her hands are not her best feature, you can see she chews her fingernails which are badly painted, but other than that she's an angel sent to save me from feeling sorry for myself.

She places her hand on mine, measuring.

'You a fuckin' giant, man.'

'Fi fi fo fum I smell the blood of a Puerto Rican girl.'

Her hand is taken away, it's like a privilege being removed.

'What's that shit? You being fuckin' racist?'

'It's from *Jack and The Beanstalk.* It's a fairy tale.'

'It's a fuckin' weird tale, if beans can talk.'

'It's about a giant.'

'OK.'

She puts her hand on mine again, she lets the heat of her go into me, and it is an antidote to the falseness of everything under the sinking sun. Then she narrows her amazing Natalie Wood eyes.

'He have a room, this giant?'

'Uh-huh.'

'Nearby?'

'Madison and 57.'

'This giant, he nice?'

'Very.'

'Not gonna to get rough, is he?'

'No.'

'Not gonna want any fuckin' crazy shit?'

'No.'

'Good.'

Her name is on a chain around her neck *Lucia* has a smile which is a secret weapon, she can use it to alter the mood; in a funny way she really is a weather girl.

'So this giant, he have money?'

'Uh-huh.'

'Cash-money?'

'Uh-huh.'

'Kay. What we waitin' for?'

She stands up. The marks of the bench are embedded on her upper thighs so she spits, then runs her imperfect hand along the tops of her legs which are smooth and hairless. Just like that, the bench marks are gone.

'How much do you think it's going to be?'

'You wan' me stay for a while?'

'Yeah.'

'You wanna go out for dinner first, maybe?'

'That'd be nice.'

'Make like it's a date?'

'Yeah.'

'OK. Dinner. Maybe a movie, we'll see. Then back to the giant's crib. We can talk money then.'

She wants to know why I'm laughing, so I say the idea of a giant with a crib is kinda weird, and she says, 'So are you,' then she adds, 'but weird works for me . . . It's like, you go into a store OK?'

'OK.'

'And there are all these carrots or vegetables, whatever. The carrots are all regular size then you find one that's a funny kinda shape, it don't mean it ain't gonna taste right, I mean, maybe the other carrots are the, you know, ab-normal ones.'

A lot of the time you just agree with people without really knowing what they're banging on about, it seems this super-market theory is extremely important to her so I just say 'yeah absolutely,' I even list off a few more vegetables, just to show I was listening.

Lucia explains that *technicolor-speaking* it's her day off, but she saw me earlier on, she really liked the way I stuck my hand up without looking, in fact she thought it was really cool the way I fucked-up their frisbee game, yeah, those two were major fuckin' assholes, they been giving her a lot of shit axe-ing was she Mariah Carey after she lost her record deal and put on weight an' all. I tell her Mariah Carey wouldn't get a look in, and in the distance you can hear softball applause as she lifts the sleeve of my T-shirt she seems to be checking me for tats.

'You a soldier?'

'Nope.'

'Navy-boy?'

'Nope.'

'What are you?'

'I'm a Companion to a Boy with Muscular Dystrophy.'

'A Companion?'

'Yes.'

'Like, some rich kid pays you to sit with him and read fairy tales about beans an' shit.'

'In a manner of speaking.'

'Shit. Where can I sign up?'

She laughs and links my arm, and far as I'm concerned there is no difference between us and the people pretending to be in love in the leaking boats on the silting lake. And maybe the reason Americans advertise their emotions so much is, if you keep telling yourself something over and over and over again, then eventually you'll start to believe:

It's OK to sleep with a hooker. It's not sad. Or lonely.

'Is it true you don't kiss?'

'You wanna kiss me?'

'Yes.'

'Go 'head.' Her mouth is an invitation to a perfect day. I kiss her, the park spins, and when I open my eyes there's this great big shiny black mare staring down, *Jesus.*

The guy says forty-five bucks without being asked and she says for forty-five she'd pull the fuckin' thing round herself, what he needs to 'preciate is the horse is the one with blinkers on, not her, OK?

He laughs and says, 'OK, whatever, hop in,' as she does she gives him the thigh-treatment, and that's when he looks at me as if to say *You lucky fuckin' bastard.* And I have to say it's nice to be complimented, even if she is a tart, and I know it's a turgid movie full of really sentimental shite but I can't help but think of *Pretty Woman*, especially when she climbs up beside the driver, laughs, and takes the little whip thing in her hand.

Some people are incredibly easy in themselves under the exaggerated skyline I believe I already indicated I sometimes feel a bit queasy, but the more Lucia shouts the faster the horse trots, and the more the guy beside her laughs the further Ed, his mother, and the claustrophobic room fall miles and miles behind.

Dana too is fading in the neat clip-clop of hooves even the high smell of horse-dung has its compensations.

A boy's sweet voice inside says, *This is the best day off so far, best day off ever.*

She's one of those people I told you about like my Ma she doesn't feel the need to be serious all the time we're walking she keeps saying stuff like, 'What's the weather like up there?' and 'Hand me down the moon' and when she puts her hand inside my combatpocket she pretends to be very concerned and says, 'You're pretty tall for your size no, maybe not, shit it's growin' some already . . . '

She takes me to this steakhouse where the Puerto Rican waitress knows her well, and the handsome little guy who brings the drinks knows her even better. He touches her lips with two dark fingers, and she kisses them with her eyes closed; you just know that for them the whole room disappears.

The steaks are nice and big. They come with a strip of well-done, a strip of medium, a strip of rare. We have a pitcher of beer and she leans across a lot to wipe my mouth, and once, when I get my mouth ready in an 'o' she just pulls my nose instead, which might sound stupid to you but I find it pretty fuckin' funny. In fact Lucia and I laugh a lot, mostly at the state of the other diners, how serious they look, how little time they take to register what the other person has said; I mean, some of them have their mouths open waiting to jump right in while others don't even bother to pretend they're listening, they just look around the room till it's their turn again. One flip-flop guy waddles to the salad bar, his wife mid-sentence.

Lucia says she's seen a lot of life, she doesn't think much of the human race, she does like kids however. Or anyone who takes the time or the trouble to make her laugh, which isn't much trouble at all.

We share a hot fudge sundae with sparklers on top, and we have a pretty interesting conversation about how you laugh maybe one hundred times a day when you're five, then twenty years later it's dropped to once or twice a day *if you're fuckin' lucky.*

Outside the restaurant she kisses me very strongly and thanks me for dinner and I can't stop laughing at Mabel's voice in my ear, *Make sure you treat yourself to something nice now, you hear?* And even though she hasn't a clue what I'm laughing at, Lucia just joins right in which is a little bit disconcerting since it reminds me of the bum outside the shoe store, but it's not like we're getting married now is it?

A power-walker flits past; Lucia falls in behind her for a whole block we do exactly what the power-walker does, including the mad elbow thing.

We stop for breath. We laugh. Her eyes are deep pools.

You can dive in and get lost, for a very long time.

A frighteningly beautiful Japanese girl in white goes past on a mobile phone; black mascara streaks are destroying the pale perfection of her face, her billboard eyes brim over with tiny, belladonna tears. Lucia says 'Oh shit' and squeezes three of my fingers, tight. Then she says, 'Let's skip the movie, huh?'

Which is exactly what I was thinking; I have to say, if I'd known it was going to be this nice I'd have been at it donkey's years ago.

She is sorry to leave *really*, she wishes there were more people out there like me, I'm gentle, kind, I'm really sorta special. And I know it's ludicrous but there's a lump in my throat when she tells the elevator-guy to look the other way she kisses me with her foot hooked around my leg, and the sensation of her sweet, soft mouth nuzzling mine, plus the lift descending, makes me very fuckin' giddy.

She can feel it in my mouth, the laughter rising, and as she kisses me the last thing she whispers is, 'That was a nice day-off from the world Trevor, thanks.'

She wiggles her perfect ass as she passes Barney who takes off his cap and scratches his head as if to say, *Jesus, ya'd nearly have to.*

Then the elevator-guy steps out of his box, it's the first time I have ever seen him smile. He says, 'I think I just died an' went ta Heaven.'

For a little guy his voice is incredibly deep and rumbly. Then the three of us watch her walking away, the great thing is she puts on a hell of a show.

One by one I light the scented candles in his room, to be honest I feel like Jesus pouring warm water into the bowl.

I wash the china-feet, then softly towel them dry. I get out the baby-oil, massage the baby-feet, pull the crooked toes which make a soft *crack,* like when you were a kid and pulled the wishbone of the roast chicken with your Ma, only not so loud.

I do the same with his hands and fingers gently as I lift him from the chair onto the waiting bed his hair is falling back like a little Indian squaw and I don't know why I feel the sudden need to kiss his head, but when I do, he isn't shocked, just pleasantly surprised.

'What was. That. For?'

'The hell of it.'

He smiles, and I realize it's been a while since we sat in the dark like a captain and his co-pilot, him calling out 'bedpan?' me saying 'check'; 'a bendy straw?' 'check'; 'decongestant, poured out in a paper cup?' 'check'; 'my inhaler under the pillow?' 'check'; 'panic-button?' 'check'; 'within easy reach?' 'check'; 'the little Sony recorder?' (in case he thinks of something for the book about his life), 'check.'

He knows what I'm thinking about the book and the tape-recorder because he sees me swallow, and I feel a bit guilty, so when his eyes close I gently brush the stray hair from his face. And that's when he asks me would I mind staying *just a little bit longer.* And I say, 'Isn't that a crappy-hippy song?' and he smiles and we sing it together softly, 'Oh won't you staaay, just a little bit longer?'

246 · LORCAN ROCHE

And sometimes singing is an act of absolute defiance. And as we sing we rise up, slaves in the cotton field, we are showing the colonists and the city (and maybe our fathers) that they may control us, but they will never ever own us.

Ed is a really awful singer, he sounds like a kitten being strangled and between the catch in his chest, his bad breathing and breath it's quite an ordeal, but we're in this together, we're singing out loud and it's magic.

He stops. Exhausted. He swallows. I hope he isn't going to cry because if he does then so will I.

He smiles. Then he asks me do I think Dana would have a nice voice, so I tell him yes I think Dana would have a beautiful voice, it would be clear and light, it'd be a wonderful thing to hear in the morning while you were shaving and she was in the shower washing her bits. And I start banging on about how, if he and Dana lived together, they'd be late for work every other day. And sometimes things click into place, he laughs out loud and I'm thinking *Why does it work on certain days? What do I bring into the room?*

Of course, the better question is, *What do I leave outside?*

Ed wants to know is there any way I could talk him to sleep like I did before, and I feel suddenly small inside because it only happened once, when I was making sure the job would be mine.

'OK. Imagine yourself floating on your back with your arms outstretched in calm blue, bath-warm water.'

'Where?'

'I dunno. Somewhere off the coast of Thailand. Ko-Samui.'

'OK.'

'The moon is smiling down and you've just made love to a brown-skinned, rose-lipped, soft-hipped twenty-one year old . . . '

'A girl?'

'No Ed, a twenty-one year old fuckin' sail-fish, jesus.'

'OK. OK.'

'A brown-skinned, rose-lipped twenty-one year old girl whose first-cousin was Movita, and whose nipples you can hang wet duffle coats off . . . '

'Who's. Movita?'

'She was in the original 1935 version of *Mutiny on the Bounty* please don't interrupt . . . '

'Sorry.'

'Anyway, you've just made love to her third cousin twice removed, a complete babe with an ass like a peach and a pussy that tastes like one, *yum yum* and you can taste her all tangy on the back of your throat, and your skin is still tingling and the water feels wonderful as it laps at you with a million cool tongues, your heart is bursting with joy, your balls are empty of Fear, in fact they're hanging loose as a goose on the back of the warm water and do you know what you do?'

'What?'

'You let out this lovely long sigh . . . '

'Aaaaah.'

'And you just lie there, suspended. And as you look up at the moon you realize the only thing in the whole wide world you have to worry about is . . . '

'What?'

'Not getting salt in your eyes.'

The door was open the whole time Dana was standing there listening; there's this weird look on her face, it's as if she is transfixed or transformed or something tells me when I lift the teatowel tonight there'll be more than blueberry 'n apple pie waiting.

It's weird that she has come to me now, weird that the day after I made love to another woman, the day after the kinks in my neck and my shoulders unravelled, the day after the knot in my stomach unfurled, there she is, *staring*.

It's as if she knows something's been altered inside.

Feels like I'm lifting the Turin Shroud, not a tea-towel.

I tell myself it's *very important to read the information slowly* because in the past I've gotten things all screwed up by getting the details wrong; this one time I had a date outside Bewley's Oriental Café and I stood like a spare prick in Westmoreland Street for an hour while the girl stood outside a different branch, or so her friends claimed after.

Here it is. Remember Clever, make sure you get her laughing, Love, Ellie.

Dana's mobile number, *Jesuschristalmighty.*

S he is an apparition in white. Drawstring linen pants, with this little tight sleeveless polo on top. Even from a distance you can see the thin, corded veins on her biceps like Linda Hamilton in *Terminator 2: Judgment Day.*

She has no jewellery, just a delicate chain round her wrist and on her perfect feet she has these tiny, golden sandals. The burnt copper of her hair is making other women green as we sit she says, 'There are black circles under your eyes, Trevor. The job is obviously gettin' to you.'

I say nothing for a while I just look at her, then she tells me there's no point pretending I'm one of those big, strong, silent types, she already knows I'm not. But I'm unable to think of anything to say so we just sit in silence, which is killing me.

After a while she says sorry, she didn't mean to be rude, she's just concerned is all. And it's not that I'm trying to be mysterious, it's just that I've dreamed of sitting opposite her for such a long time now I can't believe it's happening; I mean, the whole way over here the rhythm I was walking to was—*If she's not there, it's not the end of the world, if she's not there, it's not the end of the world.*

She says 'Let's start over again' so I stand up and walk away a bit. When I come back she says 'Hello stranger' with a big smile; it makes all the other stuff go up in smoke. And I remember when I was in sea-scouts we were sitting around this open fire singing like little Joseph Locke's, '*We'll make a bonfire of our troubles and we'll watch them blaze away,*' except my voice started to break and this grizzly old fucker who used to take us canoeing told me I'd have to think about leaving, which I didn't want to because I quite liked sitting there with my cares going up in smoke, but everyone was staring. And all the way home I sang out loud like a goose honking, till finally I had this brand new voice; I'll tell you one thing, it took my old fella by complete surprise.

She asks me to tell her all about myself, but I'm not a fuckin' eejit, so I say 'You go first' and she says 'OK, let's see, I'm focused, I'm hard-working, I'm dedicated, I guess I try to stay, you know, emotionally detached,' then there's a pause before she adds 'with my clients,' and I can feel my balls descend, like the wheels of a jetplane coming in to land.

She says she is probably a little bit serious. She likes men, but for some reason she can't quite understand, they seem a little bit afraid of her.

Still I say nothing, and the longer you leave it the harder it becomes.

She smiles and asks me what I did on my day off this week so I tell her 'Not a whole lot, just walked around looking at stuff in art galleries and shop-windows, nothing to write home about really.'

'I love to window-shop. Did you see anything you like?'

'Nah, not really.'

'Nothing at all?'

'Well, there was this one thing.'

'Tell me.'

She leans in a little, perfume overpowering.

'You know that Hare Krishna thing in the glass box, on the inside there are these clay figurines of men and women who eat meat, people with pig-heads and pig-faces and little pig-tails uncurling from underneath these excellent little pinstripe suits?'

'I've seen it. Why?'

'Well I just fuckin' love that yoke, I don't know why. Anyway I tried to buy it but the Harries were having none of it. One of them got quite upset actually, he started doing that waving-away thing like . . . '

She's smiling and shaking her head she says I'm avoiding my part of the deal, she wants to know *something concrete* about me and I have this overwhelming desire to say *I am not like you, I am not made of stone*, but I don't, obviously.

'OK. Where do you want me to start?'

'Family?'

'Not a good place to begin.'

'Why?'

'I don't particularly like them. Except my mother. And she's not with us any longer.'

'You're parents are divorced?'

'She's not with us. As in, she's dead.'

'Oh shit. I'm sorry, Trevor. You nursed her, right?'

'Right.'

There's a long pause as she pours herself a glass of water the cinnamon stick inside the jug swirls, like turd from a big fat eel.

'Let's talk about things that make you happy . . . '

'Alright.'

'Well?'

'I like finishing work and having somewhere to go, you know, somewhere *specific.*'

'OK.'

'I like counting out clean new notes at the bank.'

'Hey, who doesn't?'

'I like putting on a pair of old trousers and finding money in the arse-pocket, but I suppose everybody likes that too. Eh, I like putting on a new white shirt, especially if I have a hangover. My mother used to say, *A close shave and clean white shirt fools nearly all of the people all of the time.*

'OK.'

'I like animals, except, you know, moles, voles, weasels, stoats and ferret-like creatures. I especially like the smell of puppies. Eh, I like people who are a little bit different, you know people who don't spend their whole life trying desperately to fit in with the so-called "normal" ones.'

And I nearly do that awful inverted-comma thing where your fingers turn into squiggly caterpillars and you look like a prick with ears.

She lowers her voice and looks straight into me.

'What else do you like?'

'Eh, I like beautiful women who don't necessarily want to go out with beautiful men . . . '

'Corny. What else?'

'Physical work. The kind that makes you really tired and sore in your arms and back and shoulders. But not in your brain, do you know what I mean?'

'Yes. Unfortunately, however, with my work, the brain can get very taxed too. 'Specially after a session with *you-know-who*.'

'Right. Sorry. Eh, working outdoors. Burning stuff, you know logs and felled trees.'

I'm losing it a little here, I'm thinking of my second-last day in Ireland where I cleared my mother's overgrown garden; I worked from dawn till dusk and ended up with a bottle of my old fella's vintage wine watching cowboy-sparks ascend from a bonfire, I swear I saw her face smiling down, I swear I heard her whisper, *Remember to turn the moment round.*

'Where was I?'

'Feelings you enjoy.'

'I enjoy the peaceful feeling that floods through you after you've pushed yourself hard in the gym.'

'You've been working out too much.'

'How can you work out too much?'

'You're holding your head at a funny angle which means your traps or rhomboids are stiff, which would indicate you're lifting heavy weights, tearing muscle-fibres, then not giving them time to repair. Take a day off, do something different. Go for a swim. You can swim?'

'I can swim a mile in rough sea in less than thirty-five minutes.'

'Only because you have *those*.'

She looks down at the table, I'm hoping she will place hers on top like she did when we met for the very first time, but she just runs a finger down one of the veins, suddenly I feel like talking again.

'I like old people who sit beside you on the subway or the bus and make you laugh. I like people who make you forget.'

'*People who make you forget.* You like books?'

'Of course.'

'What's your favourite?'

'*As I Walked Out One Midsummer Morning.* It's by a guy called Laurie Lee and it's a wonderful evocation of childhood. What's wrong?'

'You sound like you're two hundred years old. An *evocation.* How old are you anyway?

'Old enough. What's your favourite book?'

'Guess.'

'*Wuthering Heights*?'

'No.'

'*Catcher in the Rye?*'

'No.'

'*Captain Corelli's Fuckin' Violin*?'

'No.'

'Tell me, for fuck's sake.'

'It's *L'Étranger* by . . . what's the matter, you don't like Albert Camus?'

She's one of those people that say *Al-bear* as opposed to *Al-bert*, if it was Ed it would be totally unfuckinforgivable.

'I can't stand Camus. Especially *L'Étranger*.'

'Why?'

'Because of the first sentence.'

'Which is?'

'This an exam?'

'No.'

'"*Mother died today or was it yesterday.*" End of interest in main character, I mean how could you not know when your mother died?'

'I think that what Camus is trying to . . . '

'Bollocks. All that existentialist shit, it's pretentious twaddle. Sartre, Beckett, Baudrillard, Lacan, Derrida, Barthes, Merleau-Ponty, all the fuckin' beret-wearers, they do my head in.'

'*They do my head in*. Can you elaborate as to why?'

'I'm just not into that whole *benign indifference of the universe* shite-ology.'

'So what do you believe?'

'For starters, I don't believe for one second that we're specks of dust, pointless dots. I believe we're major miracles, marvellous accidents, miniature gods with reason, logic and understanding shot into our core.'

'Really?'

'Really. I believe it's all out there, the spectacle of life, the wonderful, absurd, amazing theatre of existence. I don't mean traffic jams or promotions or who you're going to consume your corn-fed Thanksgiving turkey with, I don't mean tiny lives of barely suppressed rage and eternal nagging doubt eating away at your soul and cricks in your neck from looking over your shoulder to see who is coming up behind you on the fast-track to fuckin' nowhere. I believe it's our duty to burn bright, I believe it's a pity we eek out these miserable little existences in air-conditioned offices and cars and fast-food restaurants where everyone's always pissed off, or in some sort of permanent relationship meltdown.'

It's possible my voice is carrying a little because all of a sudden she is looking at her Roman-sandals, *fuck her*, she asked.

'I believe it's a tragedy that we spend our lives glued to Lazee-Boy recliners watching crappy game-shows hosted by cheesy guys who probably cheat and beat on their wives. Or else dream of having sex with pre-pubescent Scandinavians. I believe in Chance and Fate and Destiny, but maybe they're these really ancient old guys who don't have great eyesight anymore, and they can't tell us apart, and unless you're standing on top of Macchu fuckin' Picchu shouting out your name, unless you're at the bottom of the ocean laughing at the twisted colours of tropical fish, unless you're in Alaska on the longest day of the year and the light of the Aurora Borealis is making fat-fuckers in plaid trousers whisper softly as if they were in Chapel, or better still in Love, unless you're out there *doing things*, experiencing *Life,* helping people, unless you're actually *living* instead of sitting there in your black beret smoking *Gitanes* cigarettes sipping *absinthe,* screwing sad prostitutes and slowly *dying,* then nothing new, nothing exciting, nothing fuckin' terrifying will happen, now will it?'

She's muttering something about not realizing I'd been to Peru or Alaska, except she's saying it quietly, as if she doesn't want me to continue and in the corner of my eye I see this pokerthin guy with a dodgy cravat at the next table; he leans in to whisper something to his partner, Dana sees it too.

All of a sudden the skinny guy stands up, he starts to applaud and the elegant black lady sitting with him says, 'I believe I recognize that speech, it's Edward Albee, is it not? Are there any tickets left? We were also wondering, Have we seen you in something before, we have, haven't we? My husband believes it was Clifford Odets' *Rocket to the Moon*? Last year? Off-Broadway.'

Her cool hand is on top of mine suddenly she is laughing with them now she is patting my hand as if I were her possession, *good boy, heel.*

And I should dislike her intensely, but for the life of me, I can't.

She smiles and takes her hand away. She says: 'You need to understand something, Trevor. OK?'

'Shoot.'

'Nothing is going to happen tonight. I'm very old-fashioned and when I say old-fashioned, I mean *old-fashioned.'*

'That's OK.'

Strange thing is, I mean it.

For someone not much bigger than a bird Dana is a really good eater, you can see she really enjoys her nosh although she's one of those ridiculously careful chewers which means each forkful of her key lime pie takes an age and I'm finished nearly ten full minutes before her which kind of puts the onus on me to be the Light Entertainment Committee (weird the way routines establish themselves right away in relationships, not that we have one, alright?)

She pats her mouth with her napkin, five, six, seven times.

'Tell me about your mother.'

'No.'

'Why?'

'Because I could easily dissolve into a lump of goo. That's why.'

'You guys were close?'

'Peas in a pod.'

'And Ed? You and he are very close now. His mother says she's never seen anything like it, she says he . . . what?'

'Can we change the subject. Please?'

'OK.'

A long silence during which I'd love to have some wine to lower.

Eventually she says: 'Have you ever been in love?'

'Once. I loved this actress. I saw her in Berkoff's *Salomé*?'

'Sorry. Over my head.'

'It's a play based on a story from the Bible. She played Salomé, the daughter of Herodias who dances for the King and when she is asked what she wants in return, she says, "The head of Jokanaan".'

She says, 'I see,' when it's obvious she hasn't a clue what I was talking about.

'So, you like bloodthirsty women?'

'The dance is called The Dance of the Seven Veils. It's not easy for an Irish girl to do. Very Eastern, very exotic. Actually Ken Russell made a weird movie called *Dance of the Seven Veils*.'

'Don't you mean Kurt Russell?'

'Eh, no.'

Jesus, we're in trouble here.

'But the girl, the actress, she *pulled it off*?'

'Yes she did. I went backstage and I left her a note, and when the show finished a few weeks later, she rang me.'

'Wow. What did you say? In your note.'

'I told her that when I was watching her up there on the stage I forgot my name, my problems, my nightmares, even the fact that the bloke in the seat behind me was sucking boiled sweets.'

'And?'

'And you never know with a really good actress, because say you're dancing to Lou Reed's *Transformer* and she smiles up, it always feels like a performance, plus in the scratcher you're never really certain, you know all that *You're the one Billy-Bob*.'

'Sorry?'

'*Midnight Cowboy*. When Jon Voight's character is in the scratcher with his girl . . . '

'What's "scratcher"?'

'The sack. Bed.'

'Oh.'

There's another pause.

'So, what happened with you and the actress. Salomé?'

'I became confused by her. And in the end I felt she took something from me. We were on this beach and I was building a sandcastle and . . . '

'But are you sure it was love?'

'Yes.'

'How do you know?'

'Because a year after it ended I met her on the street and she put the heel of her hand on my stomach, she said I'd lost way too much weight, and the spot where she touched me, it burned for a week.'

She picks up her white wine, then stops the glass at those perfect lips.

'I guess that proves it then.'

'What?'

'I've never been in love.'

She tells me about this one guy, a really dark, handsome, super-successful endo-fuckin-crinologist in a Jewish hospital where she works three and a half days a week. They dated for a while but all he could do was talk about himself, his 911 Porsche and his turbo-charged career.

She goes quiet for a while then she looks over at me, she has a weird glint in her eyes.

'I never burned when he touched me. Sometimes, I used to feel quite cold. Like he was, I dunno, *dipping me in ice.*'

There's a strange sensation in my balls and toes and just behind my ears, it's if someone is whispering shit I can't quite understand and I can see the old Mayo man in the twilight of the pub he's like a soothsayer this time the lips beneath the grey moustache say, *Now me bucko, it's over to you, make sure she burns when you touch her, make sure the whole hayloft goes ripping up in flames*, and I'm thinking, *Take it easy old-timer, for fuck's sake*, but at the same time I'm thinking Dana is one of those women who says one thing and means another one entirely.

No. Maybe not.

It seems nothing really is going to happen, but that doesn't mean I can't pretend as I walk her home I put my arm around her. She doesn't come any closer, but she doesn't exactly move away either and when we get to her house I'm thinking *Fuckit, might as well be hung for a sheep as a lamb* so I try to kiss her gently she puts three little fingers on my chin to prevent me.

I'm about to apologize when she stands on the steps of her building and starts to kiss me back; her tongue darts to and fro in my mouth, sharp and silver, like tungsten.

When my eyes are fully closed, I hear this old woman's asthma voice rattle, 'You guys make a perfect picture, I wish I had my camera.'

When I open them, there's this shrivelled old bag with blue hair and an ancient blue poodle, she just keeps standing there with her tobacco-stained teeth she smiles and says, 'You two ever have kids, they'll come out just right!'

She says this while her hairdo-dog tries to crap, except it's so decrepit it can't, which I think is hilarious, but Dana doesn't even smile at the woman, she just stares into my eyes and naturally I have no idea what she is trying to tell me, so I just kiss the top of her head instead.

I'm wondering what will happen as the old lady slips away talking to her dog when Dana takes my hand and leads me up the surprisingly steep stone steps.

Straight into the fairy tale.

I thought it would be all Japanese and minimal, but it's very 1950s Americana; the bedspread is like something from *Little House on the Prairie*. There are all these ancient dolls with cracked porcelain faces on high-up shelves they stare down balefully. In the corner, a Balinese puppet hangs uselessly; it's as if the dolls had him executed for saying something stupid like *I love you*.

The bed has the crispest, cleanest sheets you've ever been pushed backwards on, and I'm thinking: *Man, I'm actually going to hear her singing in the morning.* She sits up on my chest, when she pulls her sleeveless top over her head her hair tumbles down, it is like nothing I've ever seen in my life.

I ask her one hundred times 'Is it OK?' and she whispers in a really soft voice 'It's more than OK, Trevor, it's more than OK.'

I can feel her slowly open herself up, like a flower.

Then I feel her hot breath hard in my ear, this time when she speaks it's like Linda Blair in *The Exorcist,* you know the bit where she goes, 'Your mother sucks cocks in hell.'

She rasps: 'Fuck me *harder*, Trevor. I'm not a little girl, fuck me *harder.*'

It's weird for a minute I come to, when I open my eyes the room is bathed in blue, it looks terribly cold. The Balinese puppet smiles and says, *Relax an' let go bro'.*

I close my eyes. I let go.

And that's when she starts to mutter, 'That's it, fuck me like a woman.' She's really riding me now she is hurting me with her nails digging into weird places behind my knees she starts to scream as I lift her clean off the bed she draws her hand back to slap me, except, when she sees me staring up, she just smiles down, lazily.

And pulls back her hair instead. Her voice is soft and warm when she asks: 'Did you come with me?'

'No. Sorry.'

'Don't apologize.'

She starts to move up and down on me like a practised poledancer she is doing it really slowly now she reaches underneath, grabs my balls and squeezes them, hard. With her thumb and index finger she checks to see if the condom is still on properly, then she puts her palms flat on my stomach, she starts to lift herself up and down, up and down.

She presses the top of my head, she says, 'I want you to look at yourself going in and out of me, OK?'

'OK.'

She grips my cock with her pussy now she is asking me, 'Is that nice? Is that tight?' and I'm thinking, 'Jesus christ I'm out of my fuckin' league here,' but in a nice way, obviously.

She starts going faster. Then she says, 'I want you to come now, I want you to come inside me, OK Trevor?' And because my name is on her lips I have no choice now I start to moan as she shoves her sharpest nail right up my ass. That's when I explode, *fuckin' hell.* And it's one of those ones that gets ripped from your heart and your legs shake like jelly on a plate and you just know something's been exposed or stolen, something you were probably trying to hide.

Strange sensation in my chest, it's like shutters in a French chateau opening really wide after a war, or a plague. I feel I've just learned to breathe properly. *Jesus, I wish I could pass this on to Ed.*

I can hear my heart in my ears again the room spins, silver blue and gold.

She lies beside me laughing. When I open my eyes I realize, *Aah, I was Dana's stepping-stone.*

She kisses me on the eyes and forehead, like my mother did

the last time I saw her alive, except obviously my mother wasn't saying shit like 'You fit me perfectly, God, you felt so GOOD inside, you really knew what to do.'

She bounces up on her hunkers with her pussy open, *jesus christ* it's glistening, like a just-opened shellfish.

She tilts her head to one side and sighs as she stretches her corded arms wide she says, 'I need to dance!'

I've never been crazy about the word *need,* especially the way it sounds emanating from her American mouth, which no longer looks so picture fuckin' perfect. And isn't it weird the way you can be staring at someone for months and not see the treasonable details? Her lazy tongue, too fat and heavy for her tiny mouth, and the real reason she speaks so little and so very, very carefully; her overarched spine, the knots of which are way too visible like the wooden beads you see draped over cab seats by fat Egyptian drivers; her ribcage way too wide for her body, and which stops her from having a waist; her pencilled-in eyebrows; the pinprick pupils that light upon you now, so cold, so scientific, so thoroughly fuckin' modern.

I know by the porno way she arches her pliable back, I know by the sly way she draws men in with her upside-down eyes that Dana has been released from the burden of being *old-fashioned.*

My heart is cold. I can't find the rhythm in the salsa music I'm thinking, I'd rather be uptown with Jerome dancing to a disco beat, or holding Lucia by the warm brown waist, or even kissing the sad WASP girl I used to share an apartment with, *fuck it,* I'd rather sit alone in The Subway Inn and drink cheap malt, *jesus christ* I'd rather be at home with with Ed, at least if he came back from the toilets after twenty fuckin' minutes he wouldn't keep sniffing through his upturned nostrils saying pathetic shit like, 'Hey Big Guy, I've been looking all over for you. There's some really neat people I want you to meet.'

She knows the manicured Latino men with their bottles of Piper Heidsieck are watching like sparrow-hawks, so she leans all the way back now, her mermaid-hair scrapes the floor while her bony pussy grinds against me, hard.

I wish I had balls enough to drop the bitch, right on her cokedup little head.

Who the fuck says *neat* anymore?

At the steps of her building she says she doesn't want me to sleep over. 'It's not a question of like or dislike, it's just that when people sleep together, it immediately moves into that Zone. Right now, I just need to have some space, right now I need to have some fun OK?'

'Would that be old-fashioned fun?'

'Don't be angry with me, Trevor, please, it's been a very difficult year for me.'

'Don't worry. I'm a very easygoing type of bloke.'

I don't even bother pointing out that I never fuckin' asked to stay, or that she's about as far removed from the concept of fun as exhibit-Ed when he's lying lifeless on his bed sucking on his machine, and mucous crap from his lungs is bubbling up through the pipes, and the museum windows haven't been prised opened in days.

What's the point in saying anything? It was a transaction, she got what she wanted, I got what I deserved.

Just as I sit down to tell her about Dana, Ellie announces she's quitting.

She's been trying to tell me for quite some time, she says, I don't really listen anymore.

Then she does The Sermon on the Mount again. She says I need a holiday, I need to get laid (which you have to admit is kind of funny), I need to do this and that, you'd swear her life was perfect; I mean, I really was on the verge of asking where exactly her kids and her ideal fuckin' husband were, but I just took a big deep breath and stood up instead. That's when she took one of my hands in hers.

'Listen to me, Clever: Ed ain't the only person dying in this fucked-up place, ya hear?'

But Ellie doesn't understand, she doesn't feel it turning.

When Dana passes me in the corridor she's like a stoat who's had you in the instrument of its jaws, but decided to let go.

She makes a point of touching me on the flat of my stomach; it does nothing but underline the fact that we are not lovers, we are not even friends.

We are two people who fucked once upon a time now we are moving down the narrow corridor, to where the sick people wait.

Doors open, doors close, happens all the time.

September 30th

Ellie left today.

When she hugged me I started to cry a little and so did she, then we started to laugh. She told me she was going to miss me, that the only reason she'd stayed so long, and here she raised her voice, 'In this goddam pig-pen, this shit-hole, this motherfucking hopeless Hell-Hole,' was 'cause of me.

I told her all about Dana and she said, 'Shit, that skinny white bitch a real cold-fish Clever, don't you know you need someone warm, don't you know you need a woman with soul? Listen to me, there ain't much hope of meeting her in Ed's stinky room, now is there? Maybe I'm wrong Clever, maybe she in there right this very second hidin' under his special bed,' and I'm shaking my head laughing and crying at the same time I'm saying, 'No, there's not much chance of that, no, you're right Ellie.' Then she said she always right, and she kissed me hard on the mouth, for five seconds.

And as she walked down the corridor with her pots and pans jangling I realized I was saying *no* to myself quietly *No, don't go Ellie, don't leave me here alone.*

And it was as if she could hear me, because she stopped and looked over her shoulder, and she whispered that she'd left some real nice shit in the kitchen. 'Only use a little bit at a time, Clever cause you ain't black, OK?' Then she asked, 'You sure you goin' to be OK without me?' and as she stepped in to the elevator, she laughed out loud and said, 'Course, you could come wi' me if you wanted.'

The elevator guy is talking now, his deep rumbly voice saying he'd miss her too. Big time. And then Ellie, 'Well you know where I'm going to be at for the next three days and nights, you could come visit, shit, don't be pretendin' like that Hector, you been thinkin' 'bout me that way for years.'

Elevator doors closing slowly for the very last time Ellie's cello laughter playing down and out the ghosted corridor.

BOOK THREE

Lies are usually caused by undue fear of men.
HASIDIC PROVERB

1.

Fall/Winter

I hear Ellie's laughter falling in the corridor sometimes when I'm carrying his OJ or his bedpan. But to be honest, the kitchen in the quiet of an evening is where I experience it most.

2

We order in a lot now. Compared with the muck that passes for Irish take-out the presentation is pretty good and the dishes are tasty enough.

But there's no love sprinkled in on top, that's for sure.

We got Chinese food last night. Ed's cookie had no fortune inside and we had a good laugh about that. It was nice because the laughter had this restorative power in it and when I put my hand on his head to say it was good to see him smiling again, I could feel it, returning.

Then his mother rang. She wanted me in her room *immediately*—the reception on one of her TV sets had gone all fuzzy, she wanted me to swap the sets around.

You avert your eyes from hers, from her rumpled bed, the Tracey Emin trays. With your back turned, you can hear her hands moving under the sheets: fat, white kittens in a silk drowning sack.

You try to leave without looking.

You try not to stare at what the sick bitch is doing *right in front of your eyes*.

In the bathroom after, with your face against the cold white tiles, you are telling yourself as you breathe in through your nose and slowly out through your mouth, *You do not have to endure this goes way beyond the call of fuckin' duty.*

She calls me in again, smiling, like a satiated lover. Under the covers her legs remain splayed like colossal tree trunks.

Baobab.

The fingers of her left hand are working away on her nipple while in her right she holds a bar of half-eaten, Belgian chocolate. In her fake Southern accent she asks, 'Want some?'

'No.'

'Suit yourself.'

'Is that it?'

'No, it's not. Fetch my négligée. It's in the *bureau*.'

It has to end. Here and now, it has to stop. I speak and watch as the old cunt's Blanche du Bois impression gets stuck in her throat, a stick trapped in a weir. Suddenly she is an amateur actor at an audition who forgets her lines. Her boneless face wobbles in disbelief, her neck-chin collapses in. Her mouth is open wide, the piggy-eyes blink off and on.

'I'm afraid I will not bring your négligée from the *bureau*. Nor will I carry tea from the kitchen, nor ancient magazines from the hall. The contract I signed with your husband states categorically that I am not expected to accede to any such requests. For the record, I am a Companion to a Boy with Muscular Dystrophy. I am not a companion to anybody else in this house, or any other house. So, do not, I repeat, do not *ever* call me into this sick, sordid room again.'

There's a pause. I'm not sure I've said this. I mean, I've been rehearsing it for so long now that it sounds like someone else, but it is me, yes, it is.

Wow.

She makes no sound, none whatsoever, just a kind of whimper is all you can hear, like a bulldog that's been kicked solidly by Bill Sikes in *Oliver*.

Then, as I walk out, there's the sound of Death breaking his shite laughing in the corner. The surprising thing is, he has this really thick Dublin accent.

Nice one, pal. Took a while, but it was well worth the bleedin' wait.

When the little phone rings, I pick it up.

'Put Ed on. Now.' I hand it to him. He listens to her screeching and says absolutely nothing; but in the weak, watery eyes something is changing.

He puts the phone down.

'Sorry, Ed. I don't know what came over me.'

'She takes. Ad. Vantage. This changes. Nothing. Between you and. Me.' We sit in silence, then he says, 'Can you. Get me. Some. More. Juice. Please?'

'With ice?'

'Yes.'

'No problemo.'

I am his iron-shod creature, his to command, his only.

3.

The house has borders now. Separate countries exist under one roof; it's like one of those old black and white films where uniformed civil servants shove little markers around a war-time map of Europe.

When Dana sits in the kitchen, I leave her to her own devices; when I wheel him to the door of his mother's rancid room she turns away in disgust, her piggy-nose all scrunched up as I bring him closer to the piled-up bed her silence is a protracted scream I can feel between my shoulder blades.

It reminds me of when I started going into pubs in Dublin: I could see things raftered in smoke-light and laughter, *seriously*, I could feel their thoughts falling on my shoulders and ears. And I'd often end up walking in and out of public houses for hours until I found the right place which was usually full of pensioners with Curly Wee hairs in their ears. But once you got used to the idea that there was no set routine for Saturday night, that there was no rule stating you absolutely had to be swilling warm cider in wet fields waiting for locked, fat girls leaning against trees to decide would they or wouldn't they, then there was a kind of peace descending. In this one place I found, the barman would carve a little shamrock on the head of your pint—I thought that was really nice . . .

His breath is impossible to withstand; his hair gets greasy in a day; he eats like a bird that flew in, but will never fly out. Red, watery spots have appeared on his chest, his elbows and in between his fingers and toes.

When I insist he get up out of bed, he just sits wordlessly in his chair. He hasn't got the energy to lift his dark, defeated head. When he tries to talk, he needs his inhaler right away. His finger points like a spectre, *over, there,* the deflated lungs gasping for air, *over, there.*

With the grey plastic tube in his mouth it looks like he's giving Death a blowjob.

I call the doctor. Ed is given laxatives for his bowels and dimesized tablets for the thrush in his mouth and all the way down his throat. The spots on his chest are thrush-related too: *candida vulgaris.* The doctor says it's because his immune system is breaking down right outside his door she uses the word *irretrievably.*

When I tell her to lower her voice please, she looks at me as if to say *And who the hell are you?*

In my whirling mind I answer, *I am his friend, I am his companion, I am the only one who cares.*

I time the doctor when she goes in to visit with the Judge; it lasts exactly one minute, twenty-seven seconds, a little longer than it takes to slide open a well-oiled drawer and slowly write a cheque, fake concern etched upon your tortoise fuckin' head.

We are not supposed to live like this.

We are not supposed to sit in sealed-off rooms, waiting. We are not supposed to surf from one channel to the next in subdued silence. We are supposed to say something, *anything,* as images of distraught fathers lifting children from debris flicker in front of our eyes we shift uncomfortably as we realize: *We are the ones who are remote-controlled. We are the ones who have been switched off, years and years ago.*

4.

A Russian with assassin eyes came for an interview today. She sat with me in the kitchen, silently smoking. When the little phone rang I picked it up, turned to her and nodded. As we walked down the corridor I was thinking, *I don't know why, but I feel very comfortable with this one.*

When I knocked, Ed's mother said, 'Come' in her fake voice, then before she stepped through the Russian touched the back of my neck, lightly. Her hand was startlingly cold, but it still felt really, really nice.

The Russian remained with Ed's mother all of four minutes.

When she came back for her handbag and coat, she was shaking her head. She said, 'You seem to me like nice young man. I like to work with you, I think. But that fat woman is *fuckink* crazy, and this whole place, it stink of shit. And human *fuckink* misery.'

She muttered something under her breath. I was going to quote old Fyodor, was going to tell her all about how *man can get used to everything*, but she already had her coat on, and was marching out the door.

By the way, Dostoevsky was wrong: Man gets used to everything, except being lied to. And being all alone.

5.

I open my mouth to speak, but he lifts his wrist on the handle of the chair. He swallows, then looks down at the pedals. He chooses his words very carefully. He says I'm a good guy mostly I make him laugh, but he doesn't want me to say anything now; I speak too fast sometimes his head spins, plus, he doesn't really understand a lot of the 'Euro-pean, references.'

Then there's a pause. When he looks up he is crying and my heart is starting to break into at least four separate sections.

'What are. You going. To. Do. After?'

'After work?'

'After. I. Die.'

'Ah, Jesus, Ed.'

'Tell. Me.'

'I don't know.'

'Have. You saved. Any. Money?'

'Yes.'

'Did. He give you. The last. Raise?'

'Yes.'

'And. All the. Over. Time?'

'Uh-huh.'

'Will. You. Travel?' Crooked, coursing tears leave streak marks down his face, white- and pink-striped candy.

'Maybe.'

'Will you. Go. Home?'

'I don't imagine so.'

'You. Should. Think. About it.'

'We'll see.'

'Do you. Never call. Them?'

'No. Well, once. Just after I started working here.'

'And?'

'My sister picked up and asked me how I was.'

'And?'

'She didn't wait for an answer. She said my dog had died, probably from being too fat because no one had the time to walk it.'

'What. Did. You say?'

'I said it wasn't an "it," it was a he.'

'And. Then?'

'I hung up.'

'Shit.'

'Yeah.'

'Life. Sucks. Trevor.'

'Sometimes.'

'Mine. Sucks. All. The time.'

This is the moment we've been moving towards forever, this is when it will all come tumbling out. I need to be strong now.

'I'm. Tired.'

'I know.'

'Tired of. Being. Fuck-ing tired.'

'I know.'

'Tired of. Being. A-lone.'

'I'm here.'

'Yes. You. Are.' He smiles. It rips a cord in my chest, like a parachute attempting to open.

'I'm tired of. Fighting. I mean. What. For?'

'Life. That's what you fight for every day Ed and I respect you greatly for it.'

'Do you?'

'Yes I do. I love fighters.'

'Yeah?'

'Yeah. Jack Dempsey, Jack Doyle, Rocky Marciano, Rocky Balboa, Apollo Creed, Cassius Clay, Sugar Ray, Iron Mike, Prince Nassem. And you, Ed.'

'Yeah?'

'Yeah.'

'You know. One time. I had a. Temperature. Every Day. For. Seven months. She'd come.'

'Who?

'That. Bitch. That. So-called. Fucking. Doctor.'

'If she was a he, I'd take his head clean off. One blow.'

'I'd pay. Per. View.' He smiles again and so do I.

'She used. To. Leave all sorts. Of. New tablets. Clinical trials. At the. Start. She. Seemed. To. Think I was a. Chal. Lenge. Now she doesn't even. Bother. Writing. New. Pre. Scriptions.'

'Get rid of her.'

'Can't.'

'Why?'

'Jewish. Mafia.'

'I'm sorry.'

'I know. You're one. Of. The. Good ones.' He is looking straight at me now, the yellow of his bloodstained eyes watering.

'Trevor. Can I tell. You. Something?'

'That depends. If you're going to tell me you're gay and you want to tongue-sandwich me, or have me slide in behind you in the bath . . . '

Tears of relief and release begin to flow. Slowly he wipes the streaks away with one fist, then—when it eventually obeys the brain—the other.

'It's hard. For. Me. To look at. You.'

'I know.'

'You remind. Me of. The horses in. The Bud. Weiser. Ad.'

'Clydesdales.'

'Do you. Never. Get. Sick?'

'No.'
'Why?'
'Good genes.'
'No. They're. Mother. Fucker. Jeans.'
'Yeah, well, fashion wouldn't be my strongest card.'
'You. Should get. Clothes. Made for. You. Silk suits. In Hong. Kong.'
'Maybe I will.'
'Do me a. Favour.'
'Name it.'
'Think of. Me. From. Time to. Time.'
'You're not gone yet.'
'And. If you. Find. What's. Her. Name?'
'Movita.'
'Yeah.'
'I'll kiss her for you.'
'Don't. Be such a. Sap. Get a. BJ.'
'OK.'
'Hey. Trevor?'
'What?'
'Thanks.'
'For what?'
'Putting. Up. With. Me. My moods.'

I hold his bony face in my hands his cold white mask of death. He relaxes his neck muscles and lets go the feather-weight of his head.

'It's been my privilege, Ed.'
'You. Always know what to. Say.'

I'm thinking, *I always know what to say, but I don't always know what to think*, and I may formulate the right sentence in my head, but do I have the right thoughts to begin with in my heart do I have the right feelings, *fuck it, do I have the right?*

'I'll be back in a minute Ed, don't go anywhere, OK?'
'OK.'

This is how I felt watching my mother disappear in the mirror I tell myself, *I won't drink tonight, not a drop, I won't smoke any of Ellie's leftover weed, I'll go down the Y, I'll sweat it out, I'll make sure I'm strong in my body and clear in my head I'll make sure I'm ready.*

Out in the corridor, the intercom buzzes briefly.
He needs me.
I walk towards his door, *I need him to need me.*

6.

Since we spoke about it—since he said straight out he was dying—he has changed: he is like a white flower placed in a vase by a closed window he has opened up, and maybe you're right, maybe it is for the last time, but he has stretched inside now there is space for other people's music. And the long day doesn't begin with a shopping list of high, whining demands. It begins instead with a gentle, yawning question:

'What. Do. You. Want to. Watch. Today?'

And he's learning too late in his life about *sacrifice*, about putting someone else first; he doesn't use the panic button unless it really is urgent, unless he needs the dropped inhaler right away, unless he can't find the strength to elbow-prop himself on his side to breathe a little easier, unless he thinks it really is true, there really is someone standing over him, unless he feels his tiny bird heart genuinely has stopped, that he needs his oxygen, his mask, his Companion.

He has learned too late not to be seized by panic, he has learned to breathe and think through it, he has learned that the oozed, stale aftermath of his body sweats doesn't need to be sponged away at half-past four in the morning he has learned to let me go.

A little.

And some days you can see in his terrified eyes that his dream of being pulled under by the shadow that stands over him at night is back. And God love him, he tries to keep it to himself, he tries to be heroic and stoic and silent, but it's there in the shaking badly hand, the trembling voice, the childish choice of DVD.

'No. Not *Sunset. Boule-vard*. OK?'

'OK.'

'How. About. *Star Wars?*'

'Again?'

'*E.T.?*'

'I dunno Ed, I think I nearly know it off by heart. How about *Terminator 2: The Director's Cut?*'

'Cool. Set it. Up. With the new. Surround. Sound.'

'No problemo.'

'Thanks. Man.'

And none of this will last, all of it will pass, but that doesn't mean it shouldn't be acknowledged, if only because you get an inkling of what Ed might have been, what he maybe briefly was before the universe began plotting in dimly lit corridors, before paediatric nurses began to scurry past with charts and useless pills, before a sense of foreboding began to grow like a black narcissus in his father's stopped, forever-startled heart.

Ed doesn't get up much anymore so I just sit beside him, listening.

He says his childhood was a series of sharp needles and cold people prodding, black orderlies lifting him and patting his ass to see if he had soiled himself, *Jesus*, how he used to wish he were much heavier, how he used to want it to be a *fucking chore* for them to heft his arms and legs.

But they hoisted him as if he wasn't really there.

Then a chorus of young Jewish doctors would come to stand around his bed at night he often thought, *Maybe I'm not here, maybe this is all a fucking dream.*

When he was five, silent men in white coats filmed him over the course of an endless indoor day. They woke him and massaged him, they stretched him out until it hurt, they placed him upright in a straight-backed chair with straps around his sunken chest and crooked waist—then they walked away and left a camera on him.

They wanted to understand precisely how it happened, how the blood began to coalesce and slow, how his head became so heavy and low, how it looked as if he were dying, over and over again.

In the end, he decided to stay alive, *just to fuckin' spite them.*

'Jesus Ed, I'm so sorry.'

'Don't get. All fuckin'. Weepy. On me.'

We laugh. He bows his head. I kiss it softly.

If someone opens up to you, Nature dictates that you must open up to them, *forget about the dam bursting,* so I tell him a bit about my family, but not about the door being hammered shut, then a little bit about my mother, how light she used to make me feel inside, how easily she could forgive, how readily she could make me laugh even on a dark day, how, if my old fella corrected her grammar or her *syntax,* she'd smile coldly at him and say, 'Why don't you take a long walk off a short fucking pier, professor?'

How sometimes she'd wait until one of my ugly sisters was finished banging on about her latest thesis, her latest dialectic, her polemic, then she'd wink at me and say to whichever one had just been droning on, 'I never hear you talk about your feelings, darling. It might be nice if once in a blue moon you let your mother know you actually had some.'

Ed looks at me the whole time I'm talking, which is hard for him because I'm standing and walking and he is lying flat on the bed and has to follow me and his neck hurts, and in the end he interrupts me with a fake coughing fit, his way of saying he is too tired to concentrate anymore.

Finally he smiles and says, 'I'd like. To have. Met her, she sounds. Like. Ex-cellent crack.'

I'm thinking, *But I'm not finished, Ed, there are other things I want to tell you*, when a low voice says, *Careful now, you cannot open up completely, you cannot overwhelm.*

It's true, there are things I can't tell Ed. Things I want to tell you, things you need to know:

In the Cathedral, no Jesuit sat listening. There was no confessing, no blessing, no fire fighter's hand pressing. Down.

In The Subway Inn no Mayo man, advising.

And in the piss-stained lane as polished black boots and white fists came raining in, the truth is I lay there making no effort to protect myself. Truth is, I laughed out loud because at last, at last I was feeling something again.

And there *was* a court case, but it was *them* who brought it against me because they became afraid as I lay there, spitting teeth, grinning up and saying shit like, 'That all you got, huh, that your best shot?'

And yes, you're right, in my swirling world every teeming thing gets repeated, over and over again. And when they walked off shaking their shaven skulls searching for words to fit the sudden confusion in their coward hearts, I rose up.

I rose up and stumbled, I tumbled headlong into them, bleeding and breathing through black, blood-blocked nostrils. And I knocked all three over like skittles. Then I kicked, I stamped, I jumped, I broke pencil bones I snapped inside I dislocated.

I saw gaps in time. Saw where their skinned red hands were going, got there first. Predicted how they would scuttle sideways like crabs. Saw how they would move again to protect their faces, balls and bald heads, covered now like old people in an underground bomb shelter.

Saw myself being recorded by a CCTV camera in another lane, in another time, in another minute now I'll stop disappearing into the folded moment where there exists no camera, no committee, no rules, no explanations, no verdict.

Where I can get lost. Where I can feel at home.

'Stop. Fuck's sake. Stop.'

'Please. Stop.'

'You made your fuckin' point, pal. Stop.'

I did not stop.

Instead, I fell from a great height on Blue Eyes' barrel chest. I took his fat knacker neck in my hands and squeezed slowly I started really *concentrating*. And I didn't let go, I couldn't let go, even as they pulled and punched, even as they were kicking me in the kidneys screaming his name at the top of their scorched lungs I didn't let go completely, no, my hands did not stop what they were doing.

Until the silver keg was raised, like a new moon dawning.

Pagan, I worshipped for a moment before it fell I hoped and prayed it was the end. Of this, my fake civilization.

Then there was the hospital, and the ignorant, Indian doctor asking what I had done to make the men so very, very angry. I told him I had simply been myself. My father. Refusing to sit in the plastic orange chair. Drawing the ringing curtains briskly asking me was I proud of myself. Again.

No Lucozade or grapes, Dad? No get-well card or After Eights?

And yes, my mother, sitting with me, holding my two good fingers. And once again it was too easy to tell the truth to someone who wasn't there.

What else do I need to tell you, what else do you deserve to know?

That for a while there had also been the miracle of the actress talking and dancing after making love in her Portobello house to Lou Reed's *Transformer*. And I was transformed. I was free from my mother's dying, dishonest room, from the inheritance of doom and the expectation of family failure.

Then there was me, becoming first confessional, telling her stupid, stoned things I should never have admitted about school and swimming coaches and city shrinks and country doctors and thin-ribbed kids behind bicycle sheds, and slow country boys with cigarettes waiting for their whole world to turn.

Changing rooms.

Me telling her about Ma, our songs, and our garden growing brighter and greener than anyone else's in Wicklow.

Telling her about Mother's Day, and Ritual, telling her about the mirror in the morning.

Swallowing hard. Waiting for her judgment.

The actress holding me like the American woman who does not exist, her holding me and telling me it was OK, let it out, let it all out.

What precisely am I supposed to let out? What exactly is my soul supposed to secrete?

Then me becoming obsessional, turning up, uninvited, at her casting sessions with red roses and yellow sunflowers, *Good luck, I know you'll get it, no one is as beautiful as you.*

Me texting her. Morning. Noon. And night. Closing in on her, choking her air, her space, her light. Knowing I was doing it, feeling myself, watching myself.

Not being able to stop.

Then there was her smiling reluctantly instead of laughing openly, her nodding patiently. Her, walking away on Dollymount Strand and not looking back even when I willed her with all my fuckin' might to turn and say: *It's OK, you can try again, just try a little less harder.*

The rank insult of her spitting pips and laughing with my mother in the lilac room, and later the heel of her hand upon my stomach and the fake concern we reserve for people we've already left miles and miles behind. 'You've grown too thin, you really need to stop worrying Trevor.'

How? How do you stop something you've been doing from day one?

The theatrical Judge said the bouncers had possibly 'o'er-stepped the mark,' my considerable physical presence notwithstanding. Then he turned his attention to me, he swallowed and said, 'However, your retaliatory behaviour clearly *emanated*'—which is a word for a smell, isn't it?—'from some dank, abhorrent place,' that I clearly was to be feared and not be trusted, that I had showed no restraint, had demonstrated no control. That in my blind fury I had extended towards these men not one single ounce of compassion, not a shred of human pity.

And we were back in school, and he could have saved himself a lot of time and said, *Look, look at the sheer bloody size of you.*

I needed a lesson taught. Pause for effect. A custodial sentence he feared would simply unleash whatever darkness I had buried in my heart. He had read carefully the letters from the doctors, the school, the Probation Service; these had greatly informed his decision. Pause for effect. This was a person who needed to be restored to society, not removed from it, this was a person who had lost his will and his way. But who still had something to offer.

How, he wondered, did 'three hundred and fifty hours community service sound?'

I said it sounded like an awful lot of hours considering what I'd already been through in hospital, but he just looked over at the bouncers, their broken bones, the ludicrous sticks they carried in their bandaged hands.

He called me up to the bench, he cupped the curved microphone with his hand, he said, 'You need to wake up to the facts here, Trevor Comerford, a man has been brought to within an inch of his life,' which I thought was a very good description of what had taken place.

Then he waved me back with his pale hand, and out loud he asked me to promise I would never appear before him again and I let out a nervous laugh because of course I was thinking of Kirk and the transporter room.

And that was how I fetched up at the Clinic. And The Captain was right to wonder what I had done to end up in a creaking, leaking shed at the edge of the world with a load of helpless hopeless people, and no letters after my name, and no halfway plausible stories about how I'd managed to arrive there.

7

For a while the Clinic provided a kind of healing, and a peaceful growing inside, a balancing.

Act.

But like the Committee said when they fired me, I didn't know where to 'draw the line,' I didn't know where to stop, which really was a crying shame because the class had loved me. And I had loved them back with all my confusion and all the pieces of my broken heart.

Then she died, and I had to ask myself all over again, how, how do I stop the tadpole-thoughts increasing?

By way of a nailed-shut door? By donning a pair of unopened Nikes? By running away? By way of a formula delivered with fake enthusiasm by a man with a carefully modulated, over-educated voice? With a country doctor's pat on the knee? With a nod and a wink? With breathing exercises and visualization, with trees, roots and water flowing? With a bitter pill swallowed in the turning morning, 'Take it with your juice and cereal, better still take it with your vitamin C.'

No. I will take it staring straight at myself in the mirror, *thanks all the same.* I'll let that action dominate, let that image set the tone for the day and the month and the year to come asunder. That will be the theme music for a life of trying too hard to decipher which feelings are real, which are imagined, which memories are to be trusted, which whisperings, which voices, which chemical choices, which lies.

What?

Did you really think the voices that drift across my sky like rain-clouds, did you really think they tell me just the names of faded movie stars, forgotten TV serials?

They undermine me.

They knock me down in my sleep they roll me over like a clumsy drunk I am very nearly awake as they de-construct me then attempt to rebuild me, hastily, except one of them will always snidely, cruelly disagree, disavow. And that is how they allow the door to niggling Doubt to be kept ajar in your head at night you get so uptight before you drift off, so pent up anticipating the moment when they crash dreams and sack joy, when they plunder and tear asunder your unwound strips of *possibility*.

And that is when you find yourself dwarfed, awake, heart thumping beside a foaming fountain beneath looming bank buildings where booming, ordinary decent people sit.

And manage to fit in.

Yes. Of course there are days of plain sailing, days off from yourself, days when your sneaker laces don't suddenly snap 'cause your feet have been sweating so much, when even the ordered-in food you consume tastes uncommonly good and the sound of children laughing in the park becomes, frankly, *inspirational*.

When Dana's footfall in the hall costs you nothing, not even a casually destructive thought.

When you are granted respite, when you earn a reprieve, when you can enjoy all these.

Music as you walk, run, and exercise; evenings alone in your little room with a good book; the gentle hand of the waitress as she leans in to pour; nights when two cold beers will suffice, no whiskey, no subway, no staring; weekends when you leave the bag of weed to one side, when you laugh along with the warm audience at the cinema, when you don't lie awake, when you fall asleep happy you're making a difference.

When things are normal, maybe even mundane.

The straw bending towards his cracked, smiling lips; weights steadily racking up in the Y; *The New York Times* stacked neatly in the lobby, a carefully folded copy left for you on his tilted desk by Jerome because one of the residents is away; his massive mop leaning, the polished floor gleaming; the steaming, rain-released city running alongside you laughing like a friend introducing new side-streets, new sights, new smells, showing you somewhere you might sit and sip Colombian coffee, somewhere you might relax and read *Empire* magazine, somewhere you could spend a peaceful hour. Or two.

Your mother's voice, warm, smiling: *Tomorrow, Trevor, you can come back here, tomorrow, it's true you know, you can easily be happy two days in a row.*

8

Silence is easier in winter things are naturally falling asleep.

Ed asks about my father, so I tell him, 'Well, he's the sort of guy who notices details but misses The Big Picture,' like when I was a kid and they'd take me out for a drive in his Jaguar and he'd be pointing out all the different trees and clouds and rock formations, using words like *deciduous*, *cumulo-nimbus*, and *fissure* when I was only fuckin' five. And when we got back there'd be this informal examination on 'What We Saw Today' and he'd sigh out loud and say to my mother that clearly I'd inherited her powers of recall, not his.

Then there would be dark mutterings about the poet and the prison. I think. But I don't really know.

But here's the thing: I can remember the *moods* in that car vividly. I remember the music. I can recall the smell of leather, and any sweet words that passed between my parents in the front. I can still see the curious way he looked at me in the rearview.

Most of all, I recall how he put his hands on my shoulders as we stood in a clearing in the woods at Lugnaquilla: I remember thinking how delicate his tremulous fingers were, almost like he were playing music on me, not distractedly pulling at the stitching on my T-shirt.

Stop Dad.

Stop undoing me, stop pulling me asunder, you're making me feel like I am made of straw.

The pier at Greystones, walking with my mother and father slowly. Her entire weight compressed in her hand holding mine.

Her picking steps carefully, him picking words in the same slow, halting way whenever we encountered his college cronies: 'And this—this *monstrosity*—this is the blacksmith's grandson.'

He could just as easily have said, *This is Trevor, this is my son.*

9

Washing his hair carefully—the roots these days don't seem able to take the pressure of the hose, even with the heavy brass tap screwed halfway back.

'You know if you wanted . . . '

'What?'

'I could get you a red-head.'

'How?'

'I could pay her.'

'A. Hooker?'

'*Hooker. Escort. Companion.* Who gives a fuck?'

'What. About. My. Folks?'

'What about 'em? We'll sneak her in some night when your Dad isn't here and your Mom is watching one of her game shows.'

'Jesus.'

'A red-head. In a nurse's uniform.'

'What?'

'Sorry, Ed. Schoolgirl?'

'Fuck!'

'If you like. But first time out, I'd go for the blowjob.'

He reaches out, he takes a hit from the inhaler which sits like a talisman on the side of the bath. He can no longer even wank without a wheezing attack taking over.

'You. Speak. Ing. From. Ex-perience?'

'There was a guy in the Clinic who, well, let's just say he had become sexually-frustrated because his girlfriend had left him after this pretty horrific accident on a farm, and he asked me would I get him a hooker.'

'Did you?'

'Yes.'

'And?'

'And, it cost me my job.'

'Why?'

'She came to the chalets at the Clinic. She was doing her thing, but there was this other little guy in a wheelchair, he hid in a corner of the room under a load of coats and I guess he started making noises or jerking off or something. Anyway, the hooker spotted him or heard the motor of his chair whining and she started screaming her lungs out, so they called the night watchman in and there was this big Lieutenant Columbo-style investigation and . . . '

'Did it. Take long?'

'The investigation?'

'No. Did it take. Long. To. Find. The. Right. Person?'

'Yes. It did.'

A pause. He flicks the water with his crooked fingers, three times.

'Why?'

'Some of them are just these hard-hearted people who the world has been pretty cruel to, and they don't exactly have a lot of milk of human kindness left. But if you look long and hard, you can nearly always find a nice one.'

'A whore. With a. Heart?'

'It's possible, Ed. Someone gentle.'

'And. Good. Looking.'

'OK.'

Another pause.

'My. Age?'

'I'll see what I can do.'

'You'll need. Some. Ex. Penses.'

'I probably will yeah, I might have to buy one or two of them a drink.'

'You should. Start. Right. Away.'

'OK.'

'Dry me. Off. Then. We can. Grab. My. Cheque. Book in. Side.'

'OK, Ed. Hold out your arms for me, that's it. Ooops-a-daisy, there we go, careful now, make sure your feet are on a dry patch, good. We're going to have to do something about those curly toenails, OK?'

'OK. But. Later.'

I dry his hair gently; white towels are not a good idea when someone's hair is falling out. He doesn't seem to notice, he's writing the cheque as if he was the head of an elite commando organization.

He finishes and it sits there for a moment we both stare at his indecipherable signature, aware of the burden of expectation.

Then I sense it inside, another kind of revolution rising. And it makes me light in my head. It's happening quite a lot these days: as I knead his bones at night or softly sponge warm water down the blades of his back in the bath he'll say, 'That's really, nice, thanks man,' and I'll feel it, *the ability to lift spirits*.

And it's based on communication, isn't it? On kind words and gestures, a shy eyebrow raised before a game of cards commences, a long evening sigh that tells you, *The Simpsons will not suffice tonight you must try harder, you must reach down inside.* And it's about understanding, it's about *divining* what the other person truly needs, it's about slicing open the razor-backed shells we've placed in precise rows in our hardened hearts in the mistaken notion that keeping things clam-tight helps us to be *focused* and *hardworking,* like that cold cunt Dana. And I know I'm getting carried away, but seriously I'm fuckin' glowing here man, I'm on fire, and like I said before *it fans all encounters along the way.*

Ed feels it too, he looks up at me smiling he says, 'You. And. Me. Bro. You. And. Fuckin'. Me.'

There is nothing I cannot do for him now, nothing.

10

Out under the sea a sponge is filling, carefully. With new-found weight and anchored purpose it begins to dance with the persistent tug of tide.

It moves left, then slowly right.

At times you'd be forgiven for thinking it was going to prise itself free from its bed, but you'd be wrong: it has put down strong roots, very strong roots indeed.

ay the words 'dystrophy' or 'wheelchair' and most of them start squawking like parrots in a terrifying aviary. Then they're swinging their loud bags shaking their frightful-looking wigs. Some take the time to explain it's really not their thing, they stand with their hands on jutting Mick Jagger hips trying really hard to think of someone who just might oblige . . . 'Let's see. There's that Marcey, yeah she white, used to be a nurse, jus' couldn't keep her hand out that medicine cabinet.' And, after telling you where Marcey lives and where she hangs and what she looks like, they say they haven't seen her for a while.

'Shit. Maybe Marcey dead.'

The dangerously thin ones, the lost girls from Ronkonkoma and Syosset, the ones with the Far Rockaway look in their overdone eyes who put you in mind of trapeze artists in a tacky, ailing circus, and whose mouths have lost the ability to produce saliva, these ones say, real slow, 'No, Mister. I don't go in other people's houses. Don't matter if it's Madison or the fuck-in' Vatican. That's how girls like us disappear.'

After they touch you with a drugged fingertip that slides up your crotch in the manner of a snail, you say 'No thanks' and they very quickly get bored like chimps who've run out of cheap crockery. And they wave you away down the watching street, their voices like warning bells: 'Don't go wasting nobody else's time with that pervert shit, *a'wight?*'

And why do they insist on putting their palms upon you in

302 · LORCAN ROCHE

sticky doorways, why in steam-filled greasy spoons do they stroke your lapel, or your cheek, without first asking permission? And they're in and out of your pockets, like monkeys in Gibraltar, and you have to keep checking every second or third block, *Shit, is the cash still in there burning?*

I hope it's worth it in the end I hope he will be happy.

One of them looks like an extra from *West Side Story,* a very tall Jet, she shrieks, 'Ooh my god' when she takes hold of my hands. She is this terrible actor who you know right away is a *he.*

She has a kind heart, however.

She takes one of my cigarettes and makes me light it for her, then she says she'll put her 'thinking cap' on and we both laugh because of the stupid-looking hat she's wearing; to be honest it looks like something Carmen Miranda would have declined.

She can't think of anyone, no, not a single fuckin' one. 'Sorry, baby.' She suggests I try the magazines and agencies, 'because really and truly Hands, the street caters for a different type of *client-tell.*'

Then as I walk away she yells out after me, 'Hey, Hands! That dive bar there, yeah. Go on in, she has red hair, her name is Sophie, she jus' might do it.'

Red hair, silver-green *Celtics* jacket. Sitting alone, which is good.

I watch her as she finishes her drink I ask would she like another but she says, 'Thanks, it's been a very long day, I'm off duty.' Then she puts her hand above her head to *click* off an invisible sign, like on a yellow cab heading home.

I laugh, so does she, and while she's laughing I scoot up two stools.

Sophie is English. She has soft eyes and quite a lot of style because she lets me finish my entire sales pitch before she interrupts; plus she takes care to turn her head away to blow her smoke out comes this little gold notebook. She writes down the address with this little gold pencil, then the proposed date—Saturday, Oct 22—Ed's name and the word *virgin,* underlined three times.

She closes her book, she says I am a very thoughtful fellow but seeing as how it isn't exactly your common or garden request she wants 200 bucks, fifty upfront, 'if you didn't mind too much, thank you.'

'Sure. No problem.'

She puts the money in her bra, like they do in movies. Then she says that I needn't worry, Ed will sleep like a 'babe in the woods' and perhaps after if I'm not too pre-occupied I might buy her a cocktail, that's a very nice part of town unfortunately she doesn't get up there that often.

'Sure. Why not?'

The way she looks right into me says she can think of about three million reasons why not.

12

Sat 22nd

Only after I have washed his hair, and lifted him from the bath with disposable gloves on do I tell him she is coming. He immediately develops this instamatic fear in his eyes, he says, 'Fuck man I've just whacked off'—as if I hadn't noticed—'Why didn't you. Fucking. Tell me?'

I say when he sees this girl it won't matter if he has whacked off a million times.

'Why?'

'Why do you think?

'Is. She. Hot?'

'Very.'

'Is she. A. Red-head?'

'Yes.'

'Fuck. What. Colour. Eyes?'

'Nearly black.'

'Jesus. Is she. My. Age?'

'There or thereabouts.'

'Is she. Irish?'

'No. English.'

'Wow.'

'That would sum her up, yeah.'

I wrap him in the towel he is shaking with excitement, his whole body quivering like an arrow that's just acquired the target. I hope to Christ he doesn't go into spasm, I hope this goes according to the plan.

Ed looks good in as much as it is possible for a guy who weighs less than six stone and has God only knows how long to live. I've blow-dried his hair to give it more life, I've shaved the annoying bits of bum-fluff on his pointy little chin, I even squeezed some blackheads. I've given his teeth a good going over, I made him rinse out with Listerine five times until all the blood from his pyhorrea gums was washed away. And as I scoured the sink I was thinking, *Weird how Buddhists believe people like Ed are paying for the sins of a previous life, Jesus he must have been a fuckin' war criminal,* except I don't believe he was; I believe the soul that's trapped inside poor Ed cried out to be born so badly that when the Gods heard him and looked down at the clouded idea of him forming they said, *See, it wants it so badly, it is spinning like a top, almost willing itself into existence.* And then, like old Palestinian or Jewish women who have seen too much and understood too little, they shrugged their shoulders and said, *What do we know of it, anyhow? Let him live!*

Then the Judge came inside the whale, like Jonah.

Like a good and faithful manservant I have placed a single, longstemmed flower in a porcelain vase by the closed window. A white orchid, it looks incredibly beautiful. When I brought it in Ed went to say something about his allergies, then he just stared at it for a while, and finally when he looked at me it was one of those occasions when you're absolutely certain what the other person is saying with their eyes: *Go ahead, I trust you. Completely. You are my friend, you are my Saviour also.*

It's like this Marx Brothers movie, you know the Big Opening Night with the tuxedoed orchestra warming up in the pit of your stomach. And expectations are running ludicrously high, I mean, it's not like she's going to provide a miracle cure, now is it?

And Barney, who I had to let in on the act, keeps ringing up saying, 'She's late Trevor, she's taken your money, you'll never clap eyes on the whore again, never. And Trevor, while I'm at it would you ever stop leaning out that *feckin'* window shouting in the evening? You're driving the residents at the front of the building insane.'

Sophie has a fun-fur on when she arrives I'm a bit nervous and my sweaty palm sticks to her elbow as I guide her past the kitchen into Ed's newly hoovered room.

I can hear my heart, like Billy in *Midnight Express* where he's just about to board the plane. Man, it's really booming.

He's heard us in the corridor; as we walk in he pretends to be busy, you know like, *Oops, here I am just putting away my stupid old clipboard.*

The blood in his cheeks is rising like mercury, it's as if he were a character in a children's pop-out book, at last someone is colouring him into life. His tiny pigeon chest is rising. And falling. Too fast.

Nothing happens for a while—it's quite an awesome silence, there are all kinds of cables and wires running through the air. When he finally speaks his voice is thick and slurred as if he's been asleep for a long time and is unfamiliar now with the mechanism of speech.

'*Henno*. I'm Ed.'

'Sophie. I've been looking forward to meeting you. Edward.'

He smiles. She can hear his gums stick, she can hear his throat click as he swallows she can feel tremendous fear in his white mouse-heart.

She's a whore, which means she's an accomplished actress, but if you didn't know better you'd say Sophie was one of those truly talented people who *genuinely* don't see the chair. She goes behind him, she strokes his hair gently, she whispers something in his ear that makes his eyes close, as if he were in pain. Then she takes off the coat and throws it out on the carpet, like a lion tamer.

She has a school uniform on. The skirt is very short, the blouse very tight.

Sophie's legs are unusually long and white, they are parted really wide. She spins his chair round; she's stronger than she looks. Ed's eyes are huge like Mr Magoo he cannot focus and when he finally sees what she's not wearing, his head goes halfway 'round in one direction, then all the way back the other. He swallows hard. His head jerks back as if she had slapped him, or as if his thoughts are too much to cope with.

His head shoots forward again, staring at her crotch. He's a carved bird in an ornate, old-fashioned German clock. *Cuckoo.*

She prances around on her incredible legs and white high heels like some exotic, near-extinct creature the Victorians captured on 42nd Street. Her eyes are wild with power and the ability to control, and I know if I sit with her later in The Subway Inn her life will be a tale of callous creatures taking things from her carefully, like apples from a tree.

Love. Innocence. Faith in other people.

'I don't think we require an audience, Edward. Do you?'

'Nnnno.'

'Why don't you tell him to leave, darling?'

'*Leaf.* Please.'

I take the flower and, as I close the door softly one loose petal falls, it floats gently towards the floor.

Six minutes later I hear Edward scream this really high-pitched girly sound, *Aaahoooh.* Now he's the one who's had something ripped from inside.

I pop a beer. I light a tiny joint. Through the smoke I can see Ellie shake her head, 'That young whore after sticking something up his boa-constricted ass, probably torturin' him with some giant black dildo.'

'No, Ellie, Ed has the electric eels again, only they're the nice ones this time, they move through you coiling and uncoiling you darkly. There's nothing to be afraid of, nothing at all.'

13.

The kitchen is hushed, just the sound of me sipping and smoking. I'm thinking, *That scream meant Ed was truly alive*, but it also means he's closer now to Death: an oyster recoiling in a restaurant as someone squeezes three piercing drops of lemon over him.

When Sophie appears in the kitchen door smoking a cigarette she looks like an angel and a devil at the same time.

'Is he OK?'

'He's out for the count, but you should go in and check. His neck might get sore, the way he was leaning back over the edge of his chair it reminded me of this old person with her mouth open on a plane, when we landed they couldn't wake her up. Shit. Sorry.'

'It's OK. I'll go in now. There's beer, if you like.' I stand up to fetch one, she doesn't move out of the door, however.

'May I have the rest of my money. Please?'

'Of course. Sorry.' I hand her the cash, it's nice the way she doesn't count it.

'So, are we still on? For cocktails?'

The word sounds weird, which you have to admit is perfectly understandable considering what's she's just been doing. And when she takes a sip from my beer she seems to be washing out her mouth, which doesn't help sell the idea.

'I better sit with him, you don't mind, do you?'

'You work away, darling.'

She mutters to herself as she turns—'Didn't think so, not for one minute'—then she struts away on her high heels and she doesn't look back as she steps into the elevator I call after her, 'It's just that tonight he needs me more than ever.'

When I lift him onto the bed he still doesn't wake, not even when I slide off his new, anti-fit Levis, still unbuttoned at the fly.

His dick is all curled up like a little slug it's still moist and there's a lipstick stain on the wizened nub and pink particles in his thinning pubic hair. *Christ,* she hasn't used a condom, she's sucked him dry, which you have to admit is both charitable and despicable.

As I'm tucking him in he opens one eye as if it was glued shut, then the other. He starts to laugh, he can't stop, neither can I.

He holds his wire hanger arms aloft, so I lean in, and when he hugs me there's a bit of strength and a lot of love in the embrace. As he kisses the side of my face, he smells of Sophie's perfume.

'I thought. The. Top of. My. Head. Was going to. Pop. Off. When I came. I saw. Stars. Collide. There were black. Holes. Opening.'

'Did she come?'

'*Eh*. Jesus.'

'I'm kidding Ed, OK?'

'OK. Yeah. Jesus.'

He laughs again—it's a really beautiful sound—then he asks me, 'Is it like. That. Every time? With things ex-ploding?' and I say, 'No, not every time unfortunately.'

He says he's going to have to do it again, then he sighs, he closes his eyes and whispers, almost to himself, 'You're. The. best. Thing. That ever hap-pened to. Me, Trevor. No. You're the. Best. Thing. That ever. Hap-pened to. This city. I'm reck. Commending. You for another. Raise in the morn-ing. OK?'

'OK, Ed. Thanks.'
'Hey, Trevor?'
'What?'
'Truly. You are. A. Giant. Among men.'

14.

Truly that is how I feel when I take the pillow I can feel my heart explode, like a stained-glass window a heavy leather ball's been kicked through, *boom-tinkle.*

His eyes are closed. He is smiling. His hands lie perfectly flat on the mattress. They make no effort to circle around like wings, they just do the accordeon-player's dance for a while, feebly.

Then the whole house is ticking quiet, just the sound of the breathing-machine gurgling away in the corner.

Could've sworn I plugged it out, but I don't remember my hands on the socket or the switch, I just remember them on his crooked pillow after, like large birds finished fishing.

And I think I remember the steady beat of white-tipped wings making their way out over water, a faint, hot wind rising. But to be honest, it wasn't much of a wind, it wasn't much of a wind at all.

Walking towards my servant-room at the corner of the uncoiling corridor I run my fingers along the flecked wallpaper, the tips begin to singe and burn.

The handle then is beautiful, cold.

I open the door, slowly.

I am not surprised: it is no longer my room, it belongs to someone else, someone whose old-fashioned suitcase lies overflowing in the middle of an unmade bed.

In his battered recliner I sit.

To the shape of him, I adjust.
I breathe in.
Close my eyes. It's true:
I turned the moment round.
I watched Ed's spirit soar.

ABOUT THE AUTHOR

Lorcan Roche, born in Dublin in 1963, is a journalist, playwright, travel-writer, magazine editor and one-time male nurse. His works include award-winning plays for radio (*Angel of Suburbia*) and stage (*Him and Her, Whatever Happened to Joe Magill,* and *The Old Fella*). He lives in Dublin with his wife and daughter.

Helmut Krausser
Eros
"Helmut Krausser has succeeded in writing a great German epochal novel."—*Focus*
352 pp • $16.95 • 978-1-933372-58-7

Amara Lakhous
Clash of Civilizations Over an Elevator in Piazza Vittorio
"Do we have an Italian Camus on our hands? Just possibly."
—*The Philadelphia Inquirer*
144 pp • $14.95 • 978-1-933372-61-7

Lia Levi
The Jewish Husband
"An exemplary tale of small lives engulfed in the vortex of history."
—*Il Messaggero*
224 pp • $15.00 • 978-1-933372-93-8

Carlo Lucarelli
Carte Blanche
"Lucarelli proves that the dark and sinister are better evoked when one opts for unadulterated grit and grime."—*The San Diego Union-Tribune*
128 pp • $14.95 • 978-1-933372-15-0

The Damned Season
"De Luca…is a man both pursuing and pursued. And that makes him one of the more interesting figures in crime fiction."
—*The Philadelphia Inquirer*
128 pp • $14.95 • 978-1-933372-27-3

Via delle Oche
"Delivers a resolution true to the series' moral relativism."—*Publishers Weekly*
160 pp • $14.95 • 978-1-933372-53-2

Edna Mazya
Love Burns
"Combines the suspense of a murder mystery with
the absurdity of a Woody Allen movie."—*Kirkus*
224 pp • $14.95 • 978-1-933372-08-2

Sélim Nassib
I Loved You for Your Voice
"Nassib spins a rhapsodic narrative out of the indissoluble
connection between two creative souls."—*Kirkus*
272 pp • $14.95 • 978-1-933372-07-5

The Palestinian Lover
"A delicate, passionate novel in which history and life
are inextricably entwined."—*RAI Books*
192 pp • $14.95 • 978-1-933372-23-5

Amélie Nothomb
Tokyo Fiancée
"Intimate and honest...depicts perfectly a nontraditional romance."
—*Publishers Weekly*
160 pp • $15.00 • 978-1-933372-64-8

Valeria Parrella
For Grace Received
"A voice that is new, original, and decidedly unique."—*Rolling Stone* (Italy)
144 pp • $15.00 • 978-1-933372-94-5

Alessandro Piperno
The Worst Intentions
"A coruscating mixture of satire, family epic, Proustian meditation, and erotomaniacal farce."—*The New Yorker*
320 pp • $14.95 • 978-1-933372-33-4

Boualem Sansal
The German Mujahid
"Terror, doubt, revolt, guilt, and despair—a surprising range of emotions is admirably and convincingly depicted in this incredible novel."
—*L'Express* (France)
240 pp • $15.00 • 978-1-933372-92-1

Eric-Emmanuel Schmitt
The Most Beautiful Book in the World
"Eight novellas, parables on the idea of a future, filled with redeeming optimism."—*Lire Magazine*
192 pp • $15.00 • 978-1-933372-74-7

Domenico Starnone
First Execution
"Starnone's books are small theatres of action, both physical and psychological."—*L'Espresso* (Italy)
176 pp • $15.00 • 978-1-933372-66-2

Joel Stone
The Jerusalem File
"Joel Stone is a major new talent."—*Cleveland Plain Dealer*
160 pp • $15.00 • 978-1-933372-65-5

Benjamin Tammuz
Minotaur
"A novel about the expectations and compromises that humans create for
themselves."—*The New York Times*
192 pp • $14.95 • 978-1-933372-02-0

Chad Taylor
Departure Lounge
"There's so much pleasure and bafflement to be derived from this thriller."
—*The Chicago Tribune*
176 pp • $14.95 • 978-1-933372-09-9

Roma Tearne
Mosquito
"Vividly rendered...Wholly satisfying."—*Kirkus*
304 pp • $16.95 • 978-1-933372-57-0

Bone China
"Tearne deftly reveals the corrosive effects of civil strife on private lives and
the redemptiveness of art."—*The Guardian*
400 pp • $16.00 • 978-1-933372-75-4

Christa Wolf
One Day a Year: 1960-2000
"Remarkable!"—*The New Yorker*
640 pp • $16.95 • 978-1-933372-22-8

Edwin M. Yoder Jr.
Lions at Lamb House
"Yoder writes with such wonderful manners, learning, and detachment."
—*William F. Buckley, Jr.*
256 pp • $14.95 • 978-1-933372-34-1

Michele Zackheim
Broken Colors
"A beautiful novel."—*Library Journal*
320 pp • $14.95 • 978-1-933372-37-2